RIDING
Hard

RIDING
Hard

BENNETT BOYS RANCH, BOOK TWO

LAUREN LANDISH

Montlake
Romance

Text copyright © 2019 by Lauren Landish
All rights reserved.

Published by Montlake Romance, Seattle

www.apub.com

Amazon, the Amazon logo, and Montlake Romance are trademarks of Amazon.com, Inc., or its affiliates.

ISBN-13: 9781503903517
ISBN-10: 1503903516

Cover design by Eileen Carey

Cover photography by Wander Aguiar

Printed in the United States of America

RIDING
Hard

CHAPTER 1

KATELYN

Beep, beep, beep . . .

My alarm wakes me up with its incessant noise, and for a split second, I'm annoyed. Actually, I'm annoyed most mornings. I bought this alarm clock specifically because I sleep like the dead and need the world's nastiest-sounding alarm to get out of bed.

I almost slap the snooze button, but then I remember—it's my first day on my own as the new events coordinator at the Mountain Spirit Hotel and Resort. The idea of starting my dream job has me popping out of bed like there are springs in my butt, and I almost run to the shower.

I can't believe it—first time out, and I land my dream job! I mean, I've had jobs before, but this is the first time I'm taking a step out on my own, the first step of many toward the life I've always wanted. Even as I soap up in the shower, I'm doing a shimmying happy dance of joy and shower karaoke-ing my ass off.

I do my best to sing "I'm Coming Out" by Diana Ross, giggling at my antics. Getting out, I dry off before dancing my way to the kitchen for coffee, thanking God for automatic timers, and stirring enough sugar in my cup to cause a toothache.

Popping a waffle in the toaster, I take a moment to think about my life. It's a huge change from just a month ago. I'm in a new town—Great Falls—in a new job that I never ever thought I'd get so quickly, and I'm in a new apartment, a pretty little one-bedroom place. Everything's still so unknown, all a fresh start.

So far, the bloom isn't off the rose just yet. I mean, I'm still figuring out my way around the grocery store, and even finding the best place in town to get my hair cut is sort of exciting.

My waffle pops, and as I put it on my plate, a twinge hits my gut, more nostalgia than regret. Every morning at home I'd start my day the same way, with a waffle. Sometimes with Nutella, but almost always a waffle. Some things change, but some things stay the same.

I think about the life I left behind . . .

. . . comfortable family,

. . . comfortable friends,

. . . comfortable boyfriend.

Well, Seth is an *ex*-boyfriend now. But the point is, it was all so easy, predictable. *Comfortable.* I could've followed all my friends back home, happy with a gold wedding band and an MRS degree. I'd have probably popped out two kids before I turned thirty and been content with life.

But I wanted more than content, and maybe that's what was slowly choking me. So instead, I'm chasing this job and the brass ring I've been reaching for my whole life. It's a little scary. I'm worried that this is all a bit bigger than I can probably handle, but at the same time, I'm hopeful that the Mountain Spirit Hotel and Resort will make me grow to fit it. Now that I'm free, I can already breathe more fully, like I'd slowly shrunk my being into too tight of a space, and now I have room to be me in a way I never have before.

And damn, I'm already learning so much. I started working with Brianna Adams only a week ago, but it feels like I've been pedal to the metal this whole time.

After my first day, I completely understood. She's been the de facto events coordinator for a few years but is ready to move on from the day-in and day-out craziness, and things around the resort seem to function at a low level of crazy as the status quo. She's needed as an owner more now that the place has really grown to its potential. Plus, she's a mom and wants time with her football-star-turned-resort-owner husband and kids.

Even so, when I got hired to be the events coordinator, I was shocked. I know I'm a good event planner, and I've done more than a few events flying solo, even if it was under my mentor's company umbrella. I just wasn't sure that would qualify me for . . . this. But she must've seen something in me, and after a week of training wheels, today I'm on my own. The wheels are off, and I'm the captain of my own destiny. Not that I'm jumping onto a bucking bronco my first ride out. She said today's calendar is straightforward, just a couple of walk-throughs with potential brides and a rundown of a corporate dinner being hosted in the newly expanded fine-dining restaurant, which I'm sure is going to be rated five stars before the end of the year.

Still . . . the meeting I have today has me jittery. All the tours, all the sales pitches can be stressful. But this is the big one, one last chance to fuck up a booking before the bride and groom sign on the dotted line and give the resort their cold, hard cash. Or credit card, as is usually the case.

Normally, that'd be easy as pie. But this isn't any old bride and groom. Oh, of course not, that'd be too simple, and I'm being thrown straight to the wolves with this one even if Brianna did say today is straightforward. The little insecure voice inside me says that it's got to be a test of sorts. I mean, who would give up being the events coordinator of a resort the very same day that the reigning, defending, and retiring bull-riding champion of the entire rodeo world, James Bennett, and his bride-to-be, Sophie Stone, are coming in to put their names on the contracts?

A rodeo celebrity seems like enough pressure. But, I remember as I try to finish my breakfast, Brianna casually tossed over her shoulder last night that Sophie's matron of honor is a very close friend of the family.

Just a regular old appointment on any regular old day, I tell myself sarcastically as I put my plate in the dishwasher and try to calm the butterflies in my belly.

Except, I don't think those are butterflies. Maybe more like hummingbirds? Thousands of them in a windstorm? Yeah, that's more like it.

Deciding I've had enough sugar and caffeine, I dump the rest of my coffee down the drain and get ready to tackle the day. As I get changed, I keep telling myself that I can do this. In fact, I'm going to rock this job.

All I've got to do is book this wedding to solidify my place and settle the question once and for all if I can handle life on my own. Not for anyone else. For *me.*

Spoiler alert, to anyone who's looking down on my life and wondering—I damn well can.

Or at least, I'm going to try like hell.

In the bathroom, I get ready carefully. A heavy dose of mascara on my long lashes to frame blue eyes that are my best feature, a swipe of pink gloss on my puffy lips, and a quick curling iron to the ends of my blonde hair complete my look.

I decide to play it safe with a blush pencil skirt and my usual sky-high heels, but I can't resist the allure of my lucky black-and-white polka-dot sleeveless chiffon top. It's perfect for the heat of the summer, although polka dots are usually a love-them-or-hate-them pattern.

For the record, I love them. And people who hate them can just get to the back of the line.

I'm still a bit nervous when I get up to the resort, but I do my best to look confident as I stride into the lobby, letting the opulence surround me. I grew up loving the old-style architecture from the past generation of hotels, the ones you don't find these days because dark woods, chandeliers, and brass accents aren't considered "stylish" anymore.

But this place shows that old-school class never goes out of style and has done it perfectly. The wood-paneled walls are all local cuts, stained beautifully in a way that gleams mellowly, while plush patterned rugs around the multiple fireplaces dampen my footsteps, and green-globed lights remind me of an old gentlemen's parlor where rich men would sit and smoke cigars while making business deals.

But it's not *totally* old-school. It's been updated, with nods to the ski chalet resort the building replaced. The main hallways are all rough-cut mountain granite, able to take any amount of snow that careless guests might dump on their way in from a day on the slopes, and the high ceiling looks almost like it was taken from a giant log cabin, with windows that let in plenty of mountain light.

Ducking into the coffee shop, I grab two muffins, one for me and one for my new assistant, Marla. While I've been shadowing Brianna, I've been watching and learning, and I've noticed that Marla eats a muffin every morning, a reward for drudging through her morning emails. And simply put, this job is big enough that I'm going to need her on my side—and sometimes that comes from a boss just giving a shit enough to notice that her worker likes muffins at nine.

I almost knock before entering, but then I remember that it's my office now and open the door slowly instead, making sure to give notice that I'm coming in.

"Good morning, Marla," I greet her chirpily. "Got you a muffin. Apple crumb, right?"

Marla grins widely at me, obviously surprised at the gesture, and she nods, her dark curls bouncing. She's been all smiles and sunshine from my first day of training. "Yes. That's so sweet of you, Ms. Johnson. I have your coffee for you. Café special, dash of cinnamon with a double dose of sugar?"

I smile, and we do an oddly funny switcheroo, trading a muffin for coffee. It breaks the tension, letting both of us laugh at our attempts at making a good impression on our first real day. Today feels different to me and probably to her too. Before, I was the new girl, the trainee who spent most of her time talking with Brianna and shadowing, asking questions, and letting myself be pointed in the right direction.

Now I'm the new boss.

Holy crap. I'm the boss! I think, taking a sip of coffee.

Deciding quickly that I want to be more friendly than superior, I think fast and set my cup down, offering a smile. "I think we can call that a tie. Want to make that our daily routine? I bring the muffins, and you bring the coffee?"

Marla laughs, visibly exhaling. "Deal. Shake on it?"

She offers her hand, and we shake. "Oh, and please, call me Katelyn, or I'll never answer you because I'll be too busy looking around for my mom."

I wink, and she dips her chin. "Sure thing . . . Katelyn."

I pick my cup back up and take another drink, clearing my throat after I'm done. "So, not that I've been obsessively going over my schedule in my brain all morning, but other than the signing, two walk-throughs, and the corporate gig . . . anything I need to know?"

Marla looks impressed that I've got it together so far, and I think to myself that if she knew about the ten thousand hummingbirds in my belly, she might not be so impressed. Instead, she'd be ripping the caffeine out of my hand.

I sip at it anyway, not wanting to be rude, and enjoying the nectar of the gods.

Marla takes a bite of her muffin, sighing happily after smacking her lips when she's done. "Nope, sounds like you're ready. I'll let you know when Mr. Bennett and Miss Stone get here. I'm going to have to inhale my muffin in record time, though, so I can brush my teeth first. I'll be damned if I'm letting James Bennett come through here with apple chunks in my teeth."

I laugh at her confession. The sharing feels nice, like girlfriends gossiping about the cute guy at school, and I appreciate that, because friends are one thing I'm in short supply of here, considering I'm new.

"Is he that cute?" I ask, wondering if I'll need to brush my own teeth, mostly so I don't have coffee stains. "I'll admit I don't follow professional bull riding, so I have no idea what he looks like."

Marla tsks at me. "I don't follow rodeo either, but I'd follow that Bennett boy anywhere he'd lead me. Only makes it that much sweeter that he is head over heels for his fiancée. Seriously, it's been the talk of the town. The man has no idea anyone else is even in the room when they're out together. Awwww."

She sighs happily like they're a fairy tale come to life. I grin, and part of me hopes to see the sweetness the way Marla describes when they come in. Every girl could use a dose of hope that maybe the fantasy really does exist.

Lord knows I've never seen it in real life, so maybe today's the day.

CHAPTER 2

MARK

Shuffling the papers on my desk for the hundredth time, I finally find the one receipt I need. Right in the stack I've already searched through three times. Why a feed and grain receipt is in the middle of the water testing reports I don't know—I'm not that kind of disorganized. One of my brothers has probably been messing with my filing system again.

My growl isn't audible, but it's definitely clear in my head as I enter the information into the ranch expenses spreadsheet in front of me and save the file. A little presto magic with the mouse, double-clicking a few spots, and the columns start lining up. Everything is right with the world once again. Spreadsheets updated, bank accounts reconciled, budget balanced, files in their place.

I nod. That's the way things are supposed to run around the Bennett ranch. Get it right and get it done.

Well, not *done*, because the work around here is *never* done. It's only ten in the morning and I've already put in four hours of work, and by the time I'm done around sundown, I'll have put in more work than some people do in two days. But things are different on a ranch, and it takes a different kind of man. The kind that most people aren't anymore.

By sunrise, I was helping in the barn. After breakfast, I was checking on the cattle in the west pasture. By the time most folks sit down at their desks, I was doing the same, but I'd had a decidedly full morning of physical labor to show for it. No slow rolls into the office around here. The animals and my family wouldn't stand for it, and it's ultimately all my responsibility.

All one thousand acres of the Bennett ranch fall on my broad shoulders. They have for a while now, but I can take it. For years, I was right here, learning every in and out of not just the land, not just the physical labor that's needed to run a ranch, but the business side of things as well. While my brothers chased their dreams on and off the ranch, I've never had to run. My dream is right here at home.

Although I figured I'd be working at Pops's side for a while longer. He made sure I was ready for everything when he was gone, even if that was so much sooner than any of us had imagined. But that was Pops, making sure everything was covered, a plan in place for every contingency.

He did it well too. I'm only thirty, and running this place is second nature, the one thing I've never questioned. This ranch is in my blood, and this job is what I was born for. *Thanks, Pops. Because you're still here—looking over my shoulder, I'm sure.*

I lean back in my chair. It's comfortable, well-worn wood and leather, the same one Pops sat in for damn near thirty years. I hope to sit in it for even longer, although I guess at some point I'll have to replace it—chairs don't last forever. Of course, the one second I take a break and let my eyes close for even a moment is the one time I get totally busted.

"*Ahem* . . . lazing around like a dog in the sun, are we?" an amused voice asks, mock crossly.

I crack one eye open, refusing the impulse to jump, and see Mama glaring at me, hands on her hips. She's still lean, and she wears her hair pulled back. Her slim body is dressed just like her sons, in a work shirt

9

and jeans. Mama's only nod to her age is that she wears sneakers unless she's in the yard doing her own work . . . where she puts on knee-high rubber boots to make sure she doesn't come into her house tracking any filth.

Without moving, I answer her, giving her *just* a little sass. "Nope, just thinking. Closing my eyes helps me focus."

Mama's been around the block a few times and doesn't get fooled easily. "Humph, don't make it worse by lying. What are you doing here?"

With a sigh, I set myself upright in the chair and blink to clear my eyes. "Just working, Mama. I just finished updating this month's spreadsheet, and everything looks fine. We're in good shape."

Even though we've already had a birthing season and our first stock sale and things are running fine since Pops passed, every once in a while Mama gets nervous that the ranch isn't doing well. And since I'm the rock around here now, it's my job to reassure her that we're fine.

And we are.

In the past few months, both of my brothers, James and Luke, have pulled more than their weight around the ranch. Both of them willingly contribute to the family coffers, to the point I nearly had to fight James about his desire to hand over his whole world championship payout to the ranch. And Luke's been getting so much work with his horse breeding and training programs that the Bennett name is getting famous in quite a few circles.

It's gotten to the point we've hired a ranch hand, Carson, to fill in for Luke since he's away from the place so much. But with the money he brings in and the fame he's producing for the ranch, he's paid for Carson five times over already. Even if James does give Luke a good ribbing, calling him "Dr. Horsecock" when they're going at each other—and Mama's not around, of course.

Mama gives me a hard look, complete with a good country woman stink eye. City girls just can't measure up there. "Son, I know we're fine.

I do get the mail before you do, you know. I've seen the bank statements. What I meant was, what are you doing *here*? And not in your truck, already halfway to town?"

My brows knit in confusion. "Town?"

Mama throws up her hands, looking to the heavens as if I might need the help of angels to prevent my brains from falling out of my head.

"It's June sixth, Mark! It's signing day at the resort for James and Sophie. You didn't forget, did you?"

Shit. I forgot. Well, I didn't forget about their signing day, or the wedding, or the craziness that's about to hit our whole family—I just forgot what day it is. That's easy to do out here when every day is so full and relatively repetitive. Animals need to eat every day, fences have to get checked, and bills need paying. Rinse and repeat, rain or shine, holiday or weekend. Simply put, I'm the machine that keeps all that running, whether I'm the actual person who does it or just the one who follows up to make sure it was done.

My goof must be visible on my face, at least to Mama, who's been able to tell if her boys were lying since day one.

"Mark Thomas Bennett! You did forget! Boy, you'd best get your butt in that truck and get to the resort before Sophie or James pay that bill themselves. You know your daddy and I always planned to pay for these things, and I aim to do so even if James is some big rodeo star and he's marrying a girl who comes from more money than God Himself."

I grin at her theatrics. Well, I don't grin because I'm me, but the corners of my lips twitch up a bit. That's about equivalent to a wide, teeth-flashing smile in my repertoire of expressions, or lack thereof. "I know, Mama. Who decided the groom's family should pay for the reception anyway?" I grumble. From what I remember, it's the other way around, although I'm no expert. Mama's right about one thing, though. Sophie Stone's family could buy and sell our ranch three times over before sundown and not miss the money. Sometimes I think it's a miracle that she's so . . . normal. "I'd like to see the rulebook."

Mama's eyebrows lift toward her hairline, and she crosses her arms in that way that tells me I'm pushing the line. "The rule comes via Ms. Emily Post, September 1982, if you must know. But more importantly, me. Only one power higher than that in this matter, and He agrees with me."

Now I know she's making it up. I can see that she's fibbing by the look on her face, but I know better than to argue. She's still right about the second part, and I won't argue the third. If Mama wants to pay for it, we're paying for it. Hell or high water, especially considering she's already had this conversation with James and Sophie. I give James credit—he gave me plenty of pained and bashful looks during the whole dinner that we discussed this, and even Sophie wasn't sure how to react.

"Shit, I'm going." I grab my hat off the hook, hoping she missed the slip of cursing. I may cuss like a fucking sailor at times, but we all know better than to do it in front of Mama, and God help the person who dares let an off-color word pass their lips at her dinner table. No dessert would be the least of your worries if you did that. There's a reason Mama has a collection of half a dozen wooden spoons . . . just in case.

Besides, no one in their right mind would ever risk missing out on Mama's nightly dessert. I sometimes think folks intentionally make their visits out here at dinnertime just to get invited for a slice of pie or some cobbler or whatever it is Mama's put together.

No dice. I can see Mama's chin tilt even as I adjust my hat. "Son, this may be your office now, but don't you dare go around speaking filth in here. Your father would have your hide."

I silently chuckle at that, knowing that most of the bad language I know, I learned at his side, starting when I was barely knee-high. Pops's diatribes against a difficult steer would have seen him not getting dessert for a decade if Mama heard them. But he also taught me when it was okay to speak roughly and when to keep my mouth shut.

His biggest rule was simple: no rough language around Mama and any ladies. I amend that thought—any ladies except Sophie. She's damn sure proper, maybe the finest young woman I've ever met, but that woman has a mouth on her strong enough to keep my wild youngest brother in line, so she can handle a curse here and there without a flinch.

Not that Mama cares about that. "Sorry, Mama," I say contritely, dipping to kiss her cheek as I head out to the truck. "I'll get there in time."

"Apology accepted," Mama says, following me out. "As long as you get there and pay that balance before anyone else does. Oh, and here's your lunch."

I realize she's got a big lunch pail cooler in her hands, and I take it thankfully. Some guys might be embarrassed to have their mother make their lunch at thirty years old. Well, they don't have my Mama making them huge sandwiches full of chicken and fresh vegetables, strawberries from the garden, and cookies warm out of the oven.

It's how she shows her love and takes care of us. Even in the years when the money was tight, Mama made sure her menfolk ate right. So I'm damn glad to accept her love in whatever calorie-laden form she wants to give it. I need the fuel for the long days on the ranch.

"Thanks," I reply. "I'll make it there and take care of everything."

Thirty minutes later, I've broken the speed limit most of the way up the back road, but I make it, pulling into the parking lot of the fancy Mountain Spirit ski resort that brings a ton of tourists to Great Falls.

It's off-season, so instead of white-capped peaks teeming with snow bunnies, the mountains rise up behind the huge building in shades of green and brown, the trees creating a jagged line reaching toward the sky. It's beautiful, but populated with tons of people.

There are just too many people scurrying in and out, wheeled suitcases and children lagging behind them. It makes my skin itch. I'm not antisocial; I just prefer a slower pace of life than the hustle and bustle of our local tourist destination.

I park my truck myself, the valet not even an option that I consider, and stride with a purpose into the fancy monstrosity in front of me. I've been here before, but I still think my first thought about it is unmatched—the whole resort looks like the Waldorf Astoria fucked a log cabin and this resort was the baby they produced.

The lobby is grand; that's the only word for it. Huge log beams, sanded smooth and stained dark, rise up at least four stories, and there's a grouping of wingback leather chairs surrounding a tall stone fireplace that roars with orange flames despite the heat of the day outside. It's a waste of good wood, but I guess people like the look.

I head up to the front desk, planning to ask where to find the events office, but the desk clerks are all busy doing check-ins and check-outs. Just my luck too. All three lines have people in front of them who seem to want to argue about something on their bills. With a sigh of annoyance, I wander until I find a directory by the elevator.

I see where the events office is located and set off, mad at myself for not remembering and being here sooner.

After two wrong turns, I finally find the door marked EVENTS and push it open in a hurry, determined to find James as soon as possible. Unfortunately, I didn't realize that someone is on the other side of the door.

As it swings open quickly, I see a flash of polka dots and pull back, but it's not enough. Everything plays out in slow motion in front of me as the door bumps a woman standing on the other side, causing her feet to slip out from underneath her. The ridiculous heels she's wearing don't help matters as her arms flail about.

Luckily for her, my brother didn't inherit all the athletic talent in the family. I've got reflexes that more than once have served me right in a tussle and enough strength to wrestle an ornery steer down with just the right wrench on its horns. This time it's a lot less difficult, and as a cry of surprise escapes her lips, I reach out automatically, catching her around the waist and pulling her to me.

Time freezes as I look down at her, feeling a zing of electricity rush through my body. It's been a long time since I held a woman this close—and fate has dropped one into my arms who would make an angel weep she's so beautiful.

Her blonde curls are dipping back over my arm, soft and smelling like roses. Her blue eyes are wide, her pink lips rounded in an *O* shape. Her breasts press against my chest for a split second, and I'm struck with the sudden ridiculous urge to dip her lower and take her mouth.

Instead, I set her right, releasing her reluctantly but still feeling the searing brand of her skin on mine. "Sorry about that," I apologize, my voice twanging almost painfully in my ears. God, I sound like a bumpkin, nothing at all like a man a woman like this would be interested in. "Was looking for someone and got ahead of myself."

She smiles, white teeth dazzling me, but she still looks a little shell-shocked as she responds with a friendly tone. "Well, who are you looking for? Maybe I can help."

"James Bennett," I reply. "He's supposed—"

She interrupts me, nodding and eager to help. "Oh! Mr. Bennett and Miss Stone just stepped out to tour the grounds one last time. They're deciding on a ceremony space and wanted a few moments to themselves to discuss the options."

I know my brother and soon-to-be sister, and I can say without a doubt that they're not debating this clearing or that. They're likely fucking somewhere on the grounds behind a tree, the same way I've accidentally busted them half a dozen times on the ranch.

We've all learned to whistle before we go to the pond now because if you come over the ridge unexpectedly, you're likely to see something you don't want to—either James's bare ass or Sophie's tits.

James almost punched me for that last time, but it was their own damn fault. Thankfully Sophie wasn't upset, and it was her joking about a whistle warning that started the whole thing. Girl's got a head on her shoulders.

"Okay. I guess I don't need him anyway. I just need to pay the balance on their account."

"And you are?" the angel asks, still looking up into my eyes with a smile and a twinkle, her body filling out her ridiculous-looking polka-dot blouse in a way only one woman in a million could—and making me think polka dots aren't that childish after all. I feel like each one could be a target for me to kiss, especially the ones centered right over her chest.

I know she's prompting me to introduce myself, and I'm tempted to tease her, but I fight the urge. It seems James being around the ranch so much has gotten under my skin in more than pure annoyance. Somehow, the filter doesn't quite make it to my mouth, though.

"*Rodeo USA*," I reply, making up a magazine name off the top of my head. "Thanks for confirming Mr. Bennett and Miss Stone's venue for us. Any other details you'd like to share? May I credit you, Miss . . . ?"

I let the question of her name hang in the air, watching as her face flushes before horror slowly overtakes her features. She covers her face in her hands, shaking her head as she mumbles.

"Oh my God, no! I did not just spill the beans about our biggest wedding of the year on my first freaking day."

My eyebrows lift at that, and a seed of guilt wiggles in my gut. Teasing a pretty girl like this is one thing, but I pushed it a bit too far. And that's exactly why I don't and shouldn't even try it. I can't pull it off like James or Luke can. I take pity on her, keeping my voice low as I chastise her.

"I was just joking, and I'm admittedly not good at it. But folks around here, we do protect our own. And yeah, those two got plenty of outsiders interested in poking their noses where they don't belong. I'd obliged if you'd be a little more careful about my brother and his bride."

I can see the relief cross her face before her eyes harden and she stands tall, indignation giving her an extra couple of inches that still puts her at shoulder height to my six-three frame, and that's in those ridiculously high heels.

"That was mean-spirited. However, I apologize for speaking out of turn," she says, her blue eyes flashing. "Perhaps we should start over? I'm Katelyn Johnson, the events coordinator for the Mountain Spirit Hotel and Resort. How may I help you today?"

It's cute the way she says the whole title, like I don't know where the hell I am. But I got the important info, like her name and that she's in charge of James's shindig of a wedding. She offers her hand and I take it, shaking it slowly as I keep her locked in my gaze.

She doesn't flinch, which I take as a good sign, because most folks turn away when I focus my full attention on them. I get it—I'm tall with deep-set, intense eyes. And while I guess girls can have a resting bitch face, I have more of a resting asshole face, serious and cold. More than one person has told me I'm intimidating. I'm not gonna apologize for it.

"Mark Bennett, James's brother and the one paying for the reception," I introduce myself, letting her hand go reluctantly. "How much do I owe you for his party?"

I see her swallow, her lips parting ever so slightly, and I have to fight back the imagery the simple action brings to mind. It's been too long, it seems, since a woman has looked at me that way, but my body hasn't forgotten what it feels like.

She steps back, not fully breaking the connection between us, but the added space at least turns down the magnetism enough that we can both breathe again. "Nice to meet you, Mr. Bennett. Please, come into my office, and I can get that figure for you."

She turns, walking through a doorway off to the side, never once looking back to see if I follow. Honestly, I don't for almost four steps because I'm watching her hips swish in her curve-hugging skirt.

Suddenly, her shoes don't seem so ridiculous if they make her ass pop out like that, like it's begging for my hand to smack it, caress it, grab it firmly as I pick her up and wrap her legs around my waist.

But that's enough of that. I'm in my work jeans, and they're not loose enough to handle me getting out of hand. Besides, I learned a long time ago that thinking about a woman in anything other than purely emotionless, functional terms serves no purpose. I'm not much of a casual sex guy, and I'm damn sure not marriage material. In a world with three billion or so women, I'm the sort of man that women might *think* they want—right up until the long days, the tired muscles, the cornhusker's lotion, and the hard work ruin everything. And that's before we even get to my personality, or lack thereof. There's only so much Pops's baby-blue eyes can do for me, and it's not enough. Especially for a woman like Katelyn.

Better to not think about it, about her—especially like that. A soft, feminine woman like this would never be interested in a man like me anyway.

Instead, I take the few steps into her office, noting with sly amusement that she starts to close the door, then thinks better of it and leaves it open instead.

Smart woman. She must sense that the tension in me has changed, even though I'm damn near a pro at hiding my thoughts and feelings, always keeping tight control on everything. Instead, Katelyn walks behind her desk and pulls up something on her computer, nodding.

"Down payment and deposit are due today," she says, her eyes darting between me and the computer screen. "Considering the quick timing, there would typically be a rush surcharge, but Brianna mentioned something about extended family and to waive that. However, we will have to include the additional charge for staff coverage due to the size of the guest list."

Her voice is crisp, professional . . . and fake. I both hate it and appreciate the instant distance it places between us. I'm feeling unusually out of control, but I can appreciate that she seems to have things well in hand.

"How much?" I say, reaching for my checkbook. It's probably quaint nowadays; so many people just handle things online or with plastic. But for some reason, I prefer checks for things like this. She gives a total cost that doesn't surprise me at all, and I'm prepared to make out a check for the whole amount when she continues.

"If that's too much at once, you can split it up into three payments," she says helpfully, looking up and smiling. "So one today, one halfway between today's date and the wedding, and the final payment due the day before the event is usually customary."

My hand pauses, and for some reason I don't quite understand, I'm agreeing to split it into three payments. "Let's do that. You do take checks, right?"

Katelyn nods, smiling. "Of course, Mr. Bennett."

"Right. Of course you do," I reply, writing out the check for one-third of the cost, ensuring that I'll have to make two more payments and admitting to myself that it's so that I can see her again.

Even if nothing can come of it, it's worth the drive to come up here to see this beautiful woman again—and I guess maybe I'm allowed to do a foolish, self-centered thing every once in a damn while.

Just the thought of seeing Katelyn Johnson, events coordinator for the Mountain Spirit Hotel and Resort, two more times gives me a buzz akin to being tipsy.

And though I hate being the slightest bit drunk, the buzz she's giving me feels good.

Good enough to tempt danger . . . two more times.

CHAPTER 3
MARK

The sunset is just fading over the horizon when a now familiar truck pulls up around the back of the house, and the fifth member of our family hops out. Sure, she's not *officially* family yet, but in everything but the letter of the law, she's as much family as any of us.

"Thanks for inviting me to dinner, Mama Lou," Sophie tells Mama, giving her a hug.

All three of us boys are already perched on our seats, ready to dig in with freshly washed hands. Another of Mama's rules, and it's one we always follow. You show up at her table dirty, you just might find yourself eating on the porch. James hops up for a second to pull out Sophie's chair, and Luke rolls his eyes at me.

I lift one eyebrow, letting Luke decide if I'm agreeing with him or telling him to cool it. Truth be told, we all love Sophie, and if James wants to treat her like that even for a casual dinner at home, he's welcome to have at it. He's certainly become more of a gentleman than I ever thought he'd be, and it's sweet. Probably.

If I knew what *sweet* was.

For a moment, my brain replays a flash of Katelyn's pink lips, and I think grimly that she's probably as sweet as Mama's iced tea. But she definitely seemed like the type who would expect manners like pulled-out chairs—and that's decidedly not my style.

I'm not saying that I'm the kind to just grunt at my woman and ignore her unless it's time to eat or fuck, but I certainly am more in the "sit in my lap so everyone knows you're mine" camp.

"Mark, can you say grace?" Mama prompts. It might sound like a question, but she's not asking.

We all bow our heads, and I say the same quick prayer Pops used to say before every meal, the connection to him and the routine somehow more important than the blessed words. As we boys all grab the platter closest and start heaping small mountains of food on our plates, the ladies carry the conversation as usual.

"How are you really feeling?" Mama asks Sophie, concern etched on her face. "You know, with the baby?"

Sophie smiles as James puts his arm around the back of her chair, giving Mama a reassuring smile. "I'm feeling pretty good. Just tired, but in a good way. The nausea seems to have lessened, and those mood swings . . . ugh, I want to apologize again about that. Mostly, I think I'm still trying to adjust to the idea that I'm pregnant."

James smirks like a shithead, as if Sophie being pregnant with his baby is some great accomplishment on *his* part. I mean, props to him for being a major support, but Sophie's got the hard part in this deal. And men and women have been making babies for a million years. It's not like he discovered some new secret to life.

Truth be told, the pregnancy was unexpected, and that's saying something for hardcore planner Sophie.

But it happened, screwing up the one-, five-, and ten-year plans she'd made for James and her pretty damn well. While a family was definitely on the agenda, kids were set to happen *after* she graduated veterinary school.

Except she's got one year left and is already expecting. That's why the wedding that had been on a slow burn as Sophie gathered ideas went wildfire with a deadline of just eight weeks from now. They want it before she goes back to school and before James's rodeo friends hit the fall circuit.

Thankfully, the resort is close, and the owners are practically Sophie's extended family. They would move heaven and earth to take care of her wedding—as soon as James passed her family's inspection. That had been fun to see, watching James meet up with some of the movers and shakers who are going to be his in-laws—and I think more than a few outlaws. I think he'd have rather gotten on the bulls again, buck-ass naked.

Mama was, of course, thrilled at the prospect of being a grandmother, but without her even saying so, we all knew that James had better put a band on Sophie's finger before the baby came, or else. Frankly, if he hadn't, I'm not sure who would have gotten to James first—Mama or the Stone family.

He wasn't hurt at the new rush, though. He's been ready to walk Sophie down the aisle since November when he proposed, and he was more than a bit disappointed when she'd wanted to wait.

Seems he got his way after all. Lucky fucker.

"I did some reading in one of her pregnancy books, and it said that she should eat a pickle every morning before getting out of bed and it'd help with the nausea," James says, still slapping food down on his plate. "So I got her a whole jar, and she's been eating one and boom, no throwing up."

James is smirking again, and I can't tell if he's being serious or if he's underhandedly joking about Sophie eating his *pickle*.

I decide I probably don't want to know. "Glad you're feeling better," I tell Sophie instead, trying to evaluate if I'm hungry enough for a second spoonful of mashed potatoes and deciding I'll pass for now. "How're the wedding plans coming?"

It's an easy question and one that'll likely get Mama and Sophie on a conversational roll that lasts until our plates are cleared. Sophie grins, setting the serving fork for tonight's roast beef aside.

"Going great, actually! I went dress shopping last weekend with Mama, Roxy, and Shayanne. I spent the whole day trying on one after another, but I found *the one*."

James interrupts her, sounding mischievously excited. "Did you pick the one with the poufy skirt or the mermaid one?"

Sophie swats at his thigh and grins, shaking her head as Luke gives me a *what the fuck* look that I shrug off. "I'm not falling for that! And I'm not telling you a thing about the dress that I picked out!"

James laughs, looking eager for any smidgen of information. "Come on, Soph. Just a hint, a little clue? So I'm ready when you come walking down that aisle for me and don't pass out at the first sight of how gorgeous you'll be?"

Oh God, it's getting deep. But Sophie likes it. She bites her lip, thinking. "Okay, one little hint. The dress I got . . ." James nods like a bobblehead, but I can already see the devil in Sophie's eyes. "It's . . . white."

James groans, ignoring his food for a moment to look up to the heavens, almost exactly like Mama does when she's frustrated. "Ugh, I thought you were gonna tell me something I didn't already know."

Luke laughs loudly, entertained by his little brother and his soon-to-be sister-in-law. "I'm trying to figure out just how you know what a mermaid dress is. Um, what is that, anyway?"

James grins, looking smug. "I listen to my girl, and I've seen enough dresses on her Pinterest page to know the difference in a mermaid and an A-line. Just because you're a Neanderthal with no fashion sense doesn't mean I am."

Luke snorts, stabbing his roast beef with his fork and cutting himself a slice. "I know da . . . *darn* well you're as much a caveman as I am. Sophie is just training you right." Quickly moving on from his almost slip of the tongue, he drops Sophie a dramatic wink. "Like potty training a puppy, ain't it? You just gotta keep telling him over and over again, maybe rub his nose in it, like . . . *this* is what I want for the wedding, James."

He says the last words in a high falsetto that I think is supposed to be an imitation of Sophie. Sophie grins even though she sounds nothing like that.

Mama interjects before James can warm up a retort, turning dinner into verbal combat. "That's enough, boys. Sophie, your dress will be perfect, even if you have a little bump by then."

James gets a faraway look in his eyes, and I know he's imagining Sophie in a white dress with a baby belly. His expression is hopeful and almost satisfied, like a man who knows his perfect life isn't complete yet, but he's found perhaps the most important piece of the puzzle. He looks happy, and that's all I could ever hope for for my brother.

Mama turns her attention to me, making me set down my big glass of tea to listen properly. "And, Mark, you got everything all squared away? You weren't too late, were you?"

I look at James and Sophie, who both suddenly look like the cat who ate the canary, Sophie blushing a little. I quirk one eyebrow, barely a movement, but they both see it, and now they know that I know they were up to no good at the resort. I don't care. If they want to get frisky in nature, that's hardly the worst thing in the world—but it's fun to tease them.

That's what brothers do, at least in this family.

"Yes, ma'am. I went and met with Katelyn, the events coordinator. Seems I'd *just* missed James and Sophie, but I got the bill covered. Made the first payment. Next two are scheduled and on my calendar."

Mama frowns, suddenly concerned. "Katelyn? I thought Brianna was handling that? Didn't you meet with her before, Sophie?"

Sophie smiles, probably glad that Mama isn't questioning where she and James disappeared to. "Katelyn's the new events coordinator, Mama. Brianna showed us around a couple of weeks ago, but I talked with her, and she's fully confident in Katelyn taking over. And Katelyn seemed to know what she was doing, so I think we're all good. Right, Mark?"

I grunt something that must sound like agreement, because Mama and Sophie are rambling on again about flowers and cake. Wedding cake talk reminds Mama about dessert, and the ladies hop up to grab tonight's confection, something Sophie taught Mama for once, apparently.

As I'm sniffing, wondering what they've made, James snaps at me, getting my attention. "Hey, thanks for taking care of the reception costs, Mark. No BS."

Mama can't hear, but I still smirk inside that he says *BS* while in her house. He's trained well. I shrug, enjoying the last bit of roast beef and gravy with relish. "No problem, just doing what Pops would've done. You know that."

James nods once, leaning back in his chair. "But why did you break it out into three payments? Thought things were going well around here?"

Shit, I hadn't considered that doing that could trigger a financial concern. I'm surprised Mama let it slide. I've sworn to James a thousand and one times that he's to take that world championship money of his and sock it away for his new family, but he's still worried. I guess it shows how good a man he's grown to be.

"No, man, it's fine. Katelyn just suggested that most folks do that, so that's what I did." I shrug, hoping he'll let it go at that.

But no dice. James is way too sharp to let me pull that line of shit. "Katelyn, huh? She was pretty, wasn't she? I mean, not like my Sophie, but in her own way. Don't you think?"

I can't figure out if he's fishing or just joking. I assume it's innocent because it's kind of accepted that I'm the perpetual bachelor of the Bennett boys. Accepted by everyone but Mama, of course. She has her own feelings on my bachelor status. She wants all the grandkids she can get, but my brothers gave up years ago on me getting married or having kids. Now, looking at the other side of thirty and having the ranch on my shoulders, the odds are getting even longer. I ain't old, but I've got important responsibilities and not much time or inclination for dating.

I let out a faux sigh, really wishing I hadn't opened my damn mouth. "I guess. Didn't really notice. Just paid the bill."

Luke and James both look at me, evaluating my words and measuring my body language. But I'm a hard read for anyone but Mama, even for the people who know me best.

And though my brain is looping the visual of her swinging ass, her hair I want to fist, and her sassy backtalk, they let it go without another word when the ladies come in with dessert.

"Mama, that looks delicious," James says as she cuts what looks like a big lemon meringue pie. "It looks very sweet and . . . blonde."

He looks up, giving me a raised eyebrow. Dammit, he's smarter than I give him credit for.

CHAPTER 4

KATELYN

Friday's finally here, and Marla stands in my doorway, her bag over her shoulder and a big grin on her face. "Hey, Katelyn, first week on the books! How're you feeling?"

She smiles at me, and I can't help but return the grin as I sit back in my chair, replaying the last few days. "Everything's gone well. This weekend's wedding is all set and has a top-notch planner, so I think it should go off without a hitch. And despite my overwhelmingly big mouth, the Bennett–Stone wedding is on the books."

Marla laughs as her eyebrows pull together, and I'm reminded that she wasn't in the office at the time.

"Big mouth? What happened?"

I give her a quick rundown of my brush with Mark Bennett, carefully leaving out how I'd felt wrapped up in his arms. I don't want her to think that maybe I was unprofessional in my first week on the job.

Thankfully, Marla nods and uh-huhs in all the right places, before summing it up in her own unique way. "Well, awkwardness aside, it's booked. So winner winner, chicken dinner! Speaking of, what are you doing for dinner? No offense, but with being new in town, I'm sure it's a bit lonely. Want to grab a bite? It's fine if you don't want to. I know you're my boss and all, but I could show you the local favorites."

The hummingbirds are back in my belly, but this time they feel warm and fuzzy. I haven't really had a chance to meet many people yet, and it feels like Marla is adopting me as a friend.

"I'd love that, actually. And really, Marla, I know it says on paper that I'm your boss, but I'd like us to be a team. Friends, even."

Marla bounces over to my desk, offering a closed fist. "Done deal."

I rap her fist with mine, laughing lightly as she wiggles her fingers and pulls back, whooshing. "Booooom, and Great Falls has a new dynamic duo to deal with. Alright, Katelyn, I'm gonna make a townie out of you yet. First order of business, happy hour and dinner at Hank's."

"I thought most folks did happy hour at the bar here at the resort? Brianna said it's a favorite hangout of tourists and locals."

Marla rolls her eyes, grinning. "Well, yeah—if you're in the upper crust and are used to things like that. Not saying the bar isn't good, but when you really want to get down and see what the working stiffs like us do in town, Hank's is the place to go. You'd fit right in at the bar, but I think you'll like Hank's too. And tonight's ladies' night, so welcome to Great Falls. Drinks are on me."

I'm touched, but I shake my head a little. "Oh, that's so sweet, but you don't have to do that."

Marla lifts an eyebrow, grinning. "I don't offer often, so take me up on it. How about if I buy drinks and you buy dinner?"

Deciding that sounds fair, I nod. "What do they serve?"

"Stuff that'll add five pounds to your ass if you're not careful, but is so delicious that you won't care," Marla declares. "We'll dance off half of it before the night is over, but every time I visit, I make sure I hit the gym the next day, pay my penance in sweat on the treadmill before the carbs stick. Besides, the eye candy inspiration there is rather motivating," she says with a smirk.

I shut off my computer, curious to hear some more of Marla's insights about town. I follow Marla out, touching the brass nameplate on my door just once before hurrying after her. This week I earned that brass tag—maybe not perfectly, but overall things went well enough, and it'll only get better from here.

I'm certain of it.

∾

Marla's right. From the first moment I walk through the front door, I love Hank's.

It's like a stereotypical honky-tonk from a movie, complete with a scarred wood bar that's got a leather pad so you can belly up for as long as you want, along with a blaring jukebox that seems to have everything. As long as it's got guitars, a little dirt under the collar, and an authentic, gritty sound to it, it's there.

The crowd seems to be a good mix too. There are dirt-laden blue-collar guys gathered around a pool table, yelling out bets on shots as they pour another round of beer from a shared pitcher. There are groups of ladies obviously out for an escape on ladies' night, dressed up very clearly either to hang with the girls or to see if they can find themselves a working-class man who knows how to show a woman a good time. A few single folks are scattered here and there, some eyeing the crowd as well, while a few are slowly drowning their sorrows and staring at their drinks more than anything else. And in the corner, a gaggle of guys playing darts are already eyeballing the ladies' night group. I can almost hear them calling dibs, but the women are doing the same, so it seems fair enough.

Marla shoves her way up to the bar and orders us two specials while I find us a place to sit, scoring a rough pine table that looks like it used to be a cable spool for the telephone company. I don't even know what it is when she hands me a pink drink with an umbrella.

I sip at it, surprised at how good it tastes. "Thanks! So you were right, this place is awesome!"

Marla smiles, sipping her own drink. "I knew you'd love it! Wait until everyone gets their first after-work drink in them—that whole area becomes a dance floor."

She gestures to an area that's currently filled with tables and folks chatting, but I can see that the tables there are different, easily moved and turning the center of the place into what could quickly become a very tight dance floor.

I turn back to Marla. "So, what's your story? You said you're a townie?"

Marla nods, grinning. "Yep, grew up right here in Great Falls. The place has changed so fast. We were a small little town not even ten years ago. Still not huge, but it's growing quickly. It's home, so after going to college, I put my business degree to work at the resort. Started on the front desk, and when events got busy enough to need more hands, I applied and have been helping Brianna ever since. Now I'm helping you!"

She smiles, and it seems genuine, but I can't help but wonder something. "How come you didn't want to be the events coordinator? Or . . . did you?"

Crap, if I took her job, it's going to be hella awkward. But Marla is already shaking her head and sipping her drink before answering.

"Hell no, I like just where I am and don't want to change that. There was an in-house applicant, Bethany, but I'm a business girl through and through. Give me spreadsheets, calendars, budgetary constraints, and contracts. Hand-holding bridezillas with cold feet as they demand fresh lobster in the middle of landlocked Great Falls—that's all you."

A laugh bursts out of me totally unbidden, and I feel the lightness in my gut. She's right—event planning can be fun one minute and hair-pulling stressful the next. Just when you think you've seen and heard and done it all, someone will throw something new at you.

"Oh my gosh, that's so true! The craziest request I've ever had was back home when I was doing a wedding and the bride wanted everything to be black besides her dress. Not like a black-and-white wedding, but like a black hole opened up around her white dress. Black linens, plates, utensils, flowers, and the pièce de résistance—she wanted to arrive in a black hot-air balloon against the night sky so it would, and I quote, 'look like she was an angel floating down from the heavens to marry her groom.'"

Marla gawks open-mouthed in shock before pulling it together and laughing. "And did you make it happen?"

I nod, grinning. "I had to call in a few favors and work a few miracles with black rope and lighting to keep the silly thing tethered while maintaining the illusion, *and* I had to pry open her daddy's wallet a hell of a lot, but I did it! And it was fabulous and weird and is actually some of the best pictures in my portfolio. I've always liked the challenge of making someone's dream event come to life, no matter how usual or unusual the dream may be."

I pull out my phone and show Marla the pictures, and she grins, giving me a respectful little toast of her half-empty drink glass. "Okay, I was thinking like Goths on Parade, but that looks elegant and luxe! Way to pull that off somehow."

I smile at the screen, remembering that bride and how I'd grown from the challenge she presented me. "I think these pics helped me get the job here, really. Crazy how things work out."

"So, you were a wedding planner before?"

I shake my head, relaxing some more. "More like event planner, although the bulk of my clients were weddings. But birthday parties, dinners, wakes, bar mitzvahs . . . you want to get a crowd together and want it to be more than a backyard barbecue, I probably pulled it off. I got my degree in hospitality management while I worked for an event planner, learning at her side. When I graduated, I started handling my own events under her umbrella company. So when I heard about this opportunity and it was on the heels of some hard times at home, it seemed . . . I don't know how to describe it. I guess it just seemed right."

Marla cocks her head at me questioningly, leaning in. "Hard times at home? Like, money, family . . . a man?"

I sigh, leaning in farther until we're practically conspiring together. "Okay, friends, right? This is not office talk, so keep it between us, 'kay?"

Marla nods, but I still search her face for any sign of insincerity. It's not that I'm ashamed of my story, or that it's even anything bad, but I'm on the cusp of something here and I don't want to hit any unforeseen bumps because of watercooler chitchat.

Seeing that Marla seems legitimately earnest, I take a deep breath and start. "Okay, here's part one of the Katelyn story, starring me. Just over twenty-eight years ago I was born in Crowley, a small town outside Boise. I dated my high school sweetheart, Seth, all through college. After, we moved in together in an apartment in Boise for work. I guess everyone expected us to get married, move back to Crowley, and start popping out babies."

"Sounds normal so far."

Normal . . . good word for it. "But we just . . . didn't. We settled into this rut, and years slipped past. Seth probably would've proposed if I'd pushed for it, but I didn't. I think I was secretly relieved he wasn't pressuring me."

"Uh-oh," Marla says. "I think I can see where this is going."

"So one morning I woke up and realized I was already closer to thirty than twenty, and we were just . . . meh." I shrug. "I should have seen the warning flags sooner, because neither of us seemed to want more. It was definitely time to get out while the getting's good—and I did. Eventually. This job was kind of the push to challenge the status quo we'd established, and when I started talking about moving here for the opportunity, he didn't want to. I think we both realized that we were better friends than anything more. We'd just stuck together because it was expected and easy, drama-free, but also excitement-free. It's like everything with him was just beige and I didn't realize it. And now that I've been away from it for a bit, I've realized that I really hate beige. I want to live in all the colors of the rainbow, try new things, have new experiences and figure out what I like. Get to know Katelyn, if that makes sense. I feel like I'm twenty-eight years old and don't even know who I am, but I'm going to figure it out."

I smile, the sentiment sitting comfortably in my heart but somehow making it race at the same time, and Marla smiles back, raising her glass. "Well, to new beginnings."

We clink our glasses together and she continues. "That sounds great. The rainbow part, that is. Not the beige stuff. Funnily enough, I married my high school sweetheart, David. But he's definitely not boring. I'll happily climb that man like a tree anytime he walks in the room, or sit and silently stare at a campfire with him for hours. As long as it's with him, it's fun."

I grin at the image of Marla attacking her husband. "David . . . he's cute then?"

Marla snorts and almost spits out her drink, biting her lip. "Hell no, David's hot. At least to me, and that's all that counts. I remember the skinny boy he used to be, but he's grown up the same way I have. My growth has been a little more curvy"—she mimics an hourglass shape—"especially after the babies. But David's thick. He works hard for the county as a lineman, climbs those poles up and down all day, and then comes home sweaty and dirty and like . . . a man. Know what I mean?"

Marla fans herself, and I laugh out loud as I shake my head. "I have no idea. Seth is an engineer and worked in an office every day. But I'll take your word for it."

We chat for a while longer, and I realize the drink is hitting me a little stronger than I'd like. "I need some dinner. Some good carbs to soak up the alcohol. What was in that special?"

Marla smirks and sucks the last drops from her glass. "I don't know—rum and something punchy, I guess. They just call it the Ladies' Night Special. But yeah, let's get some dinner."

The waitress stops by, and Marla asks if she can order me the dinner special, too, promising me that I'll love it.

At first, I consider getting something that I know I'll like, something safe like chicken and veggies, but I realize that that was the old Katelyn. New Katelyn is trying new things, so I tell her to bring it on. Minutes later, I find myself looking at a platter of chicken-fried steak, mashed potatoes, and green beans while drinking a sweet tea laced with bourbon.

I think it's probably the biggest and most delicious meal I've ever had in my life, and I virtually inhale it as Marla tells me a funny story about her twin five-year-old girls' first day of kindergarten.

"And after all those tears and theatrics, by the last day of school, they were hugging their little desk chairs, begging not to leave for the summer. I had to promise them new matching backpacks for first grade to get them out of the building."

I grin, imagining mini-Marlas with matching dark curls shaking as they refused to leave school.

Suddenly, there's a big *thunk* and a pounding noise, and I look over, realizing that, as predicted, the staff is moving a bunch of tables and chairs to line the wall, creating a makeshift dance floor. People are lining up at the jukebox, probably plunking their quarters in as it gets louder, making sure they get their favorite in the playlist before someone puts something stupid in the mix.

"Let's dance! I gotta burn off the calories from that gravy before they find a new home on my ass," Marla jokes as she pulls my hand, dragging me to the floor.

I head out with her, people moving and swaying to the beat immediately surrounding us. It seems everyone was just waiting for the go-ahead to get their groove on.

I lift my arms up, bopping my hips left and right, and smile. I feel good. I feel alive. I feel bright.

Marla and I work our way closer to the center of the floor, enjoying the music. When the opening lines of a new song begin, people partner off to dance to the country tune.

I begin to head back to the table when I feel someone grab my hand. "Hey, honey, dance with me?"

I turn to see a tall, lanky guy looking at me with bright-blue eyes.

He's cute but definitely younger than me, probably part of the bro group I saw when we first came into Hank's. Old Katelyn would politely say no. New Katelyn smiles, though, while Marla drops me an encouraging wink.

"Okay, but I'm not sure I know how."

He grins, all sorts of swagger and confidence. "Way you've been moving your hips, I can teach you in no time."

And he does, gently guiding me and coaching me through the steps. He doesn't ask my name, and I don't ask his. It doesn't matter; we just move around the floor as he softly hums song after song, leading me through the basics and then adding in turns and spins that make me dizzy and bubbly feeling.

I search the floor and find Marla dancing along with another guy, and she waves at me, mouthing, "Okay?"

I nod back and ask her the same. She gives me a thumbs-up and grins.

The next song is slow, sensual, and Blue Eyes pulls me closer, still dancing, but it's more grinding than boot-scooting. Not that I have on boots, of course. I have on my favorite heels, which means that I have to work to keep my balance.

Before I know it, he's shoved one knee between mine, pressing his chest tighter to me. It's not really inappropriate . . . if we were flirting. But I'm not interested in more than dancing. I just went out to have a fun time, and suddenly I feel a bit in over my head. I pull back, putting my hands on his chest and pushing away gently.

"Hey, I think I'm gonna take a break and get a drink. Thanks for the dance."

I try to step away, but he slips a hand to my lower back, his fingers dangerously close to my ass. His voice is whiny, higher than before. "Ah, come on, honey. Don't be like that."

The implication is obvious. As if he has some expectation just because I danced a couple of songs with him. And I'm no longer over-whelmed. I'm pissed at his assumption.

I press my hands to his chest, leaning back and letting my anger show. "Like what?" I ask harshly.

Before I can take a step back or Blue Eyes can answer, a shadow falls over us, and a deep, growly voice says simply, "Enough."

CHAPTER 5

MARK

Two trips into town in one week is damn near enough to piss me off. But it's necessary since we need some parts for an ATV, and of course there's always a hundred other little supplies you just realize you have to have when you get the chance. By the time I get the truck loaded and run a few errands in town, ensuring I won't have to come back for a couple of weeks at least, it's dinnertime. I'm hungry and the heat has me parched, so stopping at Hank's for a bite and a beer sounds like a damn fine idea. Not something I do often, of course. But while I don't like most of town, Hank's is a place I'll visit when I can.

It's pretty crowded given that it's a Friday night, so it takes me a while to see her, the crowd parting like a curtain and shocking me. Katelyn Johnson's here, and she's digging into a plate of food like she's never tasted anything so delicious.

It surprises me, honestly. She looks like the kind of woman who eats rabbit food and then declares that she's "stuffed and couldn't eat another bite." But apparently, she knows the glory of a good chicken-fried steak, and that's one dish Hank's does better than even Mama—though I'd never dare tell her that.

As I work on my own dinner, I can't help but watch Katelyn from the corner of my eye, wondering what she'd do if I went over to say hi. I'm not going to; I know better than that. But I wonder what she'd do if I did.

I see her laughing, gravy dribbled down her lip in a white line reminiscent of something much filthier, and she dabs her napkin at her mouth like a lady.

She's sitting with a brunette who looks a bit older than me, but still early thirties for sure. They seem to be having a good time. No way am I going to go over there and ruin that. I finish my dinner before leaning back and sipping a beer, knowing I should head home to the ranch. If I'm too late, James and Luke will give me the third degree, but I can't leave while she's still sitting there.

As the makeshift dance floor fills, I watch as Katelyn and her friend join the crowd. I can see her, rocking and shifting to the music, and it's sexy as fuck. She's wearing another tight skirt, almost down to her knees, which should make it demure and office appropriate. But with the way she's moving and the way the smooth fabric hugs her ass and hips, I'm fixed in place. I know she's making every man in here imagine sliding that hemline up her thighs to see what kind of panties she has on. Or maybe that's just me?

Fuck. I can't do this. My cock is pulsing in my jeans, and I can't even adjust myself because I'm worried that as soon as I touch my cock, I'm gonna blow like a pubescent boy watching his first titty flick.

I won't allow that. Instead, I need to get out of here and get back to the ranch, back to my day-in, day-out routine where I'm in control and everyone expects me to be the cold, bossy taskmaster. Because that's what I am. The man who keeps shit running by sheer force of will, and that ain't always nice.

I signal the bartender, intending to ask for my check, but then I see Katelyn dancing with some skinny stud, and my mind goes blank.

"Whatcha need, Mark?" the bartender, who knows just about everyone who comes through his doors, asks.

"Another beer," I hear myself say even as my mind says I should be heading out the door. "Draft."

The bartender nods and I turn, watching Katelyn move with the guy. I can't leave now. Not when she might need me. Internally, I smirk at my inner delusional superhero complex. I'm not John Wayne, and she's not Maureen O'Hara. She doesn't need me, but I have a burning need to make sure she's okay. Besides, I already ordered the beer, and I need to take it slow so I can drive home safely.

Everything is fine for a while. They float around the floor, adding a twist here and a turn there. She looks unfamiliar with country dancing, but she's a quick study, and watching her hips swish from side to side as she gets the steps is like watching a hypnotist's watch.

But my fist clenches when I see his hand slipping around her waist as he dips her. It's totally proper, but still, it pisses me off. My hands tighten around my beer mug with the desire to be the one feeling the curve of her hip, hearing her laughter as she spins, being the one who causes her smile.

I take a big drink of my beer, forcing my eyes away for a moment, glaring at the television mindlessly as a reporter recounts the day's news. I stare through the television into space and compel my breathing to slow, my heart rate to decrease.

It works, just like it always does. Calm, controlled, cold—that's me.

The music changes to something unfamiliar, a sort of sleazy tune with a lot of innuendo even before the lyrics start, and I chance a glance back at Katelyn.

It's hard not to thump my beer down on the table when I see that the man has his knee between hers and he's pressed against her, trying to get his grind on. I'm already half off my stool when I realize the look on her face isn't one of pleasure or happiness. She looks uncomfortable, her hands on his chest as she starts to pull away—but he's not letting her. I see their mouths moving, and a flash of anger sweeps her face as she pushes him away.

Before I know what's happening, I'm looming over them, my eyes locked on Katelyn as I snarl, "Enough."

Her eyes pop to mine, the surprise apparent as her mouth rounds and her eyes widen. In the back of my mind, I have a thought that I keep making her look like that. And yeah, I like it—I like it a lot. I relish the fact that I set her off-balance, because so far, she damn sure does the same to me.

From beside me I hear a whiny voice, and I turn my head to see Mr. Stud trying to post up, probably thinking he's going to stand his ground with me.

"What the fuck, man? You trying to cockblock me? We've been dancing all night."

I don't pay him any attention; I'm too focused on Katelyn. I know my eyes are sparking with every bit of the anger I'm feeling, even as I try to squash it down and hide it behind concern, like I'm some fucking friend of hers.

"You done here?" I ask her, trying to keep my voice calm but still strong. She bites her lip, and I swear I see her neck work as she swallows, and I have a split second of doubt. Maybe this is all part of her game with this guy, and I just jumped right in the middle for no damn reason. But then she nods, and I spin her in place, my hand firm on her upper arm guiding her toward the door.

Behind me, I hear the guy shift, his voice dripping with venom. "Cocktease."

I whirl, hot fury rising up inside me like a firestorm. I haven't been in a fight outside screwing around with Luke and James since I was a damn teenager, but I'm this close to knocking this guy out for one rude word.

But this time it's different. This isn't about me—it's about her. I don't even know her. I just know that she's doing something to my insides. Something I both love and hate in equal measure.

The guy puffs up, like he thinks he can take me even though I've got a solid five inches and sixty pounds on him.

"What, you want to start something?" he asks.

I narrow my eyes, ready to uncork one on this asshole's jaw, but I hold back when I feel a gentle hand on mine, coaxing me to relax the fist I didn't realize I'd already made.

"Mark . . ." I look down to Katelyn, whose eyes are filled with questions and something else. Fear maybe? Concern? I'm not sure. But if there's even a chance I'm scaring her, I need to go. That's the last thing I want to do.

I take her arm again and walk her toward the door. I think I see her wave to her friend, but I'm not sure. I don't care, as long as she's out of this place, out of that guy's arms.

Outside, the sun set hours ago and the summer heat is beginning to dissipate. The clear air and quiet seems to still the pulsing fire inside me some, as I'm suddenly overwhelmed with just how star-studded the inky-black night sky is. None of them shine as bright as her damn eyes. As we stop, she looks at me curiously.

"Why—"

"Where's your car?" I ask, still shaky from how she's making me feel.

It must not have been what she expected me to say, because her eyebrows knit together in confusion and she pulls back, tilting her head.

"Huh?"

"Where. Is. Your. Car?" I repeat, my voice deeper than usual. I'm not trying to be a goddamn caveman, but even I can hear that I sound frustrated. I am—but not at her. At myself. And right now, I can't trust myself around her.

Katelyn points toward the door of Hank's, and I worry for a second that she's left her things inside. "It's at work. I rode with Marla. She's my friend. Well, my assistant. But she's my friend too. She's both."

She's rambling, and it's fucking adorable. She needs to stop because I'm already on edge, and I damn sure know at least one good way to shut her up. "How much have you had to drink?" I ask.

She recoils, offended. "I'm not drunk. I only had two drinks, and that's been over the whole night. That guy just went full-steam ahead on a dime—"

I interrupt her by holding up my hand, not wanting to hear about *him* or I'll likely go back inside and interrupt whatever brag session he's likely in the middle of with his buddies. "What I mean is, are you too drunk to drive? Should I take you to your car or take you home?"

I see the instant my words register and the play of thoughts that cross her face. She thinks I'm asking if she's too drunk to consent, and if I take her home would I be able to fuck her. My cock, which had finally relaxed with anger coursing through my veins, hardens again when I see that she's thinking about it, not instantly pushing me away like she did to that bastard inside.

I allow myself a moment of enjoyment before I dash her thoughts. "I just meant to drop you off. I'm not that sort of guy."

Her face flicks between annoyance and confusion, and I'm not sure what she's going to say, if she'll acquiesce and just tell me where to take her or if she's about to verbally skewer me.

The unknown is painful torture, the opposite of everything I want—predictable, expected, restrained. But at the same time, with Katelyn I sort of like it. She's keeping me on edge, and it's a little thrilling.

"Better safe than sorry," she finally says. "Do you mind dropping me at home?"

In my gut, a knot unfurls, somewhere between dread and giddiness at the prospect of seeing where she lives. I don't answer; I just escort her to my truck.

Out of reflex, I check the truck bed to see if the supplies are all there. Nobody would steal them sitting in Hank's parking lot, but I can't help but check.

The reminder that I'm responsible for everything at home weighs me down, giving me a comfortable anchor that lends me steadiness. I help her up into the passenger seat before shutting the door behind her and climbing in the driver's side. I pull out of the lot carefully.

I've got important cargo. I'm not sure if I mean the supplies or the girl, and isn't that some scary shit. She rambles as she gives me directions. Every word, every syllable, sits like a thorn against my skin, a welcome prick of awareness leading to unparalleled softness as her voice fills the cab.

"I've never even country-danced until tonight, and it was going fine until . . . well, you know. I'm so gonna have to text Marla and let her know I'm okay. She's basically my only friend in town, so I don't want to make her worry. Oh God, I don't want her to think I just left the bar with some hot guy . . ."

She stops, looking over at me as she clasps her hand over her mouth. I raise an eyebrow, my face impassive while inside I notice that she just called me hot.

"Sorry," she says after a moment. "I didn't mean it like that. Not that you're not hot, or that there's something wrong with leaving with you, but I just . . . well, I wouldn't normally leave with anyone. And a guy like you . . . I'm just gonna stop, okay? Before I die of embarrassment?"

"Okay," I grunt, still amused.

Katelyn sighs, smiling a little. "Actually, I've never left a bar with anyone. I guess there's a first time for everything." She laughs self-consciously and lets the sentence drift off while I stop at a red light, filing the admission away in my brain, although I'm not sure what for.

It doesn't matter. I'm dropping her off and going home. I'll see her for the next two payments, and that's it. Hell, maybe I'd be better off to just mail one check in for the total balance and skip the whole mess. Be a lot safer.

Safer for *her* anyway, because she's already making me think about things I have no business imagining. I pull up in front of her place, glad to see that it's one of the nice little one-bedrooms that have started to spring up in Great Falls.

Great Falls isn't exactly known for its high crime rate, but since the big pop in growth, it has risen. And of course, the increased tourist trade brings folks in droves, but that's not too bad, because they tend to stick to the hotels and the tourist traps. Katelyn's neighborhood seems well lit, though, everything maintained, and there's an overall vibe of a community that cares.

Silence descends in the cab as I shut my engine off, looking over at her. I don't think she's noticed that I've barely said a word the whole drive over. Her chatter has been plenty for the both of us. But there's a question in the air now, and I don't want to kill it off by getting out and helping her with her door.

Instead, I clear my throat and give her a nod. "Here you are." The expectation that she'll get out, that the night is over, is obvious.

Suddenly, she leans over the console in a quick movement, pressing her lips to my cheek. "Thank you, Mark."

She doesn't say what for—the ride, saving her from the guy at the bar, for not trying to go inside. It's over too fast, but I've already memorized the feel of her lips on my skin and the sound of my name on her breath. She bites her lip unconsciously, making me want to reach across the cab and crush her with a kiss of my own.

"Be careful, Katelyn," I tell her, more growled order than request.

Her head tilts, confusion stealing her soft smile. "I was . . . I was just dancing with him, wasn't even flirting. Then he took advantage and started pressuring me. I can take care of myself," she says, her voice dripping in fury. "I appreciate you stepping in, but I was handling it just fine. I'm a grown woman and can handle an asshole in a bar getting a little handsy. And I definitely don't need some pseudo-Dad lecture about how I should be more careful."

She's riled up now, interpreting my three little words as a lecture. Her cheeks are flushing pinker by the second. I can see the pulse at the side of her throat beating in time with her quickening breath, and I want to suck the skin there, mar it with a bruising kiss so that everyone can see she's been claimed.

She gets out and shuts the door, not quite slamming it, but still a little rough, and stomps up to her door. It has a wreath with roses on it. Of course it does. I watch as she unlocks the door, a newfangled code entry, which reassures me again about her safety. I wait until she's inside before starting my engine. And though she doesn't look back before closing the door, I notice the blinds twitch as I pull away. She was watching.

The twenty-minute drive back out to the ranch feels different. I can still smell the roses from her perfume or shampoo or whatever girly shit she uses. She didn't give me the opportunity to explain myself, which I guess is a good thing.

She didn't understand. I wasn't telling her to be careful about assholes like at Hank's. Or to give her any lecture. She's obviously strong enough that he would have gotten a knee in the balls if I hadn't intervened.

I was warning her to be careful with one particular asshole.

Me.

~~~

"You all set?" I ask Luke the next morning as I toss the last of the sixty-pound bales we're clearing from the loft into the trailer down below. We're hauling hay into the barn, cleaning and filling up the stalls so the horses stay comfortable, and I'm damn appreciative of the distraction because last night keeps replaying in my mind on a loop. A dangerous loop where the ending changes, and when Katelyn kissed my cheek, I didn't warn her off like a semidecent guy. Instead, I turned and kissed her, pulled her into my lap, making that damn skirt ride up her legs so she could straddle me and I could fuck her right there in the cab of my pickup truck.

While I'm lost in the fantasy, I realize Luke is talking to me. I go over and rub Sugarpea's muzzle, grounding myself and playing it cool, being myself. Sugarpea's been my horse for years, and I spoil him rotten, even though Luke is always getting on me about it.

"Hey, buddy," I whisper, reaching into my pocket and offering him his favorite, his namesake. "There you go."

I turn to Luke. "So, you ready?"

Luke nods, grabbing the cutters so we can start spreading the first bale. "Yep, fast trip this time, then a longer one later in the summer."

"Tell me again about this deal," I grunt as I pull on my work gloves and we get to it. I know the basics of what Luke does when he travels, either training or breeding horses for various ranches. But the details of this particular contract have escaped my attention. All I know is how it affects us here at the ranch. That's my domain. Whatever horseshit Luke is doing is solely his. But talking helps the work go faster and keeps Luke's attention solidly off me.

Luke sighs, tossing a big handful down into Duster's stall. Duster was Pops's favorite horse, and he always enjoyed a good ride around the pastures. He's semiretired now, allowed to run free because Luke is the only one who can get on him. The rest of us can't bear it. But we make up for it by feeding him apples and carrots, and he's started to look just a little too full, hovering between healthy and fat. But Duster's earned it.

"I'm driving out after lunch," Luke says, rubbing Duster's nose before continuing. "I'm heading to the SRT Ranch in Colorado for about a week to check the prospects on a Thoroughbred I helped them with last year. If the horse seems suitable to race, I'll have to go back next month for about two weeks to set up his training program."

"You think he'll be any good?" I ask casually.

"He damn well better be," Luke says with a laugh. "I'm the one who picked the stallion for their mare. This is the culmination of all the planning we did two years ago, and part of my great experiment."

Luke sounds like a mad scientist mixed with a proud father. To be honest, what he does is equal measures science and art, and far beyond my comprehension. But he does feel a responsibility to help those horses be their best, to make sure they're cared for appropriately, and to get their owners bang for their buck—because owning a Thoroughbred is an expensive endeavor.

I would know because we own two retired racehorses, ones that Luke selected to use as studs here at the Bennett ranch. He's the one who decides if a mare is suitable and handles the "guest visits" during breeding season.

But between the fees he charges to breed mares and his consultation costs when he travels to other ranches, his program is a big prop for our bottom line.

"Well, if you picked right, and I'm sure you did, I'm thinking you'll be heading back for that second visit." It's as big of a compliment as I'm prone to give.

Luke grins, giving me a big wink. "Yep. Shouldn't interfere with wedding stuff either way. I'll be here to help with whatever James and Sophie want me to do. And Carson can help with whatever you need on the ranch. He's a good worker."

I purse my lips, thinking about our new ranch hand. "Carson does more than you and James put together, and we both know it. As for the wedding, you ain't gonna do shit. But that's fine, I'll handle it."

He grins at the teasing dig, flipping me off. "You know damn well I outwork Carson."

"Well hell, I ain't even doing that much for the wedding, if I'm honest, just writing a few checks," I admit. "Sophie seems to have enough help with Mama, Roxy, and Shayanne."

James comes strolling in, still looking fresh as a fucking daisy with a big grin spread wide across his face. "Y'all talking about my lovely bride? Lord knows, I can't stop talking about her. Have you seen her ass in those jeans she wears? Wait, don't answer that."

Luke tosses a pitchforkful of hay at James, making it rain yellow bits and dust all around him in a cloud. "Your sense of irony—and libido—has no bounds, dumbass."

James quickly covers his mouth and nose, scooting out of the way. "Asshole. What the hell was that for?"

Luke laughs at the few strands of straw stuck in James's hair and keeps spreading hay. "Just making it look like you've worked a bit, that's all. And if Soph heard you talking about her ass, she'd have your hide."

James shakes his head, pulling on a set of gloves to get to work. "Naw, she'd get all riled up and pink-cheeked yelling at me for being improper. I'd apologize and bat my baby blues at her, and then we'd have makeup sex. Hell, sometimes I say stupid shit just to get to the makeup sex."

He's just mouthing off, showboating in jest, because if there's one thing James does damn well, it's make Sophie happy. And vice versa. For a long time, I thought James was going to be our wild child forever, but there is nobody in the world who understands him the way Sophie does. But I'm certain she could do a damn bit better than my youngest brother—and brothers don't let each other forget shit like that.

"We were talking about how we can't believe she's gonna marry you," I deadpan. "I mean, she *is* studying to be a vet . . . but vets don't marry horses' asses that often. I figure that's why you got her pregnant and are rushing to put a ring on it before she comes to her senses."

If anyone else heard me say that, they'd think I was serious and putting my brother down fiercely. He knows better, having grown up with me his whole life.

"Fuck you, Mark," he says with a laugh, shoving my shoulder. I don't budge, not because he didn't put some muscle into it, but because it'll be a cold day in hell before I let my little brother push me around, even jokingly. And I do have a few pounds on him. Still smiling, he sobers a bit, looking at the two of us. "For real, though, don't talk like that in front of her. She's nervous people are gonna think it's a shotgun wedding or some shit, like she's tricking me into marrying her. As if I haven't been trying to run her down the aisle already."

I nod, clapping him on the shoulder. "You know I wouldn't. This is just barn shit between the three of us. As far as I'm concerned, you're already Sophie's problem. She took you off my hands when she said yes."

James smiles, hearing the love in the backhanded compliment as intended. It's what we do, how we communicate as brothers. Giving each other a hard time somehow translates into "I love you, man" more than any nice words could explain. It's a weird camaraderie, but it works.

"We were really just saying that all we need to do is show up and look pretty," Luke adds, grinning. "The women seem to have everything handled."

"Well, I'll damn sure be looking pretty up at the altar. I guess you two will just have to do your best, considering what you've got to work with."

He points at us as he shakes his head, schooling his face to look sad as he flicks his eyes between the two of us like we're ugly as fuck. I look to Luke, giving him the slightest chin lift, but he reads it perfectly.

Faster than a flash, I reach over to flick James's ear hard, and he cries out, slapping his palm over the side of his head. And just as planned, Luke rains hay down on him again.

Yeah, brotherly love.

CHAPTER 6

KATELYN

There are days when I hate having open schedules, since that means no appointments, and no appointments means boring drudge work.

This time, though, I'm thanking God for an easy Monday. Marla and I have been discussing our Friday night out for over an hour. The coffee's done, the muffins are eaten, and now we're just stuffing envelopes for the promotional materials we're going to send out later this week for the state bridal expo.

"No, I didn't know the guy you were dancing with," Marla says as she pairs up the wedding service flyer with the introduction letters we're sending out. "My dance partner was a friend of David's, so nothing awkward there since I know his wife and our kids have playdates on the regular. But, uh, honey . . . I hate to tell you this, but everyone was talking about the new girl in town who got Stone Cold Mark Bennett off his barstool. That is *unprecedented*." She shakes her head like she can't believe it.

"Shit. Being a part of the gossip grapevine is not how I planned on ending my first week of work! Wait, what do you mean, 'Stone Cold Mark Bennett'?"

Marla grins, setting another packet aside. "Didn't you notice? That man has about as much emotion as a brick wall. I don't know if I've ever seen him smile. Ever. Come to think of it, I don't know if I've seen him frown either. He's just . . . steady."

She holds her hand flat, moving it in a straight line through the air.

I have no idea what she's talking about, remembering the man I shared a ride with in his truck. "Mark Bennett, emotionless? Are you serious? He's like a volcano on the verge of eruption."

Marla smirks, shaking her head. "You must have let those drinks go to your head, Katelyn. He's cold as ice, zero heat in that man. Just a blah, boring Boy Scout."

"We might have to agree to disagree on this one. He's quiet, for sure, but I think he says more with one eyebrow lift than most guys say in a whole sentence."

"Does this mean you're gonna see him again?" Marla asks, grinning. "The grapevine wants to know."

She mimes holding a microphone to my mouth, waiting for my answer. I push her hand away, grinning. "Well, I'll have to for their wedding payments. Which is going to be awkward as hell because in addition to my previous lack of grace, I kind of went off on him."

Marla gasps, stopping her work to fully turn to me. "You went off on him? In the good way or the bad way?"

I laugh. "The bad way, unfortunately. He told me to be careful, and I was still a bit prickly about being rescued, I guess. I don't want to be that girl, you know? Now that I'm on my own, I want to handle my own shit. I'm no damsel in distress, so while what he did was sweet and appreciated in the moment, when he reminded me about it, it made me feel like he was reprimanding me or something."

Marla hums thoughtfully, starting to work again. "Hmm . . . I can see that. Guess part of it is the situation he's in. He's the one who runs the family ranch. It's sort of all on his shoulders. But I wouldn't be surprised if you see him sooner rather than later, though."

"Why's that?" I ask, and Marla laughs.

"Come on, Katelyn—Mark Bennett finally shows he's something besides a stoic Iceman, toward you, and you wonder why? I don't know of a single woman in town that he's dated, and not for lack of women throwing themselves at him . . . because have you seen him?"

She grins conspiratorially, raising an eyebrow. I can't help but sigh, my memory replaying the way he looked down at me, his intense stormy eyes and his hard jaw. He'd been projecting power, not by his size, although he's formidable, but in a sheer aura of dominance.

Still, his hand had been gentle on my arm, and he'd reined himself in at my soft touch to his rough hand. And the entire time we were alone, he might have been a bit gruff, but he was always a perfect gentleman.

"Point taken."

"For a while, there was talk that maybe he swung the other way," Marla says. "But mostly I think the consensus is just that he's a cowboy monk."

I laugh at that because Mark practically oozes sexuality. I have no doubt, regardless of who he has or hasn't dated, that man would know his way around my body and could probably coax orgasms from me by sheer demand.

"Pretty sure that's not true. But I'm also almost certain that I sent him running back to the ranch to get away from the maniac who hollered at him after he saved her and gave her a ride home."

Marla shrugs, but I can tell she doesn't quite agree with me. "I'll still bet you'll see him sooner rather than later. I'm just saying, Mark's a tough nut to crack, but I'm curious what's underneath that shell, and I think you might be just the *nutcracker* he needs." We both burst out in giggles at her words.

The phone rings, and I nod to Marla. "Sorry, I need to take this."

She nods back and walks out, and I answer the phone. I'm immediately on alert because the bride on the other end is talking fast and breathless, obviously excited about her new idea, a "stroke of genius" she's calling it.

"I'm sorry, you'd like to take your portraits with what?" I ask in total surprise into the phone.

I sit back, my pen frozen without a single note on the pad. The bride squeals a bit, her exuberance palpable through the line. "I said I want horses. I'm coming for a destination wedding, and Great Falls is known for its outdoorsy, country nature, so . . . horses, of courses!"

"That does sound like a unique perspective. Let me look into local options for that and get back with you as soon as possible," I reply, dipping into my bag of customer service tricks. Never say no, especially not outright. Even with unusual requests, I can often talk clients down with a dose of reality, whether it's time, location, or financial restraints.

If they still insist, I still don't say no. I just explain that, of course, you can have elephants at your event, but the closest ones available are over a thousand miles away, and the fees for travel plus appearance costs are rather high. Oh, and they might take an elephant-size dump on the red carpet after eating the flowers.

Suddenly, the client goes from bossy demands to shocked dismissal of the crazy idea, and I come out smelling like a rose because I was the one willing to do whatever it took to make their dream a reality. And yes, I actually had a discussion about elephants once for a birthday party.

Horses are a new one for me, though. But since Great Falls is a town surrounded by ranches, maybe it's actually doable.

"Hey, Marla!" I yell through the open door as soon as I hang up. "Need your brain!"

She rolls into view, still perched in her office chair. "Yes?"

"So, Miss Wilson was just on the phone. She wants to do her formal pics with live horses, on a ranch. Something about sitting sideways bareback so her skirt fans out, some sunset ones with her and the groom sitting on a wooden fence in silhouette, stuff like that. Any ideas?"

Marla hums, and then her face lights up like a Christmas tree as she claps. "I know who you can ask! Oh, this is just too good. You'll love it!"

"Who?" I ask warily as she gets a glint in her eye.

"Mark Bennett!" she says. "He's your man!"

I'm already shaking my head no, about the idea or him being "my man" I'm not sure, but she runs right over my argument.

"No, for real. He runs the Bennett ranch, and Luke Bennett, that's his brother, is like a magician with horses. They've got a bunch of them, good work horses for the most part. But last I heard they've got some actual racehorses. Miss Wilson would eat that shit up with a spoon if you can deliver, not just horses, but real Thoroughbreds."

Shit. She's right.

"I can't just call up Mark after making such a fool of myself at Hank's. There's got to be someone else with some nice, pretty horses."

Marla shakes her head, grinning almost evilly. "Nope, the Bennett ranch is what you need. Everyone else around here is about cattle and sheep. I recommend starting with an apology. Ooh, and some muffins or something. Like a peace offering?"

I bite my lip, feeling choiceless. "But giving a peace offering and an apology before asking for a favor is pretty piss-poor form, don't you think?"

Marla shrugs, and I understand what she's trying to say. "Well, it's not really a favor, exactly. It's a job offer. I mean, you'll look good for getting the client what she wants, but the Bennetts are the ones who will get paid for the time and the horses' appearance, right?"

That's believable, I think. Or maybe I just want an excuse to see Mark again, to apologize but also just to see him.

I still hate that he's managed to catch me at my worst two times in a row, both literally knocking me over and having to catch me and then saving me from grabby hands at the bar, but I'll admit that he's been on my mind more than I'd like.

But if I can keep this professional, just apologize and offer the opportunity, maybe I can get through this, focus on me and forget about him. And his blue eyes, broad shoulders, and iron-hard grabbable ass.

And I definitely need to forget the way his bossy growls echoed in my ears, sending shockwaves straight to my pussy.

Marla grins, seeing my internal decision. "So, should I get the directions for you?"

～

I'm still trying to decide if this is a good idea or the stupidest thing I've ever done when I pull up to the address Marla gave me. First off, I'm on a dirt road, in a little car that should never, ever be taken off road. Second, I'm still in my work clothes, and I don't think high heels are de rigueur for areas like this.

The gate to the Bennett ranch is open, but I stop. I don't know the protocol here. Should I drive on in and follow the gravel path to the house? Or should I call first? But there's no gate box, and Marla didn't give me the Bennetts' phone number since she assured me that visitors would be welcome.

"Katelyn, they're old-fashioned, and most folks here have an open-porch policy," she explained as she shooed me out. "Strangers and neutrals get invited onto the porch. Enemies . . . the dooryard. Friends? Oh, you're gonna get invited in for a glass of tea at least. So just go."

Uncertain, I pull across the cattle guard slowly, the pipes rattling my little car so much I place my hand on the bakery box in the passenger seat, keeping it secure. No use going to the trouble of getting some of the best baked goods in town just to bounce them all over the inside of the box.

I don't see anyone or anything for a few seconds, and then I crest a small hill. It's beautiful, like a scene out of a cowboy movie, with a house in the front and a couple of buildings spread out behind it, including a quaint-looking old-fashioned red barn. I follow the dirt road slowly, pulling around the house, remembering the times I had neighbors like this around Boise. They might have an open-porch policy, but there's still wariness for folks who aren't local and a double dose of that for townies. I'm pretty sure I qualify as both.

I've barely stopped when the door of the house opens and an older woman comes out, wiping her hands on a towel. I smile at her as I wave, taking in her dirty-blonde hair, lined face, and thin jeans-clad frame. She's definitely Mark's mother; I see the same eyes and the long limbs. Although I guess he got his mile-wide shoulders from his father. But she seems to have that same sort of strength I saw in him, like she's worked hard every day of her life.

I grab the box from the seat and get out. "Hi, Mrs. Bennett? My name's Katelyn Johnson. I'm from up at the resort. How're you today?"

I see a flash in her eyes as her eyebrows jump, but then her face settles into a smile. "Well hello, Miss Katelyn. Please, come on in. Can I get you a glass of tea? Lemonade?" she asks.

"Lemonade would be great. Thank you."

I follow her onto the porch and into what looks like a sort of dining room, taking in the cozy, lived-in feel of the place. It's clean and well kept, but it feels warm and welcoming.

Remembering my manners, I offer her the pink box. "I brought these for you. They're cookies from a bakery on Main Street."

She smiles and peeks in the box, chuckling. "Oh, these are just perfect, dear. My boys will love the chocolate ones later because I made homemade ice cream for dessert tonight. It's been a scorcher, so I didn't want to turn the oven on any longer than I had to."

I nod politely, not sure how to start the conversation I came for even though I practiced the whole way here. Mrs. Bennett seems to notice, and she smiles warmly.

"So, what can I do for you? Not that I don't welcome folks anytime, but I figure you must've come all the way out here for a reason. Is something wrong with James and Sophie's wedding?"

Crap, I didn't think of that. I feel like smacking myself in the forehead, but thankfully I've got a glass of lemonade in my hand, and that would hurt too much.

"Oh no, not at all. Everything is all set for the Bennett–Stone wedding. I came out, uh . . . for something else."

She doesn't take pity on me this time, just waits for me to say whatever I came to say. "Well, you see, I'm the new events coordinator at the resort, and we have a bride who has a rather unusual request, and it's my job to see if I can make her dreams come true."

Mrs. Bennett nods. "Alright, and what's this unusual request?"

"She wants to take her bridal portraits with horses on a real ranch, and the Bennett ranch was recommended. Would that be something you would consider? I hear you have some great horses."

Another customer service trick—create a request sandwich. To do that, you compliment, make your request, and then close with another compliment. But it has to be honest, or it comes off slick and distasteful.

Luckily, this one was a no-brainer because it's all the complete truth.

Mrs. Bennett smiles, leaning back against the counter and nodding. "Well, I'm sure we can work something out. Luke, he's my boy who takes care of the horses, is out of town right now. But seeing as you know James and Mark from the wedding plans, I'm sure they can take you over to the barn to see the horses."

I feel relief wash through me. It's not a done deal yet, but at least she's not saying no automatically. I might actually be able to make this happen.

"That'd be great," I agree eagerly. "I'd love to see them. And maybe I can get some cost estimates for my bride so she can make the final decision?"

She nods her head, then chuckles. "Mark can show you, maybe even get you a ballpark figure. Let me call him and see if he can come up to the house."

Annnnd that's how I find myself sitting here, waiting for Mark to walk in and see me with his mother. I tell myself that I'll know right away by his first reaction if he's mad at me for my explosive rant.

Will his eyebrows rise a centimeter? Will they furrow together as he narrows his eyes at me?

Will he smirk like a cocky bastard that I'm here, chasing him down, even if it's for something innocent like work?

Or is he just going to collapse on the ground in gales of laughter at how out of place I look?

I guess I'll find out.

CHAPTER 7

MARK

Mama didn't say much on the phone. Just asked me to come up to the house for a minute. She didn't sound nervous or upset. If anything, she sounded rather happy, almost like she's got something funny for me to see. If it were James or Luke, I'd be worried, but this is Mama, so whatever it is has to genuinely tickle her for some reason.

I swipe my feet on the mat that's fixed to the bottom step on my way up to the porch and toss my hat on the hook by the back door, wiping my forehead with a bandanna as I go inside.

"Mama? What do you need?" I call before stopping, dumbstruck at the scene before me.

Katelyn is sitting at Mama's kitchen table, sipping lemonade, chill as can be like it's a normal thing. My eyes do a quick scan before I can stop them. She's got on another one of those tight skirts, and I vaguely wonder if she has a whole closetful of the things. I also wonder if I could get her to stand up and do a spin so I can check out her ass, but when I remember who else is in the room, I shut that thought down fast.

"Hey, Mama . . . Katelyn. What's going on?"

Mama is smiling like she's just figured out the answer on the final *Wheel of Fortune* puzzle as her eyes ping-pong back and forth between us. *Oh no . . . no, Mama, it isn't like that.* I can't let her think that. She's going to start scheming on me if she does.

"Mark, thanks for coming in. Seems Katelyn needs a little help with a request from a bride and thought maybe we could be of assistance."

I see Katelyn flinch a little at the summarization. What is it with this woman and not wanting help? Standing on your own two feet is one thing, but asking for help when something's beyond your means isn't bad—it's just the smart thing to do.

"Is that so? How can we help you?" I purposely phrase the question to further get a rise out of her, seeing if I can fluster her a little. She's just so fucking cute when she looks flustered, and it helps me feel more in control when I'm damn sure not.

Thankfully, she smiles, but it feels forced, like a professional habit more than a real smile. She explains the situation with her bride, and I nod, scratching along my jaw, feeling the near five-o'clock stubble I've sprouted.

"Yeah, we could probably work something out. I'll have to confirm it with Luke—the horses are his babies. Especially his racing sires. But I'm sure he'll be agreeable to at least Sugarpea and maybe Duster . . ."

My voice trails off, and I see Mama swallow before smiling, nodding as she thinks of Duster getting to "work" some again. Katelyn's oblivious, letting out a sigh of relief as my answer ticks almost all her boxes.

"Thank you," she says, her eyes meeting mine again and her smile more natural. "Truly."

Mama of course sees an opening and pounces. "I told her you could take her over to the barn to see them."

I do narrow my eyes at that, knowing what Mama's trying and wondering if she's maybe seeing more than she should. "Not sure you're really dressed for the barn. Might get yourself dirty."

Her chin lifts defiantly, tempting me to grab it in my hand and pull it back down so she doesn't look so haughty. "I'm sure it's fine. I would love to see them, even if I have to sacrifice my clothes."

She's calling my bluff, and the suddenly horny part of my mind sees the double meaning in her words, even if she didn't mean it that way. And she's challenging me, which despite me wanting to humble her a little does turn me on. I wait a beat to see if she'll give in, but she holds steady.

"Alright then. Let's go."

I stand from the table, and Katelyn follows my lead. It doesn't escape my notice that she does as I order, and I wonder . . . even if she's haughty and contrary, she seems to also be obedient. Is that normal for her?

Mama grabs my attention as I hold the door open for Katelyn, letting her step outside first. I'm a cold asshole, but Mama raised me to be a gentleman, and on occasion I am. "Dinner's at six, Mark," she says, pointing to the clock.

It's just past five now, and I can read what Mama wants. She wants me to invite Katelyn, but I'm hoping I can just tell Mama that Katelyn politely refused and needed to get back to town. A little white lie to save myself a heap of trouble.

"She brought cookies for dessert," Mama adds, and there goes that plan. Mama can read me like a book sometimes, even if most folks can't read me for shit. I guess that comes with the territory after you give birth to a child.

I can read her, too, and her message says I'm not sitting down at her dinner table tonight without bringing Katelyn along.

As we walk across the yard, Katelyn sticks to the length of sidewalk, a concession to her heels and fancy work clothes. She looks woefully out of place. I stay an arm's length away in the grass, but I can still feel the buzz of being so close to her.

Katelyn's eyes bounce around, taking in the ranch that surrounds us. "It's beautiful out here," she says in awe.

I grunt in response. She can't even see the pond from here, or the rolling back paddocks that are my favorite because they overlook the drop valley, which hasn't been developed yet.

After a moment, she snorts, sassing me. "That all you got? *Ungh.*" She mimics the noise I made.

The corners of my lips tilt up slightly at her fire. Most people, women especially, don't even bother responding to my grunts, taking my lack of response as a signal to shut up. Usually, they're not wrong. "Don't have much need for small talk."

"Maybe it wasn't small talk," Katelyn says with a bit of bite. "Maybe I really do think it's beautiful and was just expressing that."

Her voice is quiet, more to herself than to me, but the backtalk makes me warm inside. Of course, on the outside I stay totally impassive. Instead, I hold the barn door open, letting her go in first for a different reason than at the house. This time Mama isn't watching my every move, and I take the opportunity to let my eyes drop down to her ass. Yeah, still perfect and round and begging for my hands.

I clear my throat, and Katelyn's eyes stop their scan of the barn to meet mine. She looks nervous suddenly, and her eyes dart to the side as she works up the guts to say something.

"Hey, I'm sorry for the other night," she finally says softly. "I might've gotten a little carried away. I'm not usually an angry shrew like that, but somehow you've managed to catch me off guard, not just once, but twice. I kinda hate it because I'm not that kind of girl. But I appreciate the ride home and that you stepped in with that guy, even if I was handling it myself."

She smiles at me, a megawatt flash that says everything should be fine now. But it's not quite yet, because her words raise a ton of questions inside me. I walk over to Sugarpea's stall, the gelding already standing at the doorway to wait for me. I rub down his muzzle, and Katelyn stands beside me, watching my every move.

When she reaches out to pet Sugarpea, too, I rest my forearm on the gate, eyeing her. "So . . . what kind of girl are you then?"

Confusion crosses her face, and her hand pauses on Sugarpea's muzzle. I prompt her, "You said you're not that kind of girl . . . so what kind of girl *are* you?"

She sighs, pressing her nose to Sugarpea's in some weird version of an Eskimo kiss like she's done it a hundred times before. It's gutsy— horses do bite, after all—but suddenly I'm jealous of my own damn horse.

"I don't know. I'm just not the damsel in distress who needs saving. I want to be . . . stronger than that."

I'm not sure that was the word she was looking for. It seems like she searched her brain and settled for it rather than finding exactly what she wanted to describe herself.

"Didn't you say you're new in town, new to your job?" I ask.

"Yeah," she answers, her eyes and hands still focused on the horse. "Been here almost a month."

"Seems like you're strong to me. Takes guts to move to a new place for a new job."

Her hands drop and she turns to look at me, her beautiful face glowing from the praise. A deep part of me likes that I can have such an impact on her. She holds my gaze for a long moment.

"Thank you," she finally responds, her voice soft, like the compliment means something to her. "That might be the nicest thing someone's told me in a really long time."

"Want me to tell you more nice things?" I deadpan, bumping her with my shoulder and giving her the barest hint of a smile.

She gapes at me, then giggles. "Oh my God, did you just make a joke?"

I mock glare at her, hoping she can see the spark of teasing in my eyes. It's a test. I know it is. Most folks don't bother to look much beyond the fact that I'm not all smiles with an over-the-top personality like my little brothers. They dismiss me as mean and intimidating or cold and boring. I wonder . . . does she see that? Or does she see something more?

Fuck, I want her to see me.

It's a dangerous and scary desire, for both of us.

Finally, Katelyn laughs out loud, a full belly laugh that sounds like an explosion of happiness. "You did! Holy shit, you do have a sense of humor!"

Her teasing feels good, and before I know it, I feel my cheeks pulling up a tiny bit, and I'm unable to stop their progress. Katelyn takes a step back, her hands going to her chest like she's in shock, maybe even having a heart attack.

"And he smiles too! Will wonders never cease?"

"Maybe I was just seeing if you were really fishing for compliments. If you need some flattering words, I can definitely give you some," I reply. I mean it to continue the teasing banter we've got rolling, enjoying the lightheartedness, but my words hit with weight, and the tension is suddenly strung tight between us. Katelyn lowers her hands, backing against the wall next to the stall as I close Sugarpea's door.

"Like what?" she whispers on a soft feminine breath.

Never one to shy from the truth, whether pretty or ugly, I turn to face her fully, placing a hand on the post next to her and studying those beautiful eyes, knowing no matter what I'm going to tell the truth. That's my way.

"You're beautiful . . . ," I start, mentally preparing a list of her finer attributes.

She interrupts, sparks in her eyes. "You said that was small talk when I said it."

"It's not small talk when I mean it," I say with a low growl, boring into her with my eyes and making her mouth snap shut in shock. "As I was saying, you're beautiful, all Barbie-blonde and big-eyed, strutting around in those ridiculous heels I'm starting to like. You smell like roses, deep and layered and soft, feminine to the core and enchanting. But you're sassy as fuck, something that should irritate me, but I find myself enjoying it for some reason. You're smart—otherwise you wouldn't be in charge at work. And yeah, you're strong. Moving to a new place and starting a new job takes guts, and handling assholes like me with no problem takes even more. And if we're being honest here"—I pause, taking a moment to inhale, opening myself more—"I bumped you with the door, so that's on me, not you. And yes, you could've handled that guy at Hank's just fine, and I know it. I just couldn't stand his hands on you anymore. So I accept your apology for yelling, but I'm sorry for losing my control and not letting you deal with that situation the way you wanted."

It's more words than I've strung together in ages, but it's not enough. I feel like I barely know her and am just scraping the surface of all the ways she's amazing, and there's so much more of me that I want her to see too.

But getting deeper is dangerous. I'm not the type of man who can give her all the sweet romance she wants. I'm not the type to bring a girl flowers or to wake her up in the morning with soft kisses. I'm not that kind of man, and no matter what I might feel for her, I never will be. I know better than to chase her, even more so to tempt her to want something I can't give.

But she deserves the truth, at least, and that I will always give.

Katelyn's eyes shimmer, and she swallows, her lower lip trembling before she answers. "Wow. That was . . . wow. Thank you. I think I needed that more than I realized. I don't know what to say, but thank you."

She chews her lip, and I'm dying to know what she's thinking, so I wait her out. Finally, she puts a hand on my chest, and I read her, taking a step back and giving her some space.

"I'm trying really hard to be strong," she says, pacing for a moment before going over to the simple bench along the wall and sitting down. She's not quite perching ladylike—her knees are spread a little—but I do my best to keep my eyes from following the small length of thigh visible, considering if she's wearing white or pink panties . . . or maybe a sexy red. "It's not something I'm used to, but I think I'm doing pretty damn well. But I'll admit, since we're being honest and all, that having a big, strong man swoop in like some powerful knight in shining armor to save me, defending me against a jerk, was . . . nice. Sweet. I don't have all the words, but I liked it. A lot. And that kind of pisses me off."

I huff a small chuckle, and she cuts her eyes to me, those sparkling blue diamonds flashing as one part of what I said dawns on her.

"Why didn't you like his hands on me? And what's wrong with my shoes?"

Her questions, one seemingly obvious and one superficial, are both penetrating, and I find myself suddenly uncomfortable, risking revealing more of myself than I'm sure I can. I clear my throat, but my voice is still husky as I squat down, looking her square in the eyes.

"You know why, princess," I reply, not giving her a chance to take it all in before I launch into her second question. "As for your heels, they're impractical, like you're putting yourself at a disadvantage in favor of wobbling around with your long legs and ass on display. I hate them."

She smirks, and I already don't want to hear her next words. She singsongs, like we're five years old or some shit, "You said you're starting to like them."

I grumble, wondering how it is this woman makes me feel like I'm getting hit in the head every time she speaks. "I fucking love them," I admit. "That's *why* I hate them."

She looks down at her shoes, charcoal-gray suede pumps, turning them this way and that, like she's trying to figure out what I see in them and why they offend me so much.

"Come on," I finally say, standing up and turning around. "Let me show you the rest of the horses."

It feels like we've really made up from whatever tiff she imagined happened on Friday night, but there's more between us, some unspoken swirl of magnetism pulling me toward her even as I try to repel her.

She needs to get away from me, run far and fast, before I sully her bright new start with my working hands and dark thoughts. I know better than to test myself. There's no need, because I know exactly where my breaking point is.

And while I've been able to keep most folks at arm's length and any women far from that boundary, Katelyn is charging in, completely unaware that she's accidentally jumped into the deep end of my desire. And I'm doing what I can to dissuade her, but my fucking mouth keeps spouting off without restraint.

It's easier chatter as I tell her about the horses in the barn, comfortable as she asks questions about their temperaments and how they'd handle taking pictures with a stranger in a big white gown. She smiles at the horses, scratching along their necks, and it tells me about her.

Horses are smarter than most people know, being so high strung, and if so many horses take to her so quickly, she's got to have a lot of good inside. She just knows how to connect to every horse automatically, her nails making me imagine them raking down my back as she holds on for dear life while I ride her hard.

"Want to see Luke's pride-and-joy babies?" I ask her, desperate for a change of venue before I throw her over a bale of hay. My cock's straining my jeans, and I have to constantly shift to not broadcast what she's doing to me.

She bites her lip and nods excitedly. "If they're half as beautiful as these horses, I wouldn't miss it for the world."

"They're out in the east pasture. We can take the Gator out since you're not dressed to ride."

She looks offended, her jaw jutting out as her head tilts. Before she can say a word of argument, my mouth pops off, dangerously unfiltered for a change.

"If you ride in that skirt, it's gonna hike up so far the whole ranch will see your panties. That what you want?"

She should slap the shit out of me for saying something so crude when we don't even know each other, and I'm half expecting the sharp sting or at least a screech of her yelling. Who knows, maybe it'll be enough for her to do the smart thing and get her shapely ass into her car and send her spraying pebbles all the way back to the main road.

Instead, she only lets out a little squeak of noise, and I can't decide if she's shocked, offended, or if she liked me talking about her panties. Finally, she shakes her head.

"No, the Gator is fine."

CHAPTER 8
KATELYN

It turns out that a Gator is an ATV version of a golf cart, two-seater but more workhorse utility than Sunday tee time. I hadn't known, but after Mark's teasing and intensity, I damn sure wasn't gonna ask when all I could think about was flashing my panties to him on the way out to the pasture.

Oh, and the whole ranch, too, but mostly just to him. He could have had the entire town lined up along the road and I wouldn't have noticed, with the way he looks at me.

He's intense, just so fucking intense. Our conversation in the barn felt like the most influential moment of my life, but I've barely met the man. There's just something about him that seems to make every word, every microexpression loaded with layers of meaning, and with those layers he draws me in like a moth to a flame.

The drive across the various fields is breathtaking as Mark tells me the story of how it became his family ranch.

"So Pops was just a ranch hand, should've been on his way at the end of the season, but he met Mama in the diner where she worked as a waitress. He scrimped and saved every penny, worked his ass off for years, and bought this ranch for her. It was small then, just some land.

They didn't even have a house. But she moved here with him, sight unseen. He proposed under that big tree in the front."

He swallows hard, and I think there's more to that story, but he spins the tale off another way and I let him, not wanting to push too hard and happy just to let the rumble of his voice wash over me.

"They worked hard, bought every acre of land they could, and this is what they built. It hasn't always been easy, but the Bennett ranch is one of the largest family-owned ranches left in the area. Everyone larger is corporate."

He looks around proudly, and I look, too, taking in the waves of green grass as far as the eye can see, the wire fences the only thing breaking up the panorama until the green meets the line of blue sky far in the distance.

"I don't think I've ever seen anything this wide open before," I say honestly. "I want to run through the hills with my arms open and catch the space, let it fill me up and surround me. It feels free out here. Maybe that sounds stupid . . . I should shut up now."

He looks at me, seemingly surprised. "I think that sounds pretty accurate. I sometimes get caught up in the day-to-day grind of running this place, but I do one thing that helps. Every morning at sunrise, I stop whatever I'm doing, wherever I am, and just watch. The back porch is my favorite, but the view from the hayloft is great too. It feels like a fresh start every time. A chance to do better, appreciate more, take care of Pops's legacy."

"Oh, your dad passed away?" I reply, realizing that Marla had said Mark led the ranch, but I hadn't realized the implications of that. "I'm so sorry. The way you talked about him, I thought we might run into him out here somewhere."

He nods slowly, looking toward the hill off to our left. "Me too. Doesn't feel real sometimes, even though he passed away a little over a year ago. I ran the ranch side by side with him for almost ten years, slowly taking over more of the ropes as he'd let me. Now it's on me, taking care of Mama and my brothers, keeping the family strong and making sure Pops's legacy doesn't crumble. We're living out his dream here."

Something in his phrasing of that feels important, raising more questions in my mind. I'm chasing my dream by moving to Great Falls, so for Mark to call this his dad's dream strikes me as sad.

"What about you, though? What's *your* dream? Did little boy Mark always see himself here, running a ranch? Or did you want to be a fireman or astronaut or something crazy?"

He lifts one eyebrow, chuckling. "Nah, this was it for me. I knew that, even in kindergarten when Ms. Zeneker asked what we wanted to be when we grew up. I always said I wanted to be my Pops. A rancher."

I study him closely, trying to imagine this huge mountain of a man, so serious and confident, as a young kid excited about riding his first horse.

I can't see it. He seems like he just sprang forth, fully grown and mature and responsible, settled on a horse, with dusty boots, a slightly worn hat, and his hands already calloused from hard work. He looks like the sort of man who, from minute one, took the weight of the world on his shoulders because he was built to bear it.

"I think I'll need to see some proof that this mini-Mark existed, ranching in his blood as a little boy," I finally say with a giggle. "A pic will do."

I see him hold back a smile, the corner of his mouth twitching, and just like that, earning a full-fledged smile from this stoic man becomes my mission.

"Don't say that around Mama, or she'll pull out baby books for all three of us hellions. You'll never escape."

He says it like it's a dire warning in an old documentary from the fifties or something, but I can hear the joke in his tone. It's subtle, like the difference between ninety and ninety-five degrees. But it's there. I'm getting better at reading him.

"Maybe I don't want to escape," I toss back with a wink. "Maybe I'll just stay here forever."

The tease is a thoughtless response to his comment, but even as the words leave my mouth, I realize I went too far. We both close our mouths, my teeth worrying my lip while his lips are pressed into a tight line. He studies the horizon, his eyes squinting a little as he stares into the distance. The lightness evaporates in the open air around us, heaviness descending over us once again.

We're quiet as we ride out even farther, and I consider asking questions about the ranch again to get us back on track for polite conversation, but it seems superficial after everything else. Instead, I try to focus on the good feeling, scavenging something from the afternoon sunlight and the light breeze, letting the silence stretch.

We reach a lush green pasture, the fences making it smaller than the others, and Mark pulls to a stop, shutting off the engine before climbing out and whistling sharply, the note piercing the air.

Two horses turn and walk over, tossing their heads. I marvel at how beautiful they are. Mark reaches into a small bag at the back of the Gator and pulls out what looks like a granola bar, breaking it in half before holding the pieces out, his arms wide.

"They're gorgeous," I murmur, reaching out carefully.

Mark looks on approvingly as I rub one downy-soft muzzle. "This is Demon's Revenge and Cobalt Mist. They're retired, and Luke's studs. They're his babies."

I hum, rubbing Cobalt Mist's side. "Their names are poetic. Is that normal?"

"Couldn't tell you. But these two had already been registered under those names when we got them, and Luke kept them that way. Around here, we mostly call them Demon and Cobie."

Demon is a huge animal, much like I dreamed the Black Stallion was as a girl when I read the book. His coat is shiny and black, matching his eyes, and I know Miss Wilson's white gown will look stunning next to him. Cobie is a silvery-gray color, giving a softer look to his countenance as he looks at us with bluish eyes.

"Luke can tell you more about them than I ever could, but I know Demon was a helluva racer," Mark says. "Bred to be that way and didn't disappoint, winning a lot more than not. Cobie, on the other hand, was considered a failed breeding. He's the result of two Thoroughbreds that should've made a winner, but he came out with every recessive gene represented. Still managed to run like a machine and won quite a few races in his older years. Luke felt sorry for the fella I think, but he gets plenty of requests for him as a stud because of his lineage and race results, even with the unusual coat and eye color."

I'm shocked that he's describing such a beautiful creature as a failure. "What do you mean Cobie's a failure? He's gorgeous!"

Mark shrugs, feeding Cobie another bite of granola bar. "Not my words, and he's definitely not to me, just what they say in terms of breeding. Luke knows more than I do, but I know that gray isn't commonly something folks breed for, and blue eyes in horses have lots of myths that are hard to overcome."

"Well, he's stunning, and I think he'll be perfect for the pictures," I declare firmly. "I think gown pictures with Demon would be good, contrast his dark color against the white dress. But for Cobie, I think a misty dawn effect with both bride and groom would be perfect. Miss Wilson is going to love them!"

I look at the horses and scan the big field, the pictures coming to life in my mind, gorgeous and perfect and special. Mark is looking at me like I grew a second head, his hat cocked back slightly.

"What?" I ask, heat rising in my cheeks.

"You see them, don't you?" he asks quietly. "In your head, you can see the pictures like they're already real."

I nod my head, slightly confused. "Well, yeah. That's what I do. Bring people's ideas to life in a way they didn't even realize they wanted."

He half hums, half grunts, turning back to the horses. "You seem good at that."

The way he says it, I'm not sure if he's talking about bridal pictures. A moment later he gives the horses a good pat, shooing them away, and we climb back into the Gator. Pulling a nifty little three-point turn, we start rumbling our way back to the house.

As we crest the last hill leading back toward the house, Mark slows, turning toward me. "So . . . dinner?"

Holy shit, is he asking me out? My inner me jumps around, giddy and clapping for a second before I realize that it's probably not a good idea.

I'm not opposed to dating—definitely not in any mode of rebound after Seth, considering that was such a nonevent of a breakup to begin with—but jumping into something with someone as intense and overpowering as Mark feels like going from the shallow end of life I've been wading in to traversing raging rapids without a life vest.

I have no doubt that I would lose myself in him, happily and mindlessly giving in to his every quiet command. That sounds blissfully easy, but is it what I need to chip away the shaping done by my previous life?

Is that the excitement and experience I've been missing out on? I've been quiet too long, I realize, but Mark is just watching me have an existential crisis in reaction to his simple question, his forearm cocked on the steering wheel, one long leg hanging halfway out of the bare-bones cab. He looks like he could stay here forever, not pressuring me, not rushing me, not making the decision for me.

He sways me with his next words, even though he speaks them casually. "I don't know what Mama is making, but it'll be good. She's a damn fine cook. She said you brought cookies for dessert?"

I feel like such a dork. He wasn't even asking me out, just talking about dinner at his house, and I jumped to all these conclusions, miles ahead of myself. Saving face, I plaster a grin on my face, nodding. "Yeah, that sounds great. Thanks. I brought cookies from the bakery on

Main Street, and she said they'd go good with the ice cream she made for dessert."

It's not until after I say yes that I realize I just agreed to a family dinner. Normally, that seems like it'd be way more important than a simple dinner out with a guy. I mean, meeting the family is usually like step seven, right?

~~

My head still swirls with questions as we pile around the big table. Mrs. Bennett—no, Mama Lou, as she instructs me to call her—is on one end, with James and Sophie on one side, and Mark and I on the other. Luke, the brother I haven't met but have heard so much about, is missing, apparently traveling.

"You're lucky," James says with a chuckle. "He's so ugly he'd ruin your appetite—not that he'd leave anything behind if you don't get the platter first."

"Oh hush, James. Luke's quite handsome," Sophie chastises, giggling. "Don't be jealous of your brother. You already got me."

James chuckles, giving Sophie a kiss on the cheek. "Okay, okay. Still, I'm calling dibs on his cookie."

Everyone joins hands for grace, and I see the boys not lock hands, but put their hands on the back of the big chair at the head of the table. I suspect that it happens nearly every meal. I don't need to be told—it's obviously Pops's chair.

It feels picturesque and sweet as Mark says grace and we begin passing platters around, filling our plates with pan-fried ham steaks, potato salad, and collard greens. It's good, simple, and honest food. Nothing fancy about the looks of it, but it tastes amazing.

I listen raptly as Mark and James talk about the ranch, their conversation about pasture rotation and cattle prices floating over my head, but I enjoy their back-and-forth.

I learn that Sophie is on summer break from vet school and pregnant, something I didn't know, but I file it away. Nerves can set off any bride, but a pregnant one can usually use a few ginger lollipops and flat club soda to help settle her stomach on the big day.

I see that Marla was right about James and Sophie—their love virtually floats around them like little cartoon hearts, tangible to everyone in the room. It's not a show, it's just real, and as the first dishes are cleared away, I suspect that Sophie would've already climbed onto James's lap if I wasn't here.

"So, Katelyn, after you've listened to these two wax poetic for far too long," Mama says, "tell us a little about you. I'd enjoy my dessert more learning about you than hearing about a cow with gas problems. No offense to your rather *productive* day as a vet assistant, Sophie."

Sophie laughs about that, and as we divvy up the cookies and ice cream, I start my story, telling everyone about moving to Great Falls to chase my dream job. Mark looks impressed, even though he's heard most of it already.

"There isn't much else to say," I admit, breaking up a cookie and adding a big scoop of ice cream and some chocolate sauce. "The work part's going well. I'm just excited to get to know more folks in town."

Mama Lou smiles, handing me a silver spoon for my dessert. "Well, you know us now. Welcome, Katelyn."

I grin, wet heat in the corners of my eyes because it feels like she's welcoming me to something much more important than town. "Thank you," I whisper. "All of you. And this looks like the yummiest sundae I've ever seen."

"Well then, dig in!" Mama Lou encourages me with a smile. "Don't let the ice cream get too melted."

In seconds, we're all moaning and groaning in delight, shoveling bite after bite in without even swallowing. Sophie looks like a blissed-out squirrel. "Oh my gosh, sooooo good," she finally says when she remembers to breathe again. "I might need another bowl."

James laughs, looking to Mama. "I think we're gonna need a cookie or two to take home if there's any left. Ice cream, too, if you don't mind."

Mama grins, nodding her head. "Of course, I made extra ice cream for my grandbaby, and you can take all the extra cookies. We don't want Sophie waking up hungry in the middle of the night, now do we?"

James smirks, and something tells me that he doesn't mind Sophie being a bit hungry at two in the morning—just not for ice cream.

Mark rolls his eyes, reading his brother's mind. "James."

The one-word sentence is like a full-blown parental lecture, and James laughs anew. "Mama said it, not me."

Mama looks between the guys, but Sophie gets everyone's attention again, talking with her mouth full. "God, I'm going to be as big as a house!"

James puts his arm around her shoulder, pulling her tight and kissing the top of her head sweetly. "Just more of you to love, darlin'."

It's so tender, so warm, and I think my ovaries just exploded a little from watching them.

After dinner, Mama shoos us out of the kitchen, telling us that she can clean up herself because the boys always put stuff away in the wrong place and then she can never find it.

"I swear those two want me to think I'm senile far before I am!" she says with a smile. "Now go!"

Sophie and James take separate trucks, James grabbing the box of leftover cookies. "I'll take these with me or they'll never make it home."

Sophie pouts for a second, then agrees. "Probably a good call. I'll see you at home, Cowboy?"

They pull out, leaving Mark and me alone beside my car. "This is what you drive."

It's a statement, not a question, but I answer anyway. "Yeah, why?"

Mark shakes his head. "I should've known. Only way a car could be more Barbie is if it was a white Corvette."

I look at my baby, trying to see it through his eyes. I'd saved for years for the down payment, had felt like I'd truly made it when I drove it off the lot, and every time I see it, it makes me happy inside.

"Actually, I'm pretty sure Barbie drove a pink 'Vette. This"—I say, pointing a pink-tipped finger at my white Volkswagen Beetle—"is not a Barbie car."

Mark purses his lips. "Maybe. But it's a girly car, princess. It seems like you."

For some reason, what would come off as an insult from most people feels like a compliment from Mark. "Why do you call me that? If anyone else called me princess, I'd likely break a nail slapping them stupid."

Mark's lips twitch, and he makes an amused snort. "That's why. You're everything soft and feminine, but with a core of strength, ruling your domain with grace. It's foreign to me. Do you want me to stop?"

His voice is low and deep, and it's the first time I've felt like what I say might actually affect what he chooses to do. Most of the time, he just runs roughshod over me, in control of the conversation while I'm struggling to catch up and stay focused on something besides his full mouth and every microexpression. I should keep my mouth shut, but I can't with him, the truth pouring from me before I can stop it.

"I should hate it, it should piss me off, but I like it when you call me *princess*," I confess quietly. It changes the atmosphere between us, the pull instant. Mark moves closer to me, his body inches away from mine as he looks down at me. I lift my chin, my lips parting without conscious thought, wanting him so badly I can feel it deep in my soul.

He's going to kiss me, I know it with every cell in my body, and I lean toward him like he's the sun, knowing he's going to burn me up but not able to stop it.

I lick my lips, preparing, and I see his eyes lock on to the movement. He inhales sharply, his thumb reaching up to trace the wetness, his breath coming out as a deep, unconscious sound of longing that makes me wonder how much passion this man has—and how anyone could see him as icy.

Just before his thumb touches me, so close I can feel the heat from his skin, he pulls back, his voice a dry rumble in my heart. "Princess. Katelyn. I can't. You are everything bright and light, and I'm . . . not. I'm dark and cold, an asshole. I'm sorry. You deserve better . . . different."

He steps away, his shoulders almost shaking, and I can feel the desire coursing through his gut. I know because I'm feeling the same way. Our eyes lock for a moment before he turns and walks toward the house. He doesn't pause, doesn't look back, just leaves me standing alone in his front yard by my girly car.

I think that's the first time he's lied to me, but more troubling is that I think he's lying to himself too.

CHAPTER 9

MARK

My balls are fiery twin pokers of pain stabbing up into my gut as I cross the yard to go inside, I want Katelyn so badly. Still, I don't let myself look back, knowing that whatever emotion is playing on her face will either kill me or piss me off, and will likely lead to me going straight back to her and taking her in my arms. Instead, I walk into the house and shut the door behind me, leaning against the doorframe as I listen for her car to start. Finally, I hear her pull out, and I exhale, breathing through my nose until my body is finally under my control again.

Turning away from the door, I can hear Mama humming in the kitchen as she cleans up, and I head in to see if she needs any help, thankful for the distraction.

"Hey, Mama, can I do anything?" I ask, deciding to brave it. She's wiping down the counters, which are already sparkling clean.

"You can sit down and keep me company while I finish up," she says, smiling over her shoulder while I sprawl out in one of the kitchen chairs, watching her flit around the kitchen. It's something I've seen her do a thousand times, and it always feels like she's dancing to some tune only she can hear.

The normalcy of it is comforting, and I understand why Pops loved doing this too. On the nights he had a lot on his mind, he'd spend an hour in here with Mama, just talking and watching her. Some people learn about love from books or movies; I learned from them.

"So, Katelyn seemed nice, don't you think?" Mama asks, reminding me that while she may dance around the kitchen, she's not one to shy away from getting right down to business. You never have to guess where she stands on anything.

"She is," I agree, grabbing my glass and pouring myself some water. "Nice and sweet, but smart too."

Mama nods, her cloth never stopping as she wipes down the countertops. "Mm-hmm. You two have a good trip out to see Demon and Cobie?"

"Yeah, she thinks the pictures would be great. Luke will have to get her the financials on that, though," I reply. "I don't think he's ever had them do something like that before."

Mama stops her cleaning to turn around, her eyebrows lifted as she gives me a look. Yep, I'm in the doghouse. "That's not what I asked, and you know it. But I think the nonanswer is answer enough."

Mama grins at me, the devil in her eyes as she knows I just exposed more than I'd intended. I sigh, tilting back and looking up at the ceiling, struggling with the words that I *want* to say and the words I *need* to say.

"Mama . . . don't. You know it's not like that," I finally tell her. "We just met. She's a friend and nothing more."

Mama grins at me. "Well, I can tell you that I've never looked at any friend of mine the way you were looking at her."

I give her a pained look, silently praying she'll stop. The prayer goes unanswered as she continues.

"And she was thinking some rather *friendly* thoughts about you, too, if I'm any judge. And just so you know—I am."

"Mama, she might be looking at me as something more, but it's not happening. That's not who I am. I've got enough on my plate with taking care of the ranch. She needs to find her a nice guy in town. Something easy and sweet. Not some asshole cowboy who works from sunup to sundown six and a half days a week." The excuse sounds weak, even to my ears.

Mama leans forward, holding me immobile in her gaze. "First off, language, son. I know I taught you better. Second, don't go putting things off on running the ranch. You're doing a fine job, and I know it's a lot of work, but your daddy managed it while married with you three running around. You could, too, if you'd get your stubborn head outta your ass."

I don't bother pointing out that she just said *ass* because that won't go over too well and I know it, so I don't say anything. But when she doesn't hear any acknowledgment from me, she continues.

"Do you think your daddy and I were in love?"

The question seems out of left field, and my brows shoot together in confusion. "Of course. Everyone knows how much you and Pops loved each other. You could see it just being in the room with you."

Mama glances at Pops's chair, almost as if she can see him sitting there listening in on our conversation. "You're right. That man did love me something fierce, and I loved him back just as much. But that don't mean it was always easy. Your daddy was a stubborn, hardheaded man with a mission, and hell or high water, nothing was gonna get in his way. Least of all me. Lord knows, he led me kicking and screaming into some of the crazy things he did, like letting James run off barely outta high school to join the rodeo or investing way too much money in those racehorses of Luke's. But those crazy things always turned out for the best. Well, most of the time . . ."

Mama stops to chuckle, and I know what she's talking about. When I was ten, Pops decided to try to cash in on the big natural sweetener craze people were going through, and he figured the best way to do that was to keep bees. There was just one problem. After spending more than $1,000 on equipment and gear, Pops discovered that he was seriously allergic to bee stings.

"Those daggum bees. He had those big white coveralls and mesh hat, made him look like a dime-store version of an astronaut."

"I remember," I reply, smiling a little. "I'll never forget when he came running in the first time he got stung, his face all puffy. I swore he was never going to look the same again. After that, he wanted me to help him, but after seeing what happened to him, I was so scared of those bees, I wouldn't even go in the field."

Mama laughs uproariously, tears leaking from her eyes at the silly memory. She wipes her eyes, nodding. "It was bad. I don't think you boys knew, because you were in school when it happened, but he had to get a shot for it the second time. Damn fool was lucky. The doctor said he could've gone into shock. Then he went right out and did it again."

That surprises me, and I lean forward, shaking my head. "I didn't know that."

Mama's smile falls, her tone turning serious again. "I'm sure there's a lot you didn't know. Did you know we fought about you?"

"Me? What did I ever do?" I ask, surprised.

"Nothing, honey. You were a good boy, and that was the point. You were born right here, grew up on this land, and never went anywhere. I told John that wasn't right. You see, I thought he was putting pressure on you to take the reins. You were just a boy, and a boy should be allowed to play some, have stupid dreams and stupid loves and just . . . be stupid from time to time."

"Figured that was James's job most of the time."

Mama doesn't laugh, just sighs, and the sound is almost heartbreaking. "But he could see it in you. Knew you were destined for this life and wanted to make sure you were ready. I think he felt like he could save you some of the growing pains he went through with this place. He knew about ranches, of course, since he was a ranch hand, but working one versus owning and running one are completely different creatures. He tried to make it easy for you, step by step while he was holding your hand. He was right, and you were ready, even though it was sooner than any of us thought."

The compliment feels good, warms my soul that I'm doing Pops proud and fulfilling the lessons he taught me. "I've done my best, Mama."

"I know, but I still wonder if you've been robbed of something somehow. If you'd be different if you'd gotten away for a bit, maybe seen all the world has to offer, experienced life outside this bubble, you know? You'd have still ended up here, I'm sure of it, but maybe you would be different. Maybe married, smiling more and not a man who has the weight of this whole family resting on his shoulders alone. I feel like I should've fought John for you a bit harder."

"Mama, don't," I protest, getting up and putting my hands on her shoulders. "I'm happy here. This is the life I chose. You think Pops didn't tell me to get off the ranch? He and I talked about it a bunch of times, and I knew he would've supported me going anywhere I wanted. But I said no. This is my home, what I'm meant to do and where I'm meant to do it."

She's silent for a moment, stepping away before resting her hands on the back of Pops's chair. "Well, maybe seeing Katelyn today just reminded me that I worry about you. You are an amazing leader for this family, an example for your brothers, and you take care of us all. And you're my firstborn, so I'll always take care of you, you know that. But maybe I wish you had someone to share life with besides us, someone you choose to be on your team, by your side to share the responsibility with. I loved John, and he loved me. That's what made this life here so special. Not the acres of dirt and animals. It was our love and our family. That's the legacy Pops left you, and the one I want you to honor."

Ouch. That hurts, because if that's what I'm supposed to be doing, I'm damn sure not. And don't have any real intention of doing so either.

"Mama, Katelyn is just a friend, and barely even that. It's not like that between us. Like you said, she's nice and new to town, and I'm just trying to be . . . polite. I'm not interested in her like that, and she doesn't like me that way either. I swear it, though, I'm happy here with life just like it is."

Mama twists her lips in that way that tells me she's not convinced, and hell, neither am I. But she lets me go without further argument.

Back at my house, I get a bottle out of the fridge to enjoy one of my other favorite times of the day—the post-dinner beer.

I go out to the back porch, settling back in a chair. Exhaling hard, I watch the moon rise in the dark sky. I sit and sip at my beer.

I stretch my legs out and try to free myself of today's tension. It's harder than normal. Mama's words roll through my head, making me wish for things I can't have. It's not that I don't want a wife, and I have dated a time or two.

But I learned pretty quickly that I'm not relationship material when each girl or woman I got serious with complained about the same things. They might have been drawn to my stoic, quiet demeanor and cowboy mystique, but soon enough, they all grew tired of my grunts and one-word answers. They'd want me to smile and tell funny jokes, to head into town on a regular basis to dance at Hank's, or to get myself all cleaned up and put on a monkey suit to sip wine at a restaurant. They'd expect there to be some give and take.

But I am who I am, and that's not likely to change at this point. I remember reading somewhere that after you hit thirty, the sort of events that'll change you tend to either fall into the realms of death or birth—and I'm not planning on either anytime soon.

I try to picture walking into my little house at the end of a long day, a woman greeting me with a kiss before we sit down at the table for dinner, just the two of us.

The hazy image of a woman is quickly filled in with Katelyn, all fancy clothes and blonde curls with fire in her eyes.

I'd order her to strip, but leave her sexy heels on, and when I tell her to kneel before me, she'd do it without question, her hands automatically crossing behind her back demurely. I'd trace her open lips with my cock, making her wait to suck me until I couldn't delay another second.

And when I allowed it, only then would she take me down her pretty little throat, work me with her tongue as I held her hair to guide her, giving her more with each pass until I was balls deep.

I'd hold her there, watching her so closely for her limit and giving her breath just before she needed it. She'd bob over me as I thrust powerfully to meet her, up and down, again and again until I came down her throat.

Then I'd swoop her up and sit her on my lap, feed her dinner and take care of her. She'd nibble the food from my hand, nipping my fingers, and I'd have to spank her naughty ass until it was pink and hot as she bent over the table.

But I'd kiss it better, before grabbing it firmly in my hands, knowing it'd sting. She'd cry out, pleasure tinged with a hint of pain as she pushed her ass back, begging for more.

And I'd oblige, but not until I pulled her hands tight behind her back, holding her there as she pleaded for me to fuck her. I'd tease her with the head of my once again hard cock, smearing precum all over her pussy before filling her in one smooth stroke, bottoming out as she spasmed around me, coming instantly on my shaft. I'd hold her there, pushed into the kitchen table as I took her roughly, savagely, her feet lifting off the floor with the force of every stroke as I pounded into her.

The fantasy feels real, vibrant in my mind as I imagine claiming Katelyn like a ferocious beast.

The fantasy becomes too much, and in reality, I rip my jeans open, pulling my rock-hard thickness out and using the precum already leaking to ease my hand's way up and down my shaft. In my head, I talk to Katelyn.

"That's it, take my cock deep in that pretty little pussy. Squeeze me tight and make me come. I'm gonna fill you up, mark you inside and out so everyone knows you're mine, princess."

Fuck, the nickname does it, and I come all over my hand as I growl and shudder.

I grab my bandanna from my back pocket, wiping the stickiness off and already feeling guilty. Katelyn might not be a candlelight-and-missionary type, but she damn sure deserves better than a dirty fuck held down on a table and forced to her limits.

I'm just a filthy prick, a user and a taker. And fuck do I want to make her take me, deep into her body until she feels me there long after I've pulled out. My mark, my brand . . . my princess.

CHAPTER 10

MARK

This is a trap. I can feel it in my bones. But when your pregnant soon-to-be sister-in-law calls you up and says that her girls are getting together for a night out and need you to be the driver, what are you supposed to do? You drive the damn truck, and that's the end of that.

At least James will be there, too, and yes, I tried to bail, saying he could handle things on his own. But no luck, because I'm not that immune to Sophie's coaxing, and she insisted. At least I won't be solely responsible for keeping the wildness to a manageable level. Although I'm well aware, and James is, too, that the girls are gonna do whatever the hell they want. We're just here to, I don't know, carry the bags or something.

Our job isn't to corral them; it's to make sure nobody decides to get stupid and ruin their good time. Since we're the ones out in the country, James and I pick up Shayanne first. She lives next door, although that sounds much more neighborly than it really is.

In actuality, the Tannen family ranch is just past ours, and about a mile separates us by direct line, with the fence splitting our lands roughly halfway in between. But the fence between us isn't the only thing that keeps us apart.

There's always been tension and rivalry between our families, a tension that turned into a rather curt understanding that they don't bother us and we won't bother them after Shayanne's daddy made a crude offer to buy our ranch mere weeks after Pops died.

It was on the border of getting ugly and has resulted in a bit of a Hatfields-and-McCoys-during-a-truce vibe between the two families. But Shayanne tends to march to her own drummer, staying out of the family drama of her father and three brothers, so she and Sophie have managed to maintain a tight friendship, even though Sophie's weeks away from becoming a Bennett.

It's sort of a friendship of opposites, but it's been good for both of them. The city girl and the country girl, the planner and the one satisfied to go along with her daddy's plans. They couldn't be more different, but they've found common ground in each other, and I'm damn glad for it since I want Sophie to be happy here.

It's not altruistic. It's a bit selfish, because one of the perks of Sophie being happy is that James stays here, home on the ranch the way Pops would've wanted. I feel damn glad that's a reality now.

When we pull up to the gate at the front of the Tannen property, Shayanne meets us, hopping up into the shotgun seat, all smiles and swinging braids. She's got on a pair of tiny cutoff shorts I'm sure none of the menfolk in her family have seen because they haven't been burned in the trash fire yet, good cowgirl boots, and a blingy tank top, and as she closes the door, she blows a kiss to both of us.

"Hey, Bennetts! Thanks for the lift tonight! Daddy and the boys are over in Alvarado, so I get a whole night to myself," she begins, barely pausing to breathe. "Helloooo, girls' night out, with a bonus of it being ladies' night at Hank's. I've got my overnight bag to stay at Sophie's tonight too. Hope you don't mind me intruding, James."

She talks in one long, run-on sentence full of perkiness and sunshine. James smiles and chatters back with her, even if she carries the majority of the conversational weight.

I get the feeling she doesn't have many conversations at home and is glad for someone to interact with. Thank God it's not me. She's a nice girl with a lot of charm, but her constant babble drives me a little nuts. By the time we pull into the lot at Hank's, my hands are gripping the steering wheel so hard they're turning white.

James points as I drive down the line, grinning. "There's Sophie's truck and Roxy's car. Looks like we're last."

I glance at the clock, his words putting me on edge because I hate to be late, and he knows it. But it's straight-up seven o'clock, right on time as planned. James smirks, and I realize he did it on purpose. Fucker. We head inside, and it's already louder than I'd like, more crowded than I'd prefer, and I'm ready to leave.

But before I can open my mouth, I see the table, and my mouth closes in a snap. Oh shit. Sophie and Roxy are sitting at the big corner table they've already claimed, but they're not alone. Sitting right there with them is . . . Katelyn.

My feet stop without me telling them to as I stare at her, the images from my own imagination replaying across my mind without permission, pissing me off for no damn good reason. At her or at myself, I'm not sure, but it doesn't change the way that I feel.

Shayanne bumps into me from behind, not paying attention since she's still talking to James. "Whoa there, big man. You don't need to play a wall yet. We're over there!"

I half turn, and she shoulders her tiny way past, waving and making a general annoyance of herself as Sophie jumps up with a squeal, waving back. "Shayanne! Come here, girl!"

They embrace, and I'm reminded why I'm here. This friendship, it's good for the family, and it keeps James happy.

And fine . . . I like Sophie and maybe even Shayanne a little bit too. I've met Roxy and her husband only once, but from what I can tell they're good people. But all their noise is a buzz in my ear as my attention is drawn to Katelyn.

She's sitting down, so I can't see her fully, but her top is more casual than I've seen before, just some tiny little straps that lead down to a loose-fitting flowy scrap of fabric. Floral, of course. I smirk a bit, thinking that the feminine swath of cloth suits her.

James and Shayanne scoot into the booth, and somehow, the only spot left for me to sit down is next to Katelyn. I'd thought this was going to be a trap to help with the wedding or maybe be a bodyguard for Roxy, since in addition to being Sophie's sister-in-law, she's a big-shot pop singer. But now I'm thinking this is a setup of a different sort. The kind that maybe Mama had a hand in.

I give Sophie a suspicious glare, but she simply smiles and launches into a wedding-themed conversation with Shayanne and Roxy, James nodding his head along as she points out pictures on her phone. Meanwhile, Katelyn stops what she's doing, not quite looking at me but also totally aware of my presence. She's almost vibrating, thrumming like a guitar string, and I feel the same way. We sit silently until finally I swallow and greet her in a low voice. "Hey."

She dips her chin slightly and blushes at my greeting, and my cock is already hardening. She just looks so beautiful, and to know I make her react, too . . . my body knows what it wants.

"Hey, sorry," Katelyn says quietly. "I thought you knew I was going to be here."

No, but I know exactly who I should be blaming for that oversight, considering he's giving me sly eyes and looking like he's only half paying attention to his woman chattering away.

"It's fine."

Not wanting more conversation, I force my eyes to scan the room. If I'm supposed to be some two-bit bodyguard, I should probably make sure no one is eyeing Roxy.

"Sophie invited me," Katelyn says, not letting me go so easily. "Said she was adopting me as a new friend."

She laughs lightly, and it's sweeter music than the jukebox in my ears, but I ignore her.

I ignore the press of her thigh against mine, the bare flesh exposed in the shorts I can see now that I'm beside her.

I ignore the heady floral scent surrounding her, the one that makes me wonder if she smells that good all over.

I ignore the heat building in my gut, and lower, from her proximity until I can't take it any longer.

"I'm gonna grab a beer."

I rise, striding toward the bar, knowing that I could've waited for the waitress but that I needed a minute to clear my head, get a firm hold on my control from the unexpectedness of seeing her here. Whatever it is about Katelyn, she's like an instant triple shot of whiskey. I'm loopy whenever I see her.

By the time I return, Katelyn is fully engrossed in the wedding conversation and doesn't even acknowledge me when I sit down. I'm glad, or at least I should be, but I could've handled at least a look in my direction. Some other guy might have been able to snuggle up next to her. The thought of some other bastard trying to make a move on Katelyn riles me up anew, jealousy flashing through me even though I have no right.

The conversation rolls through dinner and a round of margaritas— virgin, of course, for the pregnant Sophie and the just barely underage Shayanne.

James and I keep nursing our first beers, trading sips with our sweet tea as we eat. I honestly have no idea what the hell they're even gabbing about, a problem I've always had with female talk. I keep hearing words like *stunning*, *elegant*, and *timeless*, and I swear they debate the validity of ivory versus cream for almost twenty minutes.

I'm pretty sure they're the same damn thing, but I keep my mouth shut and just watch the interplay between the ladies.

Katelyn fits right in, her eyes lighting up at the same moments as the other ladies, her smile flashing at each new idea as she adds nuances to improve them, her hands dainty as she uses them to illustrate whatever she's talking about.

Weddings are something she knows, so I'm not surprised, but I think she'd fit right in with Sophie and Shayanne even if they started talking about goats, something both of them actually love and I'd bet Katelyn knows jack shit about. I bet she could sing along with Roxy if she started belting out too. Katelyn seems to be comfortable with everyone, and everyone accepts her easily too. I'm both proud, knowing how much she wants friends, and jealous that she hasn't so much as looked my way in over an hour.

When the food's gone, Shayanne leans back, patting her belly. "Oh my goodness, I swear it's just a food baby, but dang, maybe I shouldn't have eaten that last biscuit."

Sophie laughs, patting her own belly, which is starting to swell a little in a good way. "Mine is not a food baby, and I don't feel the least bit guilty about my carbolicious choices. In fact, I could have gone for more gravy."

I see James stifle a laugh, and I know damn well what he's thinking.

Shayanne doesn't seem to get it, though. She grabs Sophie's hand but talks to Roxy and Katelyn, too, fidgeting as she looks for a way out of the booth.

"Let's go dance!"

"Don't forget me," James protests as he takes Sophie's other hand. He gives me a glance but says nothing as they hit the dance floor en masse, James having fun and making a general ass of himself, much to Sophie's delight.

But my eyes stay fixed on Katelyn, taking in the way her filmy shirt floats as she moves, her legs sticking out of the cotton shorts she has on, her ass looking yummier than the bacon cheddar burger I just finished.

Of course she's got on heels, but they're different tonight, a sort of sandal that I think's called a wedge, like a giant doorstop under her heel.

They're still high, and I wouldn't expect anything else on her. I doubt she owns any tennis shoes, and I bet she'd rather be dead than caught in cowgirl boots.

She's everything I don't like—fancy, girly, and prissy. And gorgeous and light . . . and mine.

No, not that last one, I remind myself. She can never be that last one.

But I don't stop staring, watching her shimmy around the floor with Roxy and Shayanne while James and Sophie . . . well, have fun.

The song changes, some dance anthem the girls are shaking their hands at turning into a country tune. Shayanne waves and finds a cowboy to two-step with as the rest of the ladies head back to the table, James trailing behind them. Roxy and Sophie plop down in the booth, giggling uncontrollably, but Katelyn stands beside me. I look up at her, the position unusual since I always tower over everyone.

"Yes?"

Her eyes are full of fire, seduction in their depths. "Hey, Mark, want to dance with me?"

The thought of holding her in my arms, leading her around the floor as she moves against me sounds like delicious torture, and I doubt my ability to withstand the onslaught. I force myself to look at my nearly empty beer bottle, my hand tightening on the glass.

"I don't dance."

James kicks me under the table, looking genuinely pissed. "The fuck you don't. Mama and Pops taught all of us."

Katelyn looks between James and me, my refusal seeming much more of a personal dismissal now. But she stands strong, unwavering.

"Alright then. Sophie, do you mind if I borrow your husband-to-be for a twirl around the floor? I just learned how, and I don't want to forget."

Sophie smiles, patting James on the shoulder. "Oh no, you two go ahead. I'm not moving for a bit. This girl needs a break and maybe a Coke."

James takes Katelyn's hand, nothing more personal than a handshake, but I'm already pissed. He casts one glance back at me, and I can read his eyes clearly. *Hey, dumbfuck, this should be you.*

They join the other couples on the floor, and I can see James coaching her as they start to move. He's polite, and there's room for the Holy Ghost between them, just like Mama used to tell us when we were little, but it's too close for my taste.

In my periphery, I can see Sophie and Roxy whispering about something, but it doesn't register until I hear them counting down. *Five . . . four . . . three . . .*

Fuck this.

I get up and stomp over toward them, hearing Sophie telling Roxy to "pay up" behind me. I don't ask to cut in; I just take Katelyn's hand from James and body check him out of the way. He laughs good-naturedly, not knowing that his life was in jeopardy for daring to touch her.

"I believe that's my cue to go get a drink. All yours, brother," he says.

The only thing saving him from an ass kicking later is that I know this dance wasn't his idea. Well, that and he's totally spun for Sophie.

James disappears and the world fades away as I look at Katelyn, putting my other hand on her waist. I just hold her for a second as she looks up at me, eyes big and blue and full of hurt and confusion as she bites her lip.

"You don't have to dance with me if you don't want to, Mark. It's fine."

I don't answer, just start to move her around the floor, and she follows my lead like she's been doing it her whole life. It feels easy. Natural. Right.

As the first song ends, I pull her a little closer, more than Mama would have approved of when she was teaching us, and I lean down to whisper in her ear. "You're playing with fire, princess. I don't know why, but I strongly suggest you cut it the fuck out."

Her hand tightens on my shoulder and she meets my eyes, looking up bravely, and I can see she's pissed off. "I'm not playing. I wanted to dance with *you*, but you said no. Actually, no. You lied to me so you wouldn't have to. I don't want to play games. That's why I chose to not dance with some random guy here. I remember how that turned out. Instead, I figured I'd dance with someone safe, your brother—your very in-love-with-his-fiancée brother. And you're *still* pissed."

I can't help but smirk a little at her mouthiness. "Not playing games? But you still got me out here, didn't you?"

She shrugs. "Begrudgingly."

I grunt, not quite knowing how to respond, and she stops in place, fighting my lead and releasing my hand. Before I can say anything, she looks at me harshly.

"Fine, I'll just go. I'm sorry for intruding on your family outing," she says sadly. "I thought . . . it doesn't matter."

I did this to her. She's been smiling and happy with the girls, and I fucked the night up. No. I might be an asshole, but I'm not that kind of asshole. Fuck that.

"No. You wanted to dance with me? Then let's fucking dance," I growl at her. I take her hand back in mine, reminding myself to be gentle with her. I pull her close to me, our bodies pressed against each other, no Holy Ghost fitting in between us for damn sure. You couldn't fit a piece of paper between us.

Her breath hitches when she feels my cock, thick and growing between us in my tight jeans. I barely resist the urge to rub against her like an animal in heat. The next song starts, something on the border-line between bluesy rock and country, and we dance, not covering the floor in sweeping turns or long lines of two-steps, but instead I sway her back and forth, curled around her tightly with our interwoven fingers pressed to my chest.

I feel the moment she gives in, relaxing against me and letting me lead her again. It feels like a victory, an acquiescence of a creature so powerful choosing to give in to my will. It's everything I want. It's everything I *shouldn't* need.

Especially not from her. I press her backward, and she takes tiny steps, staying close to me and letting me decide where we go on the floor. It should just be a dance, maybe a bit of foreplay and naughtiness, but it's bigger than that and we both know it. Neither of us speaks as the growling guitars ebb and flow like the tension building between us.

I don't know about her, but I'm scared to break the spell that's woven its way around us, afraid she'll turn skittish on me if I press her too far, so I hold back, letting go just enough to satisfy the dark urges rushing through me to claim her, mark her, and make her mine.

I hope the song never ends.

CHAPTER 11

KATELYN

The music is pulsing, not with electronic bass but an older, deeper pulse, and my head is spinning.

Does he hate me? Does he want me to go away and leave him alone?

Even though we're dancing, there have been some definite moments tonight where he was giving me hardcore *fuck off* vibes. Like when I'd gone far out on a skinny limb and asked him to dance, fearful the branch would snap beneath me and I'd fall on my face like a fool.

And I had when he glared at me before flat-out lying in front of all the girls I'm trying to make friends with, saying he couldn't dance. He embarrassed me, hurt my pride by making it clear that he thinks I'm just trying to play him as a game, and I even tried to run away to mitigate the humiliation.

But then there's this, as we dance close enough that a whisper couldn't find its way between us. These moments where it feels like he wants me to stay, or maybe just plain wants me, at least judging by the hard ridge pressed against my belly.

I'm not sure why he's fighting himself so much. I'm throwing out every green-light signal I can.

I made my decision when I saw him standing there with his brother. Yeah, last time I said that maybe I need to hold back, but when I got home that night I knew that was mostly the old Katelyn talking, the one who lived in a beige little world.

But if I'm going to be the new Katelyn, the woman who wants to experience the world in all its Technicolor glory, then I have to be all-in. I've done it with my wardrobe, with my choices in friends . . . and seeing Mark standing there next to James, I realized I have to be all-in with him too. And if that means I get hurt, then that's Technicolor too. So I turned it on, and now we're here.

For all that's grinding between us, we barely move around the floor, and the feeling of being cocooned in his arms, directed here or there by his desire and whim, is heady. I feel lost in him, losing track of my surroundings, the music, and the other couples on the floor.

My whole focus is on Mark. I don't say anything, too scared he'll gain control of himself again and change his mind. Right now, he's letting me in, just a little, and it's deep and dark and addicting, sneakily surrounding me, overtaking me like silk and softness.

I want more of him, of whatever this is. Minutes later, or maybe it's hours, he lifts his head from where it's been resting against mine. He lets out a sigh, somewhere between regret and relief. He leads me back to the table and we sit, and while I'm aware that the others are looking at us, nobody says anything about our dance.

Finally, Sophie wipes her forehead, grinning happily. "Whew, I'm beat. James is going to take me and Shayanne home. Roxy, what about you?"

"I'm ready too," Roxy says, waving it off. "But I'm fine to drive myself. Don't worry about me."

Sophie gives her a nod. "Okay then. Mark, would you mind giving Katelyn a ride? I picked her up, and I'd really like to head to bed."

She punctuates the statement with a big yawn, obviously fake, but nobody else is calling her on it. She's a good wing-girl, but I don't want to push Mark too far, too fast.

"It's fine," I protest, reaching for my purse and my phone. "I can call an Uber."

Mark shakes his head, his look cutting off any objection. "I'll take you home."

Well, okay then. I guess that's that. We throw a few bills for the tip on the table and head out. In the parking lot, Sophie gives me a big hug.

"Good luck, girl."

She winks at me as they all load up and pull out of the lot. Mark jerks his head toward his truck, and I follow. He opens the door for me, offering a hand to help me climb up inside, then shuts the door behind me.

When he gets behind the wheel, the only sound is the rumble of the powerful engine as we head out of the lot. Other than the light wind coming through the open window, it's quiet, the silence full of questions.

"Is this our new Friday night routine?" he asks suddenly, his eyes still fixed on the road.

Confused, I turn to him. "What?"

We pull up to an intersection, and Mark comes to a stop. "Two Fridays in a row now. You at Hank's. Me taking you home. Should I plan for next week?"

The question could be construed two ways, but his tone definitely sounds more disapproving than asking if I want him to meet me next week.

"No, just coincidental. Celebrating with Marla, and then Sophie asked me tonight. Next Friday, I'll probably be eating pizza alone in my pj's and having a movie marathon," I say honestly. I'm pretty sure I see a hint of a smile at that, so I push it further, latching on to the joke. "But you're welcome to come over for that. As long as you don't like pineapple on your pizza. That's a hard no. Nonnegotiable."

He lifts an eyebrow, pulling through the intersection. "Pineapple has no place on pizza. Or chicken sandwiches."

I grin, surprised at the teasing tone in his voice. "Oooh, now see . . . agree to disagree there. I can totally get down with a chicken teriyaki sandwich with a slice of grilled pineapple. Mmm."

He shakes his head once, his smirk still there. "Nope."

He says it like that's the final word. In his mind, it probably is. But I'm not that easy to deter. "Well, I guess it's a good thing I'm offering pizza and a movie then and not sandwiches, isn't it?"

Whoa, this got a little carried away. It started as a joke, but am I really inviting him over for pizza and a movie? I think I am.

His eyes narrow, and I expect him to reverse right the hell out of this conversation. "What movie? And so help me, if you say some chick flick shit, I'm out."

Oh boy, shit just got real, and I feel both excited and like I'm in about ten feet over my head. I am literally negotiating a date. With Mark. And me. At my house. With pizza. And a movie . . . what movie?

"Um, let me guess . . . action?" I ask. "Cars? Lots of testosterone? Something like *Fast and Furious 35*? Or *Die Hard 10*?"

Mark's lips twitch upward, and he shakes his head in slight exasperation. "How about you order the pizza and *I'll* bring the movie?"

It's a question, but it's more of a directive. One I'm happy to follow. I know pizza, but guy movies bewilder me. "Okay."

And holy shit, I think I just agreed to a date with Mark. More importantly, and somehow less likely, I think he just agreed to a date with me. My heart is thumping away like I just ran an obstacle course. Hell, a conversation with Mark feels a bit like one, too, and I think I just successfully climbed the seven-foot wall at a Spartan Race.

We pull up to my place, and he turns the truck off. I remember the last time we sat here just like this. I'd kissed his cheek, and things went awry quickly. I desperately want to rewrite that script.

"Walk me to my door."

I take a play from his book and don't make it a question, instead an order, although my voice is just a *little* less demanding than his.

He still does as I say, getting out and escorting me like a gentleman all the way up the sidewalk and two concrete steps to my front door. I try to remember if I left a mess this morning, but it's too late to clean up now if I did.

I unlock the door and swing it open, stepping inside. "It's not much, but it's mine. Living room, kitchen . . ." I start the nickel tour, but Mark is frozen in the doorway. He's got one hand on either side of the doorframe, and though his breath is slow and steady, the tension is radiating off him.

"Katelyn, what are you doing?"

The question throws me. "Um, showing you where I live. You can come in." I wave at him, beckoning him inside.

"That's not what I mean. Why are you inviting me here . . . tonight, for pizza next week?"

His eyes are locked on me, and I realize that I'm going to have to say it. I sit on the couch, reaching down to unbuckle the straps of my sandals and kick them off, putting off the inevitable. Finally, I curl my legs under me and take a big breath.

"Look, I have this color theory. See, my life has been beige for a long time. No, that's not true. My *love* life has been beige. And moving here . . . it's like a chance to be something different. Like there's a whole rainbow I've missed out on. And you feel . . ."

My eyes drop to the floor, and I know I'm blushing. Some fucking vixen I am. "Just come in?" I plead. "It feels weird to share like this with you standing in the doorway."

He rumbles back, not moving an inch. "I feel what?" he asks, forcing me to complete my sentence.

"You feel . . . *not* beige."

It's all I can give right now, as close to the truth as I can admit when he's physically holding himself out by force, hands gripping the doorframe like it's a lifeline. I'm not sure if it's to save himself or to save me, though.

"If I come in there, princess, it won't be *beige*. That's for fucking sure." He huffs a laugh, but it's not joyful, more like he's in on some joke I'm unaware of.

"Please." I hear the need in my voice, and so does he. I'm not experienced enough to hide it, and to be honest, I don't want to. I feel like this might be one of the first times in my life I can be real, even with myself. It almost looks like he's ready to relent, but then his grip tightens on the door.

"Katelyn, this isn't happening. Not tonight and not ever. It can't."

I bite my lip, more confused by the second. He's telling me no, loud and clear and obvious. But I can see the power it's taking to force the words from his lips. He wants me, he just doesn't *want* to want me. And isn't that all that really matters?

"Oh. I guess I thought . . . You were just so . . . Maybe I misread."

"I don't do casual fucks at home. And you're new to town and figuring shit out. You don't know what you're getting into. Whatever you're looking for . . . it's not me."

I feel so confused. At Hank's, I was pedal to the metal, volume cranked to eleven and ready to do whatever it takes to not have another beige moment in my life. I wanted to live, to let my freak flag fly a little. But am I really ready for Mark? He seems to have so much passion, so much there. Mark's like skydiving. But am I ready to jump, or am I getting ready to hurl myself out of a plane without a chute? I look down, tracing shapes on my leg with my nail, trying to process what he's saying. Maybe I am jumping without a chute, I don't know. What I do know is that I like spending time with him, I enjoy the way he makes me feel, and I also like his family. I want more of that . . . of him, of them. So if that's all I can get, I'll take it. If I'm honest, I need it.

"What about a friend? I definitely need that. Can you do that?"

His brow furrows. "A friend?"

"Yeah, you know . . . friends. Like people who hang out and send each other silly text messages. Okay, so maybe the silly ones will have to be from me, but you can send me serious dad ones, like 'don't talk to strangers' and 'did you lock the door?' Friends who watch movies and eat pizza without pineapple and grab a beer on Fridays after work. Like that."

I'm rambling because I'm nervous. Like he doesn't get the concept of friendship. He turns, leaning his back against the doorframe and crossing his arms. I studiously ignore the way it makes his biceps bulge against his sleeves, focusing on this moment. He grits his teeth, and I can see the muscle working in his jaw. He appears to be thinking about my proposal. That's something, at least.

"Friends. That's it and nothing more. I can do that," he finally says, eyeing me like he's almost certain I'm trying to trick him. I swear he's thinking I'm going to take advantage of him at the first opportunity. That I'll be hopping on his dick like a sex-deprived maniac. He might not be wrong, so I blink and school my expression into one of innocence.

"Yeah, like you said, I'm new and figuring shit out. And Sophie's kind of adopted me, so I'm going to be around, hopefully. At least until the wedding. It'd be great if we're friends too. Less awkward that way, you know?"

He looks up, like he can't believe he's saying it, but the words come out anyway. "Fine. Friends."

CHAPTER 12

MARK

It's quiet as I take Sugarpea for a workout ride through the dawning light, appreciating the way the dark turns dusky purple before blazing into shades of orange and pink. I wish I could shine a flashlight into the dark corners of my soul and brighten them as easily, as sure as the daily sunrise. But I know nothing's that simple.

I've strode through my days, steady and solid as the sun, the one thing everyone knows they can depend on like clockwork. Everything's even, strong, and there isn't a problem I can't handle.

But inside, I know better. I know my soul isn't full of brightness. It's a dark place, twisted and ugly.

I don't know when I first realized it, probably in high school when guys would mouth about what their girlfriends had done to them or *for* them, bragged debauchery that paled in comparison to my fantasies. Never about what was done to me, but about what I would do to the imaginary woman in my mind. How I would take her, learn her every nuance, and use that knowledge to own her, not just her body, but her very soul.

Of course, I didn't have those words back then, just some vague idea that I wasn't like the other guys in the locker room. So, I shut up.

And shut down. Never bragged, never talked about girlfriends, although I did date. I learned to watch for signals, to respond the way I thought most guys would, to be sweet and easy. I thought I'd end up just like every other guy, married to a nice girl, working the ranch like Pops, and having a family of rough boys to carry on the family tradition.

Eventually, I learned the act wasn't worth it. It was too much work to pretend I'm not an asshole, and I was never a good enough actor that my girlfriends actually felt like I was present with them. So many of them ended up repeating the same words. That I was "holding back." And "I can tell there's something wrong—why won't you talk to me?" being the most common.

But I'd held strong and stayed true to my chosen façade. Until her. Nicole. With her, I'd felt more, so much more. She had fire, and for a moment I thought I'd found my partner, the woman who could take all I had and not only accept it, but give it back too—a completion, a connection I'd only dared dream about. So I'd chanced a hint at the truth, and she hadn't been able to handle it. Handle *me*.

It was ugly, awful, and that was the first and last time I ever gambled like that. Until Katelyn.

Fuck. I tried so hard, said what I could to scare her into some form of self-preservation, did asshole things to run her off, but she didn't run. No, she fucking begged me to come into her apartment, and when I refused, she agreed to take less. Friends.

As if I can stop thinking about her as something more, like this desire to pleasure her and possess her completely can be shut off like a light switch. But maybe for her it can. Maybe she's attracted to me, but it's no big deal for her to decide to not want me anymore.

I know that this is going to be impossible, a test of the very fabric of my character, but I can't help but want to be around her. She's like a light shining into my soul. And I'm just enough of a monster to take her light, steal it away to brighten the dark corners inside me. Even if for a moment. Every day's light is taken by the night, so maybe if I can get just a taste of her sunshine, it'll be enough. It'll have to be.

Sugarpea whinnies, sensing the emotions rolling through me. He's a good horse, more sensitive to me than most humans are, and he pulls at the reins, letting me know he wants to run and likely knowing that it will do me some good too.

I give the reins a slight shake as I press into his sides, giving the order he wants. "Let's go, boy. Hi-yah."

With a snort, we're off, galloping across the field faster than the wind, eating up the ground beneath us, tufts of dust and grass billowing up behind us. I direct him to the left in a big looping sweep around the pasture, feeling the rush of wind on my face. It's cathartic, a washing away of the sins weighing down my soul. But it's fleeting, only lasting until I acknowledge it, which triggers the guilt to slam back onto my shoulders with a thud.

Too rough, too hard, too bossy, too controlling, too domineering, too demanding. Too . . . everything. I heard them all from Nicole, stabs to my heart because they're true. And it's exactly why I'm better off alone, cold and stoic and keeping the depth of my ugliness to myself.

I start another lap, but then I see Luke's ATV coming up in the distance and redirect Sugarpea to intercept him. He slows, and Sugarpea moseys up to the ATV, totally acclimated to the burring machinery.

"Hey, Mark, what the hell are you doing? You okay?" Luke asks. "You said you were taking 'Pea out on a workout. I didn't think you'd be training him for Santa Anita."

I reach down and pat Sugarpea's neck. "He just wanted to run, so I figured some laps would do him good."

"You, too, it looked like," he says, leaving the unsaid question in the air.

I don't say anything, not sure what he thinks he knows and unwilling to share.

Luke eyes me suspiciously and doesn't give up. "You know, because you were working him for more and more speed, looked like you needed the run too."

I don't give him the satisfaction of a direct answer, instead skillfully dodging. "What're you doing out here? Need something?"

He squints his eyes, letting me know he's well aware of what I'm doing, but choosing to go along. "Just checking in because I noticed you were out a bit longer than normal. Thought I'd see if you needed help with anything."

I shake my head. "Nope. Just busy, so I thought I'd take Sugarpea out for a bit before settling in at my desk."

He grins, shutting off the ATV engine. "I feel ya, brother. I've got some work in the barn to make up for being gone, but I swear it seems like at least half of what I do is desk jockeying these days."

I appreciate the attempt at camaraderie; Luke's always good at that, somehow balancing his dual roles as easygoing peacekeeper with the lighthearted jokester vibe he maintains.

"At least that slab of wood won't buck you off like some of those beasts you train," I say, keeping the focus on him.

Luke grins good-naturedly. "Yeah, but not nearly as fun. A little wildness keeps you on your toes, makes life interesting."

I snort, thinking he has no idea how dangerous the smallest bit of feral can be, even if he spends time training horses to behave. Hell, maybe that'd be a better outlet for me, control the animals that need to be domesticated, since I seem damn unable to restrain myself fully. Maybe I'd understand their chafing at following rules and expectations that don't suit their nature. I'd relate to pacing like a wild animal forced to live in a box sized for its body, not its psyche.

"Got all the interesting I need wrangling you and James while keeping the ranch running. You two are worse than any high-strung horse."

"If you say so." He pauses, but I can tell he's got more to say, so I wait him out. "Mama said the events lady up at the resort wants to book some time with Demon and Cobie. Thought I'd head into town tomorrow and go see her, give her a cost estimate and make sure I'm ready for whatever she needs."

I purposefully keep my face neutral, not giving away a thing. He was gone for our Friday night outing, and unless James has been running his mouth, there's no way Luke knows about me taking Katelyn home.

"Or you could just call her," I tell him. "We do have those things called phones now."

Luke looks at me, evaluating me with every sweep of his eyes. "I knew it. Something about the way you said her name when you were talking about paying the bill. You're into her."

I huff a sigh, like I'm exasperated with him, while inside I'm praying he'll drop the whole topic. "Just saying you could save a trip to town if you called her."

He chuckles, kicking his boots up on the front fender of the ATV. "You're that fucking spun, huh? Dropping like flies. First James, now you. Once you pull your head out of your ass, tell me about her."

"Just call her," I growl. "And drop it."

I pull on Sugarpea's reins, intending to turn him around and head back out for a quick check on the cattle. But Luke's words to my back stop me in my tracks.

"You know that since you reacted like that, I'm honor bound as a brother to go meet her, check her out, and make sure she's good enough for my older brother."

There's a smile in his words, but ice runs through my veins. Just what I don't need, my brother poking around in my business and bringing to light that it's not that Katelyn isn't good enough for me, it's that I'm not good enough for *her*.

"Luke," I warn, "it's not like that. We're friends. Just give her a call with the quote and let it go."

He must hear the finality in my voice, because for once, he does as I ask. "Alright, Mark. But I'll tell you what—I'm going to do you a favor. I'll write up the quote, and you can give it to her yourself. On the phone, in person, or by email for all I care."

Well, almost what I asked. But I'll take it if it keeps him from nosing around in my business.

~~

By Wednesday, I'm officially an asshole. I haven't called her, not after leaving her with some stupid agreement to be friends, and not after Luke gave me the quote for the horses.

But really, in the scope of ways I suck, the horse quote is ridiculously minor. I'm a grown-ass man, responsible for a lot of shit, and I can damn sure make an uncomfortable phone call. Especially since I know Mama is going to ask me about it at dinner tonight . . . again. And James and Luke are gonna glare at me like they know a damn thing about what's going on in my head . . . again.

Not that I need it, but with a big breath for courage, I dial Katelyn's number. I'm not sure if I'm pissed or thankful that it's included on her business card. How many people have her number already? I mean, she's new to town and most of the guys she runs into are getting married, but the ready access irritates me.

"Katelyn Johnson," she answers, her voice professional and measured.

"Katelyn," I say, the word apparently enough of a greeting because she dives in.

"Mark! Hey! Good to hear from you. I mean, not that I thought I wouldn't, but it's been a few. I mean . . . Hey!"

She's rambling again. It's adorable. Feminine and soft and moldable. *Could she . . . ?*

Stop it, I chastise myself. *Stick to business. For her own protection,* I remind myself.

"Luke's back. I have his quote on the horses for you."

"Oh . . . okay."

I can almost hear the sunshine leave her voice, and it cuts me, but I can take it. I'll take the pain and spare her.

"It'll be five hundred dollars for the day, both Demon and Cobie, and they can photograph anywhere on the ranch. Luke will escort to keep everything safe while the bride gets the photos she wants."

My voice is robotic, like I'm reading from the paper in front of me, but I'm just staring at it, wishing it would tell me what I should really say.

"Alright, I'll let Miss Wilson know, and if you want to send me the contract, I'll forward it so she can sign it."

"Will do." There's a long stretch of silence, neither of us sure what to say, and the awkwardness stretches until it breaks, both of us talking at once.

"Mark . . ."

"Katelyn . . ."

She giggles nervously. "You go ahead."

"About the other night—" I start, but she interrupts me.

"Yeah, what do you want on the pizza? I mean, not pineapple obviously, but are you a plain cheese or meat lover's or veggie guy? I'm guessing not veggie, but I didn't want to assume. I mean, maybe you're like the first ever veggie pizza cowboy or something," she says with a laugh. "Do they even make veggie-loving cowboys? I kinda figured you guys were always meat lover's with extra bacon or something, but what do I know?"

My lips twitch. "I don't know if it's a good idea."

I can almost hear the pout in her voice. "Mark, you said we're friends. Friends have pizza-movie hangouts. We can do this."

Fuck me. I can't tell her no. It's going to be hours of torture, but if she wants to hang out, I'm gonna give in and I damn well know it, so I need to stop pretending.

"Okay, okay. Just no pineapple, anchovies, or onions and I'm game."

She squeals a little, and the sound shoots straight to my cock. "Awesome. I'll see you Friday around seven."

CHAPTER 13

KATELYN

It's almost seven, and I'm honestly not sure if Mark is coming. It's been radio silent since he agreed to come over . . . barely. And that's even after I sent him a cute GIF of a kitten riding a slice of pepperoni pizza.

Juvenile, I know, but it seemed like a safe way to remind him about our . . . *not* date.

I take a quick look in the mirror one last time. It might not be a date, but I don't want to look bad. I consider changing again, but yoga pants and a T-shirt are friend-appropriate, casual loungewear. And I am wearing a bra, so that's not too flirty. That seems like the best way to keep Mark on an even keel, nothing overtly sexy. I also decided a good reminder for myself was in order, so I intentionally chose my most granny pair of plain cotton panties, definitely not ones I'd ever show off.

My physical shields fortified, I try to prepare mentally to not jump him the instant he walks through the door. It's going to be hard, but if a friend is what I get, a friend is what I'll have. Nothing more, but hopefully nothing less if I can stick to the rules.

Right on time, I hear his truck pull into the parking lot outside. I peek out the blinds, so I'm able to see him take a few deep breaths and run his hands over his face before he walks toward my door. Interesting. Seems I'm not the only one struggling with the friends-only edict.

I open the door to his knock, giving him my best "casual" smile. "Hey! Come on in."

He steps in like he's facing a firing squad inside my little living room. He looks good, a black T-shirt stretched tight across his chest, along with slightly faded jeans that show off his thighs and bulge. Not that I'm looking, of course, because we're just friends. To cap it off, he's got on a pair of boots that are probably his "good boots," if I had to guess. Not quite ranch wear, but not fancy either.

I wonder if he spent as much time worrying about his casual clothes as I did. Probably not. Guys never seem to worry about that to begin with, and Mark definitely doesn't seem like the type to give a rat's ass about what someone else thinks of him, much less his clothes. Still, the little musing helps add a flush to my cheeks.

"Pizza should be here in a few minutes. Want a beer?"

He dips his chin once, and I disappear into the kitchen, hollering back over my shoulder, "Make yourself at home."

But when I return, he's sitting on the edge of the couch, looking ready to bolt at the slightest provocation. I decide to take the bull by the horns. "Okay, first rule of pizza and movie night . . . no shoes. Take your boots off."

He looks at me, his lips twitching. "Excuse me?"

"You heard me, boots off. Sit back, relax, and have a drink."

I hold the beer out, but when he reaches for it, I pull it back a little. "Boots, sit back, relax, drink."

We have an eye-glaring standoff contest, one I'm determined to win and somehow magically do.

"Alright, fine," he says, grumpily taking his boots off. He lines them up next to the couch and sits back, laying an arm along the back of the couch. "Boots off, sitting back, and relaxed. Satisfied? Now give me my beer."

I grin, feeling the small battle was a victory earned even if he said it demandingly and didn't ask. I hand him his beer, and he takes a long swallow. I can't help but watch the way his lips kiss at the mouth of the bottle, and an image of him laying those lips along my skin pops into my mind.

I blink slowly, willing it away, but knowing I'm going to revisit it later tonight after he leaves. I have a feeling I'll have lots of little snapshots of Mark doing sexy things at the end of the night. God, my vibrator is going to get a workout.

I clench my thighs together, looking for relief, and sit down on the other end of the couch, curling my socked feet underneath me.

"So, what did you do today?" *See? Safe and easy. Keep him talking. I can do this.*

He clears his throat. "Today? I rode out with James to check fences around the north pasture, then we moved the herd there. Then I worked in the office for a bit, paying bills and ordering supplies. Just the usual, keeping everything running."

"Does your family know how awesome you are?" I ask lightly, but I'm serious because it sounds like he does a lot.

"Definitely not. They give me shit for being boring. In fact, most people do."

I laugh, because it's either that or put a hand on his arm, and if I do that . . . I'm lost. "You are so *not* boring. I've done boring. Hell, I graduated from the University of Boring with honors. You most certainly are not."

"I can't imagine you boring either. But tell me about this boring version of Katelyn, about before you came to Great Falls."

The knock on the door interrupts us, and I take full advantage of the reprieve, getting the pizza and grabbing plates and napkins for us. But once we're sitting down again, I take a big bite, chewing thoughtfully and searching for how to tell this.

"Well, I guess I just did what I was expected to do for the most part. Grew up with good parents, went to school and got good grades so I could go to a good college. Dated one guy all through college. Got a job. And ta-da . . . boring."

"Tell me about him," Mark asks. "Mr. Boring."

"Seth?" This could be awkward, but I dive in, willing to answer his demand. "He's a good guy. An engineer. We were together for over ten years. After college, we were supposed to get married, have kids—the whole picture-perfect thing, you know? But we . . . didn't. We lived in the city, worked too many hours, and just cohabitated in this holding pattern. There was just never this big urge to take the next step. We were more like roommates who, toward the end, occasionally had boring sex. And when I found out about the job here, I thought it might be a fresh start for us together. Like learning a new city, making a new home, and meeting new people would add some excitement to our stagnancy. But when I told him about it, he . . ." I trail off, his words echoing in my head.

"He . . . what?" Mark prompts, his voice steady and giving me confidence as I share. He's listening, really listening. Not condescending, not judging, just giving me the space to say what I need to say.

"I guess you could say it was the biggest fight since we moved to Boise," I reply, shaking my head as I laugh hollowly. "God, that sounds pathetic. We barely raised our voices. He didn't want to move. He told me that he wasn't leaving the job he loved so I could *plan parties*." I mimic the sneering voice Seth had used so dismissively about the job I love. "It was the first time he made me feel like what I do was unimportant, frivolous compared to his job."

Mark's mouth pinches, and he sips his beer, saying nothing, just watching me.

"But I was so excited. I mean, this is a dream job for me, and when my boss told me I'd earned this and should go without him, the idea took hold. I applied without telling him, thinking that if I got it, it'd be a sign I should go. But if I wasn't hired, I could just . . . go on like it had been. Not rock the boat."

I laugh sadly. "But he found out and . . ." I let the words die on my tongue.

Mark sets his beer down, and while he barely moves other than that, I can see a new tension growing in his body. "What happened when he found out? Do I need to find him and give him a beat-down?"

He's teasing again, but I can tell that if I said yes, he'd probably jump in his truck right now and drive all night to do exactly that.

"No, nothing like that. He just didn't care. Told me good luck and to let him know if I needed help moving. That he'd arrange for a crew to come. It was like everything else between us—just blah. Easy and safe. No anger, no hurt, no anything. When I flew out for the second interview, I thought maybe he'd want to make a weekend out of it. I was still trying to talk him into coming with me, but he laughed and said he was having drinks with the guys after work. That weekend was when I knew. Walking around the resort and downtown, I felt sparks I hadn't felt in a long time . . . maybe ever. Like there was possibility around every corner. All I had to do was go get it. I went home with a huge smile, knowing I'd aced the interview. Seth didn't even ask how it went, and I didn't feel the need to tell him. I started sleeping on the couch that night, although it didn't really matter because we hadn't had sex in months. And when Brianna called to offer me the job, I started packing right after we hung up. It took me three weeks to handle the events I already had scheduled back home and get here. And then you walked in on my first day flying solo and literally almost knocked me on my ass."

"Hey, I caught you," he argues.

"You did," I agree. My voice is husky, quiet.

"Princess, if he didn't know what he had, that's his loss," Mark says in that tone of finality that he has. "You're not boring. You're exciting and daring, brave and strong to chase after your dream job. From what

I've seen between James's wedding and whatever weird shit your other brides want, you're damn good at it too. You should start fresh and do whatever crazy things you want to. It sounds like you've earned it after ten years of *blah*."

It's a Mark version of a pep talk, complimenting my work while encouraging me to experience life. But there's only one thing I want to experience right now—him.

"You think so?" I ask, gathering my courage.

"I *know* so. You can do anything," he reassures me, still pumping me up like the most serious cheerleader to ever exist.

"Thank you. I guess I feel stupid for settling for so long, being so stagnant and not even caring enough to realize it. I don't want that anymore. I love it here, and I've met some great people. I feel excited about the challenges of each new day, but it'd be nice to share that with someone, you know?"

Mark's eyes have gone dark, and his voice is gravelly. "Katelyn . . ."

It's my warning to back up before I get too deep, so I mitigate the impact. "That's why I'm glad I have you and Marla and Sophie too. I had friends and family back home, but it's nice to build my circle up here too."

His eyes study me, like he's weighing the truthfulness of my words. I don't think for a second that I have him fooled, so I try to distract him.

"What about you? I told you my Not-Grand Love Story. What's your deal? Did some girl break your heart, or are you a perpetual bachelor committed to his manwhore ways?"

I poke him with my foot and wink so he knows I'm kidding.

He lifts an eyebrow. "I told you I don't do casual."

I lift my eyebrows back at him. "Um, no, what you said was, you don't do casual fucks at home, so I assume you do them elsewhere or else you wouldn't have specified. So, manwhore then? I wouldn't have guessed that."

He sighs, knowing I'm not going to be deterred. "No, definitely not. I dated when I was younger, had a serious girlfriend once, even thought we'd get married. But it didn't work out. She wanted someone . . . different . . . nicer or sweeter or some shit. Hell, probably just someone who could carry on a conversation without grunts."

I laugh. "Well, you seem to have grown into that, because we're talking just fine."

I don't mention that I'm collecting every word he says like a treasure, little trinkets to help me put together the layers of enigma he's housing. He has this way of being gruff and caring at the same time, of sharing some things but hiding others. He's a mystery, wrapped up in packaging that I think very few people take the time to examine. Like a brown paper parcel tied with string, seemingly boring but that houses the best gift of all. Him. And fuck do I want him more than ever.

CHAPTER 14

MARK

The next week is full of *friendship* with Katelyn.

The very word makes my stomach twist because I crave so much more.

She sent me a picture of nail polish bottles the day after our movie not-date, asking my opinion. I told her that she should ask Marla or Sophie. I smiled when she told me I was the tiebreaker because Sophie chose Midnight Magenta and Marla chose Kiss Me Carnation. I said to go with the pink one, which seemed safe enough since they were both shades of pink.

She followed up with a picture of her cute little toes painted light pink. It made me want to kiss all ten of them and then work my way up her legs to taste her pussy. I didn't text her that, but the seal had been broken and the expectation set.

Since then, I think we've texted not just every day, but damn near every hour. Pictures of the sunrise over the western pasture, her and Marla holding up fancy glassware, Sugarpea eating an apple, the apple Katelyn was having for lunch at that very moment, too—which apparently made her and Sugarpea kindred spirits—and more. Little snapshots as we chat about what's going on throughout our days.

Every night after dinner, I sit on my back porch like usual, but instead of being alone, it's with Katelyn in my ear, telling me about her adventures around town, like the coffee kiosk she found and the fundraiser gala she's organizing at the resort. And she listens to me talk about the importance of sustainable herd health and how good it feels to have my family all back on the ranch.

While we talk, I imagine what she's wearing and picture her curled up in the corner of her couch like the kitten she told me she saved once. I can't help but wonder if she touches herself when we hang up the way I do, jacking myself off with images of her splayed out for me to touch. Tease. Taste.

Hell, two nights ago, I couldn't even wait until we got off the phone. I heard a splash of water on her end, and when she said she was in the bath, I went rock hard in an instant. Knowing that she was naked on the other side of the line did funny things to my brain, like make me want to wash every inch of her body, use soap bubbles to massage away the stress of her day until she was squeaky clean, and then dirty her up by coming all over her. I had to unzip right then and had the quietest and quickest orgasm of my life. It barely took the edge off, but she never suspected a thing, telling me a story about a frat party she'd gone to without missing a beat.

Finally, after a week of this, a time apart that feels both too long and not long enough, I'm going to see her today. Technically, the next wedding payment isn't due until Monday, but we agreed to meet on Friday and hit Hank's with Marla for dinner instead. I'm actually a little nervous to see her, afraid that whatever balance we've struck on the phone will be thrown off when I see her lush little body in person. But the temptation is too sweet to resist.

I head straight for the events office and knock before gently opening the door, having learned my lesson from before.

"Hey, Mark!" Marla says, looking up from her desk with twinkling eyes. I just bet she's getting a kick out of this. "Katelyn's with someone right now, but come on in. She should be almost done."

"Thanks." I stand there, still as a statue, while Marla gives me the once-over. It feels more like she's evaluating me for Katelyn rather than checking me out, and I can't decide if I want her to find me worthy or if it's better for her to realize Katelyn can do much better. That'd be safer. Easier.

Katelyn's door opens, and a brunette in a black suit steps out. She's pretty, but in a sharp, New York kinda way, with an air of high class. As she walks out, she tosses her words back over her shoulder. "I'll be in touch if I need anything, Katelyn."

Even her voice is crisp and clipped. She turns and realizes she has an audience as Marla and I look at her. She pointedly ignores Marla but offers me her hand, limp like she thinks I'm gonna kiss it or something.

"Well, Mark Bennett, so good to see you."

I shake her hand, definitely not kissing it because she's not the queen of anything.

"Sorry, do I know you?"

"Oh, I'm Bethany Land. We went to school together, but I guess that's been a while. I was Bethany Garrison back then. Land is my married name, though I'm divorced now."

Her voice is higher, brighter, and I dare say flirtatious because she sure seems to want to mention the divorced part.

"Oh, sorry. I didn't recognize you," I reply, sort of lying. I honestly barely remember the name at all, except as one of those girls who ran in their circle while I lived in mine.

"I'm a bit grown up since then. You, too, it seems."

She steps closer to me, and though I have an urge to step back, I hold my ground. Then Katelyn steps out, and Bethany just disappears into the background.

"Mark?"

My eyes meet hers, and all the fantasies I've had over the last week pale in comparison. Today she's wearing a hip-hugging white skirt with big pink flowers, black heels, and a black silk top. Everything about her screams sex to me. Silk, leather, and the pink flowers that couldn't possibly be as pretty as her pussy. I want to push the skirt up to check, confirm my hopes.

"Hey, princess. You ready for me?" The innuendo is unintentional, but the blush on her cheeks tells me she noticed my words, and that makes it more than worth it.

"Yeah, come on in. I'll double-check the balance amount for you."

She holds the door open for me, and in the corner of my eye, I see her give Bethany a hard look. My princess is jealous that someone else was even talking to me. Like anyone could compare to her.

Not that I'm comparing, because I'm not. Not even considering. Because we're friends.

Fucking friendship sucks. Well, I've heard friends fucking doesn't suck, for the right set of friends. But that's not us. And what we are is all I can have if I'm gonna protect her from me, keep my focus on the ranch, and be her friend.

～∽

By the time we get to Hank's, Marla's husband has already gotten us a table. He introduces himself as David, and we all settle into the booth. Despite any promises of friendship, it seems oddly like a double date, not the casual "grab a bite after work" we'd discussed. But soon enough, good food is the great equalizer, and any awkwardness disappears as we enjoy our dinners.

David actually seems like a pretty great guy, keeping the conversation light with tales of his job, and we bond over our B-shift jobs, the old adage of "I'll *be* there when the day starts, and I'll *be* there when the day ends" a reality for us both.

When the music gets louder and the waitresses clear the dance floor, I get a pit in my stomach. Is Katelyn going to want to dance again? If I take her in my arms, there will be no mistaking the effect she has on me.

We're on a precarious balance here, and I don't want to tip the scales too far, too fast. I might not be able to have her because of my own issues, but I damn sure don't want to give her up just yet.

If this little taste is all I get, it's got to be enough to last me through the lonely nights ahead. But I'm not full yet—I need more of a taste of Katelyn's presence. And if I dance with her, it's going to start a domino effect.

I realize Katelyn is staring at me, searching my face and waiting for me to ask her. I give a barely imperceptible shake of my head, and she sighs.

"David, you mind spinning me around the dance floor? I learned a few weeks ago, so I'm not that good, but I'm getting better every time."

He glances at Marla, who smiles at him, giving silent permission, and David escorts Katelyn to the floor. I watch carefully, protective and possessive of her even if David seems like a good guy. He spins her in a complicated weaving of arms that leaves her laughing innocently, like a little girl getting spun around by her father at a church dance in the park or something. I save the tinkles of her laughter in my memory bank, knowing I'll need the happy sound to brighten my day when she's done with me.

As I memorize every motion of her body and each expression that plays across her face, I hear Marla beside me. "She's not going to wait long, you know."

I turn, looking at her blankly, my patented expression. She doesn't wait for me to ask what she means, knowing that I understand already.

"You're fighting a ticking time bomb of your own making, Mark. She likes you. You like her. Why are you making this so difficult? I don't know what your issue is, but you should figure it out. Fast. She's a good woman, and some man is gonna come along, snatch her right up from under you, and give her what you won't. And you won't have anyone to blame but yourself."

I look back at Katelyn on the dance floor as I say my next words. Short, as usual. "I know."

The words are quiet, an admission to myself as much to Marla.

"I told her weeks ago that you were cold and steady. Actually, I told her you were a boring Boy Scout."

That gets my attention. If Marla is talking down about me, it'd definitely affect how fast Katelyn gives up on me. As much as I keep thinking that'd probably be the best thing for her, I don't want that. Not yet. I look at her, narrowing my eyes.

She grins, seeing that she has my attention. "Wanna know what she said?"

I lift my brow questioningly, nodding slowly, once.

Marla leans in to talk to me directly, her hard gaze not leaving any room for half-truths. "She said that you were like a volcano on the edge of eruption. That you said more with one eyebrow—exactly like you just did, mind you—than most guys said with a whole sentence. I didn't see it before, because you're kinda known for being a quiet asshole. But I see what she means now. But it only happens with her. For her."

I don't know if I've ever been this uncomfortable before. It means a lot to me that Katelyn sees that in me, but talking about shit like this with Katelyn's friend is weird.

"Thanks for telling me that. I appreciate it. A lot."

She gets up, laying money for her and David's share of dinner on the table. She slips her purse on her shoulder. "Tick-tock, Mark. Tick. Tock."

CHAPTER 15

KATELYN

"So I'll see you at work Monday, okay?" Marla says, giving me a hug at the door to Hank's. Just as I let go, she whispers in my ear, "Go for it."

I know what she's saying, but the drive home is tense, totally silent other than the rumble of the truck's engine. I can tell Mark's wound tight as a spring, his hands gripping the steering wheel in a death grip that's turning his knuckles white.

I have to fight the urge to reach across the cab and kiss them, soothe whatever tension he's fighting, but I decide that chatter might be the better course of action. Pushing him physically didn't work out so well last time.

So I fill the cab with just about anything that comes to mind that isn't girly or sappily romantic. Car movies, The Rock, pizza . . . I think I even mention my favorite flavor of Gatorade. It's so much that as we pull up in front of my place, I can't even recall much of what I said. I'm sure that it was all a bunch of rambling, semicoherent blabbing, but he seems to like that about me. Why? I really have no damn clue.

Still, he comes around like before, offering me an elbow as he walks me to my door, gentlemanly even though I can tell he's still fighting something inside.

"What did Marla say? I saw you two talking. I'll talk to her. I'm sorry if she pissed you off," I start, laying my hands on his chest.

Mark looks at me in the dim glow of my porch light, folding his hands over mine and pressing my palms against the hard planes of his pecs. I can feel his heartbeat, steady and sure, but thumping a bit fast, like the bass line in a rock song that's just about to go from steady to ass kicking.

"She said if I don't give you what you want, someone else will and I'll be alone in a misery of my own making," he finally says. His voice is sad, resigned, as if that's the only possible way the future could play out.

"Oh," I say, biting my lip and not sure what to say to that. I mean, she's probably right, but I'm not in any rush to chase someone else. Even this little bit with Mark is more than I've ever felt before. More exciting. More powerful. More sparks.

"She's right," he says fatalistically.

I don't say anything, the quiet full of the lust from my body and the hope from my heart. Instead, I let my eyes ask the question, and Mark sighs, looking down. "I can't give you much more, princess. I just can't. But I can try . . . a little more. If you think it'll be enough."

His words should give me pause. But a deeper, more primal part of my brain hungers for this, whispering that even if it's not all of Mark, it's more than I've ever experienced, and that can be enough. For now.

"Please." I hear the begging, the permission, the desire in my voice, and so does he.

His eyes flare as he steps through into my living room, like it's the final step of one phase and the first of another. In a way, I guess it is. He's been here before, but this feels different.

He shuts the door behind him with finality, like he's warning me that I can't get away now. But I don't want to get away. I want to get closer.

He crosses the room, guiding me backward to the couch, and I kick my heels off, sitting on my knees to meet him.

He cups my face in his hands, forcing my eyes to his as he locks me in place. "Katelyn?"

He's giving me one last out, but I don't want it. I rise up on my knees, getting closer to him and forcing matters on my own.

I meet his lips with mine, and with a growl of defeat, he takes over. His lips move over mine, fierce from the first touch, his mouth laying claim to mine with heat and power.

His tongue invades me, tasting, devouring. And though I move against him, kiss for kiss, there's no doubt who's in control.

Mark nips at my bottom lip and then sucks it into his mouth for a tiny nibble before soothing the sting with a lick. I moan at the sharp twinge, and his reply is instant.

"Fuck, princess."

His kisses move down my neck, across my collarbone, and he traces the thin straps of my top, following the fabric edge along my chest. The barest of touches but it feels like he's searing me, the heat a map of burning paths marking where he's been and highlighting the untouched skin I need him to claim.

I arch against him, silently begging for more. His eyes darken as he sees my nipples harden beneath the silky fabric. He runs a thick finger around the obvious tip, teasing me and not getting quite where I need him.

"You know, the only thing keeping me from this all night has been me—not some slip of a shirt."

He's right. He's the one setting the pace, holding fierce restraint even as I beg for more. Something about that makes me want to tempt him further, find the tipping point where he goes wild, just to see if I can. To witness what an uncontrolled Mark might be like.

"I know." The response is barely an answer to his comment because it's more air than sound. "Mark . . . I need you."

I can feel a shudder rush through him, and he reaches down to the hem of my top, pulling it over my head in a whoosh.

My hair settles back around my shoulders, and I watch in shock as this powerhouse of a man unfastens my bra and drops to his knees before me, his face even with my chest, a reverent look in his eyes as he runs his hands over my breasts.

"You're perfect, Katelyn. Gorgeous."

He wraps a muscular arm around my lower back, pulling me to him, and the first touch of his tongue to my nipple is like lightning shooting through me.

I cry out, pressing more of my flesh into his mouth, wanting him to taste all of me. He sucks me deep, with drawing pulls that seem connected to my clit, pulsing in time with his ministrations.

He switches to my left breast, his free hand covering the wet heat as his mouth deserts the skin of my right breast, using his saliva to slip and slide around my nipple.

"Oh God . . . yesss . . ."

He growls against me, pulling away to look in my eyes. "No. Only my name."

Happy to oblige, I breathe his name, stroking through his hair again. "Mark . . . always."

I lean back, giving more, and he holds me secure, like an offering as he feasts on me, devouring me like a man possessed. My skirt is nothing but a band around my waist, my pussy against his stomach as he covers me, and I can't stop the bucking of my hips, searching for more as I ride him mindlessly.

His fingers slide down, cupping my ass and massaging my skin. It makes me feel nearly naked and ready to take him, but he's fully dressed. The difference makes me feel sexy, like his plaything.

"I want to feel how wet you are for me," he says as his fingers tease the edge of my panties, his breath hot in my ear. "To feel your hot pussy clamp on my fingers when you get so overloaded with pleasure, you come apart in my arms as you scream my name."

None of his statements are questions, more like promises, but I nod anyway, doing what I can to encourage him. "Do it . . ."

He pulls my panties to the side, stroking my lips with a powerful, slightly rough thumb before his middle finger dives into my core, impaling me in one forceful stroke.

My breath is snatched from my lungs, my body frozen in pleasure, every muscle contracting. Not at the invasion, but to keep him there, locked inside my body. I feel my pussy wrap around him, and I squeeze him, let him know that yes, this is what I want . . . and to never stop.

"So tight. You feel like fucking velvet," Mark rasps, sliding his finger back and making me whimper. "Sin and sunshine . . . and redemption."

The poetic words somehow unlock my body, and he fingerfucks me, adding another finger, his thick digits filling me over and over as I move my hips in time with his thrusts.

"No," he orders, his arm around my waist tightening and holding me still. "Take it, princess. Take what I give you."

His words shock me, harsher than he's ever spoken to me before, but there's an edge to them, too . . . one of security. I can trust that he's got me.

I think . . . I like it. That mix of authority and care.

I stare into his eyes, meeting his hardened glare and smile. "So bossy," I say, hoping he can hear how seductive his control is.

He spears his fingers deeper into me, almost to the edge of pain, but my mouth drops open in pleasure as he gives me more.

"You have no idea."

I fight the instinct to fuck myself on his hand, to search for what I want, hoping that somehow he can get me to the peak I feel coming like a freight train. I'm used to working myself for it, either alone or with Seth.

But Mark seems to have instinctually mastered my body, telling it what it wants and my body automatically saying yes. It's delicious torture, staying still for him, but I want it to go on forever.

"Fuck, Mark. Feels so good . . . I'm close . . ."

He ups his tempo, his palm smacking my clit as his fingers plunge in and out of me roughly, curling up with every stroke to stretch and stroke me deeply. He's slamming into me so hard I think I'll split in two, and I know I'll be bruised tomorrow. Good. Because my fear is that this is a dream, just a fantasy, and I want to know he's been inside me long after he's gone.

"No, you're not," Mark says, interrupting my thoughts and pulling me back to this moment, this agonizing paradise that he's giving me. "That's not your edge. You can take more. Don't come until I say."

I cry out, every tap against my clit vibrating through my body as I arch back, thankful that he's holding me tight because I feel like I could float away without him to anchor me. "Ahhh . . ."

He freezes, his fingers grinding against my front wall, finding my G-spot easily. The change in stimulation staves off the impending explosion, feeling good but different, and my orgasm drifts away. I pout, digging my fingernails into his shoulders as I whimper, begging.

"No . . . please."

I lift my head from where it dropped back to find him watching me closely, his very being in tune with my every move.

"Take what I give you, princess," he repeats, his voice sounding like he's slightly disappointed in me, like he shouldn't have to repeat himself. "And you don't come until I say."

I nod, biting my lip to keep from begging. I've never felt like this, like something life-changing is about to overtake my body, but I want to show Mark that I can take everything he wants to give me. Because as much as he wants to give, I want to take. I want to take it all, every morsel of pleasure he can wring from me.

He keeps massaging my spot, slow and constant and unrelenting. I moan at the sensation, so different than before but driving me just as crazy, but I force myself to relax in his arms, trusting him to have me.

"Good girl, princess."

His nickname unlocks the deepest points inside me. Any hope of holding back my orgasm evaporates in an instant, and I cry out.

"Mark, I'm falling . . . please . . ."

His arm tightens around me, so tight it'd squeeze the breath out of me—if I were breathing at all. Instead, I'm hovering right on the edge, everything in my body paused as I force myself to wait. He touches his forehead to mine, his words deep and piercing me all the way to my soul.

"I'll catch you. Come for me, Katelyn."

I detonate, shudders racking through my body as wave after wave of pleasure washes over me. Stars sparkle behind my eyeballs, and I think I yell his name, or maybe I just scream incoherently. I don't know.

I've had orgasms, but I've never felt whatever he just did to my body. I don't know what to call that, because *orgasm* doesn't seem like nearly a strong enough word to describe it. It's like he took my entire body and rearranged all the cells to his liking, reshaping it the way he wants. I feel changed at a fundamental level forever.

Through the whole thing, he holds me tight, teasing every last bit of pleasure out of me until I'm fighting against him, pushing on his shoulders.

"Too much . . . mmm . . ."

He lowers me to the couch, his fingers still teasing inside me.

"Don't make me tell you again, but I'll go easy on you. This time."

My brain is fogged, so it takes me a second to connect the dots that my job is to take what he gives, and I just questioned him. Again. I have no doubt that if he wanted to, he'd take me right into another orgasm. Easily.

I don't know if I could stay conscious through it all, though, and he seems to recognize that.

"That was *easy* on me?" I ask, my voice a shocked rasp. "That was more like, holy shit, Mark. I'm going to feel that with every step I take tomorrow," I whisper incredulously, wiggling my hips a little happily. "You ride hard, cowboy."

I eye him, bleary but unable to miss the way he takes his fingers into his mouth, sucking my juices from them with a moan. *Oh shit, maybe I could go again.* Just watching the joy on his face at tasting me has my body filling with a deep desire for more.

I reach for him, trying to pull him on top of me on the couch, but he shakes his head.

"Katelyn," he says.

I wait for the rest, but he just says my name, like the word on his tongue at the same time as my flavor is a treat in itself. But his face is haunted, his eyes stormy. His fingers move to rearrange my panties before I realize what he's doing.

"Mark?" I at least stop myself before breaking his order again.

He gives me a look of satisfaction, like I did well, and though it shouldn't mean anything, just the look makes me bask in the silent praise.

Without a sound, he guides me down to lie on my side before arranging a cushion under my head, and tucks me in with the blanket from the back of the couch. It feels nice. No one has taken care of me in a long time, but I still feel like there should be more happening.

I can see the bulge in his jeans, thick and straining against his zipper. I want him to feel pleasure too. I want to show him how changed I am because he just opened my eyes to a whole new world of colors. Something tells me it's barely the surface with him too. And I want more—every hue on the spectrum. And I want to make him experience them too. With my hands, my mouth, my body. With me.

But I'm boneless, jelly from the way he worked me, and I'm not going to question him. Instead, Mark shifts, taking a single knee beside me before he kisses me slowly and deeply, the intensity maybe more powerful because it feels possessive and protective.

"Get some sleep, princess."

Before I know what's happening, he's gone, my front door closing silently as he disappears.

I consider moving to my bed or putting on pj's, but in the end, I stay right where he left me and do exactly what he said. Sleep.

CHAPTER 16

MARK

Driving the ATV back from the back pasture where I've been working myself into an exhausted mess, I thump my forehead with my palm, cursing myself yet again.

I'm a complete asshole.

For a moment there, I considered that I might have some redeeming qualities. I brought Katelyn home, I was a gentleman escorting her to her door . . . but no, complete and total bastard.

I've replayed what happened in my head a thousand times. Driving home, I thought I'd be watching the mental repeat while I jacked off, but now . . . now it just makes me cringe.

She trusted me, willing to expose her inner goodness and light, to place that soft beauty in my hands. I should have cradled it, and if I couldn't do that, I should've walked away before she got hurt. What I did was take her light and squeeze it tighter and tighter until it blinked out and she fell apart in my arms.

For a beautiful moment, I thought it was okay, that she was with me. The sass she gave me about being bossy seemed like a hint that she could handle at least a taste of me.

But with her eyes barely open after I wrung every last bit of pleasure out of her that I could, she seemed confused that I called what I'd done to her "easy." She didn't understand, had gone further than ever before, had more than she ever dreamed possible.

For me, though, it was barely the tip of the iceberg. And even before I kissed her, I knew. As much as her light called to me, as much as it still beckons me with the sweet taste of heaven, she's not the woman I deserve. I'd just dim her brightness, ruin her new and innocent attempts at independence. And though I'm a bastard, I can at least give her freedom from my destruction.

Still, I fed my needs one last time, tucking her in and caring for her, letting myself feel better that at least I left her satisfied and hoping that she'd remember the end of the night, not the way I'd been too rough with her. But even I know that not so much as sending a good morning text after being fingers-deep inside her is the pinnacle of shithead moves.

I keep telling myself it's for her own good. It worked for most of the day yesterday as I toiled in the barn, repairing the auto feeder and getting elbows-deep in a machine that was built three years before I was born and coming out blacker than midnight in the back forty.

When she calls Sunday morning, I'm too short with her, more grunts than usual, but I can't stop myself. It's so ingrained in me. And it's an easy slip into the protective facade that will hopefully keep her from seeing how disappointed in myself I am.

"Yeah?"

"Hey, Mark," she says hopefully. "I figured you'd be up, and I was going—" Her words drive a stake in my chest. She still thinks I'm a good man. Redeemable, fixable, a seed brimming with potential to be positively guided.

I interrupt her, glad I'm outside so Mama can't slap me in the head.

"Katelyn . . . I'm sorry. I shouldn't have . . ."

It's all I have. There's nothing more I can say to explain, and honestly, I don't know if I can verbalize the mess I feel inside. How fucking amazing it was, how much I loved the feeling of her in my arms, trusting me to catch her, and how sorry I am that I was too hard on her.

It was everything I could've wanted, and then, with a careless phrase, she highlighted once again that not only do I not get what I want, but that I shouldn't even want it in the first place.

"Oh . . . okay." There's less spark to her voice now, like I disappointed her.

"What were you going to say?" I ask hesitantly. I'm afraid I'm a glutton for punishment, but if I don't find out, I'll always wonder.

"I heard about the town's Fourth of July festival, and I was going to ask if you wanted to watch the fireworks together, but . . ." She trails off.

"I don't think that's a good idea," I say as gently as possible, the words acid on my tongue. Fireworks? Just her presence is fireworks in my life, and while I've always loved seeing the real thing, the town's display has nothing on Katelyn's sparks.

"Um, okay. Thanks for . . . ," Katelyn says, trying to find a reply. "I'll see you around or whatever. Bye, Mark."

Her words are stilted, softer and softer until she's barely whispering. When the line goes dead, it feels like my heart stops too.

It's for her own good, I remind myself again and again throughout the rest of the day, like it's a mantra. But protecting her, even from me, hurts so damn much.

And now, because I'm a weak asshole, I don't even have her as a friend.

After the call, I pour myself into work, ignoring the rest of the normal Sunday schedule to do outdoor work like a beast, riding myself hard as some twisted form of punishment. I'm tempted to take Sugarpea, riding out to the farthest pasture to be alone, but the kind horse's comforting presence isn't what I deserve right now.

Instead, I take the Gator, heading out to cut down a tree that's on the edge of death with an ax. It'd be faster to use a chain saw, but I want the work, the hard labor of almost futilely hacking at the dense ironwood until the sweat trickles down my back and my muscles are on fire. It's painful, and even my toughened hands develop a blister that pops and oozes a sticky mess, but it's what I need. I need to feel it.

Now it's time for dinner, and the sun hangs lows in the sky, but I don't feel any better. I park the Gator and set the ax aside, knowing that after dinner I'll be back out here in the barn, sharpening the now blunt steel and unloading the stacks of wood tied down on the ATV's bed. More work, more distraction, more penance.

I rinse off quickly, stripping down in the barn to hose off and pull on a fresh shirt for Mama's dinner table.

Dinner is slightly tense, and I'm silent, even for me. I can feel Mama's eyes on me. James and Luke both try to give me shit to lighten my dour mood, and even Sophie's story about a pet ferret's weird tricks doesn't engage me. I barely respond to any of it, not even grunting most of the time tonight.

"Hey, Mark, since you decided that training for your next career as a woodcutter was more important, you can thank me for taking Mama into town," Luke says, grinning. "You better be glad about it, too, or else you'd be eating nothing but grits for dinner."

"Hmm."

I know Luke's just teasing—he loves going into town and making a Sunday of the whole thing—but I'm busy giving myself a mental whipping again.

I'm about halfway through my dinner when I realize Mama is talking to me. Setting my spoon down, I look up. "What, Mama?"

She gives me a concerned look, but she doesn't say anything for a second.

"I said we'll head to town midafternoon tomorrow like usual for the Fourth of July festivities, right?"

I shake my head, thinking about Katelyn's phone call. "Nah, I'm gonna skip it this year."

She balks, giving me her full attention. "Excuse me? The h-e-double hockey sticks you are, young man. It's tradition."

I glare at her, but she's immune to my dark looks—one, because I got them from Pops, so she's got plenty of experience ignoring them; and two, because she remembers me as a sweet kid. It's hard to change your Mama's opinion of you, no matter how good you get at looking stern and intimidating.

"Luke can take you," I finally reply, looking back down at my plate. "And James and Sophie will be there."

Mama isn't having any of it, though. "And you'll be there too. You're going, and that's final."

She gets up from the table and heads into the kitchen, muttering something about "hardheaded boys who grow up into stubborn men" to Sophie, who trails after her. I don't argue further, knowing that once she's said it's *final*, it fucking is.

The silence at the table is long and drawn out, and I know my brothers are staring at me in utter shock. Maybe even some anger. When Mama leaves the table like that, it usually means no dessert.

Finally, James can't take it anymore. "What the hell, man? Why don't you want to go to the festival? It's one of the things we look forward to all year!"

I shake my head slowly, spooning up my beans mechanically. "Because I've been working my ass off all day and would love a chance to just sit down and chill the fuck out," I growl. "Just one day, I'd like to sit around like a lazy ass. I don't want to deal with the crowds of people, shitty food, and fireworks that are the same every year."

Luke and James stare at me openmouthed before looking at each other, big shit-eating grins breaking across their faces simultaneously.

"Bull-fucking-shit," Luke says. "Your idea of being a lazy ass *specifically* involves funnel cake and Snicker-changas. So what the fuck is up?"

Goddammit, Luke's right. I do look forward to the once-a-year treat that is the deep-fried tortilla, whipped cream, sauce, and Snickers, only available during the Fourth Festival.

"Nothing."

James jumps to the right conclusion, though. Asshole.

"This is about Katelyn, isn't it? We did herd checkups damn near all day yesterday, and I didn't see you check your phone once. Lord knows, you've been texting and calling each other like teenagers for the last week, so for her to not text you means something. Especially now that you're grumpier than usual and talking shit about the best funnel cakes ever."

I don't reply, spooning my last bite of beans into my mouth.

"And I ask again," Luke growls, "what the fuck is up? What did you do?"

"We were friends, and I fucked it up, okay?" I say in a rare moment of confession, slamming my spoon down on the table and rattling the glasses. I push back from the table, stalking out to finish my work. As I hit the door, I glance over my shoulder, tossing my farewell back toward the kitchen. I guess I should be grateful Mama was out of earshot or I'd be getting a verbal lashing on my way out. "Thanks for dinner, Mama," I call out.

I don't stop, not for her questions, not for my brothers' teasing concern, not for anything. Instead, I head out to the barn, grabbing the blunt ax and the sharpening stone, ready to get to work.

As the stone rasps over the steel, the anger builds hot in my belly as I start cursing myself again.

I should've had better control. Not only about how I just acted at dinner, but obviously with Katelyn. If I couldn't have stopped it from happening completely, I should have at least been enough of a fucking gentleman to not hurt her.

And now I have nothing. Again.

Not even a friend.

Friendship fucking sucks, but being alone feels so much worse than it did before I got a taste of her sunshine.

My hand slips, and I scrape the back of my knuckles along the edge of the ax blade. I hiss as the skin is scraped away, the physical pain sharp but nothing compared to the sick feeling in my gut.

CHAPTER 17

KATELYN

"So grab a bit and just pull. Like this," Marla tells me, demonstrating her tried-and-true method of eating funnel cakes without getting powdered sugar all over herself. It's nothing I haven't seen before. I've eaten my fair share of funnel cakes, but that isn't stopping Marla from trying her best to be a good host on the introduction to a Great Falls Fourth.

I watch her, noticing that her tried-and-true method isn't very effective, but my mind is absent anyway, distracted and wishing I could be at home alone, soothing my wounded pride.

"Your turn," Marla instructs, wiping at her cheeks. "And may you be better than your teacher!"

I grab a bit of the fried dough, ripping it off without care and shoving it in my mouth. I'm sure it's delicious, but it feels like Play-Doh in my mouth. Marla notices and smiles softly, trying to keep a cheerful front going.

"Well, you did just make a huge mess, but fried dough and sugar—can't go wrong with that."

I look down, dusting the white powder from my top. "Yeah, I guess."

Marla nods, then grabs her husband by the arm. "Hey, David, why don't you take the girls on the Ferris wheel?"

He looks from her to me as he tucks away the last of a corn dog. Their silent communication is usually adorable when they finish each other's sentences. Right now, it's another reminder of what I don't have.

Their daughters, cute as buttons, bounce up and down, eager to get away from the mopey adult ruining their good time.

"Sure, just give me a wave when you're ready to move on."

He lays a sweet kiss to Marla's lips as he pats her hip, then turns to the two dark-haired girls swirling around us, already hyped up on sugar and excitement.

"Alright, girls, who's ready for the whirling and twirling town view from the tippy top of the Ferris wheel?" he says, imitating a carny with loads of melodramatic flair. "It'll be sooooo high!"

The girls jump up and down, both squealing, "Me! Me! We are!"

He scoops them up in his arms, holding one on each hip with ease and moving through the crowd toward the big white circle reaching high in the cloudless blue sky. I smile at the sweet picture they make, wistful for my own version of Marla's happy ever after. At least something makes me smile, and Marla uses the opportunity to see if she can get a little deeper.

"Okay, hit me with it. What happened?"

I shake my head, wishing she couldn't already read me like an open book. "What? No, nothing happened. Everything's fine."

Marla snorts, blowing a small puff of powdered sugar off her upper lip and making her look like the world's cutest half dragon.

"Lie. Try again, Katelyn. Friday night you left Hank's looking like you were floating. Now, today of all days, the first three-day weekend we've had in who knows how long, you look like someone just told you you've got a dozen June bridezillas all wanting refunds and a piece of your ass. So, spill."

"Fine. Just feeling a little homesick with the holiday. You know, Fourths aren't much different wherever you are. A little fried food, a lot of corn dogs, rattling old rides . . . just giving me flashbacks," I try, seeing if she'll believe that and drop it.

No such luck. "My bullshit detector's blinking hard. What's wrong? Work? Is there really some new bridezilla you don't want to tell me about? Something back in Idaho? Mark? Did he fuck up?"

I'm shaking my head back and forth as she starts on a laundry list of sins, but something must change on my face because she realizes the issue. "Mark . . . goddamn. Okay, so he fucked up. Tell me about it so I know what I'm kicking his ass for next time I see him."

I grin a little, knowing she probably really would do that if Mark had wronged me somehow. And in some ways, it'd be entertaining to watch five and a half feet of Marla fury going banshee on Mark.

But he didn't do anything wrong. Not really. He's been upfront from the beginning that he isn't interested in pursuing anything with me, even though the chemistry is off the charts.

I should've respected that. I just thought . . . my body still aches for his touch, and I wonder if I'm ever going to have anyone satisfy me that completely, that thoroughly, ever again.

I realize Marla is waiting, and I decide that I could use some advice, even though she's the one who *kind of* got me into this mess. Alright, I know she didn't really; that blame lies solely on me for pushing for things Mark told me he didn't want to give. She might've helped speed up the runaway train just a bit, but she's my best friend around town, so who else am I going to talk to?

"Fine," I sigh before stuffing the rest of the funnel cake into my mouth and talking around the sweet mess. "So, I guess you said some stuff to him Friday at Hank's, something about not waiting forever because someone else wouldn't?"

She visibly winces and looks genuinely embarrassed. "Oh shit, should I not have said that? I was trying to help. I swear it, Katelyn."

"No, it's fine. It's the truth probably. Anyway . . ."

I give her the rundown of Friday night, how Mark had rocked my world and left me bonelessly blissed out but is now brushing me off. As I continue, I keep telling myself I'm not going to cry, but my eyes certainly feel grainy as I finish up.

"He even turned me down on coming to the fireworks. So I guess I fucked things up pretty good somehow. I'm not sure what happened."

Marla is wringing her hands, twisting her napkin to the point of it being a useless, ripped-up scrap.

"Shit, Katelyn. I'm so sorry. I feel like I might've messed this up for you."

I shake my head, blinking away my tears. "No, it's been one step forward and two steps back with Mark the whole time. He even accused me of playing games. He's flirty, then warns me off with a 'just friends' label. He wrings pleasure from me and then bolts. I just can't deal with that. If I'm going to date someone, I don't need someone too weighed down with his own shit when I'm just getting free of mine. It sucks, because I really like him. Even more because I can tell he likes me too."

Marla nods along with me but furrows her brow. "Okay, hear me out for a second . . . and I'm saying this as your friend, so don't hold it against me tomorrow morning at the office. Deal?"

I nod, even though I'm not sure I want to hear what she's going to say, considering how thick she's laying on the disclaimers. "Go ahead."

"So you were with Boring Beige Boy since the dawn of time, right?"

"Something like that. Why?"

"And it was easy—no muss, no fuss. No boat-rocking, just smooth sailing until you left and came here. Am I right?"

I nod again, still not seeing where she's going. "You know you are. We've talked about Seth, although now I'm stuck thinking of him as Triple B—Boring Beige Boy," I say sarcastically. "He's got a nickname more exciting than he is, so thanks for that."

Marla grins wanly. "It's a gift, Great Falls seems to come up with nicknames for everyone. But what I mean is that you never had to talk anything out, deal with your issues or his, fight and make up. At the first real sign of disagreement with Triple B, you did what you wanted and left him."

My jaw drops, indignation flaring inside me. "But he could've come—"

Marla holds up a hand, stopping me. "Hang on. I'm not saying you were wrong to do that. Because you did the right thing, coming here and chasing your dream, and obviously Triple B wasn't the guy for you or you'd be all torn up missing him instead of us having this conversation about Mark."

My ire settled, she gets down to the crux of her speech.

"All I'm saying is that you've never had to fight with someone you care about and come out the other side of it stronger and closer. It's not always easy, and I get the sense you don't want it to be. I think part of what you like about Mark is that he's complicated. He's a challenge you want to conquer, want to earn. So fight for it, earn it."

I shrug my shoulders, unconvinced. "And do what? Chase him like some needy, desperate girl? Isn't the guy supposed to be the pursuer?"

Marla laughs a little bitterly, but there's a hint of frustration in her voice. "Only in teenage rom-coms. In the real world, where you're an adult, if you want him, have a conversation, for God's sake. Fuck, David and I, we've had a few conversations that tore our guts out at the time, but it made us who we are today."

"From what I see, it's pretty damn good."

"It is," Marla agrees. "And maybe when it's boring in the office I'll tell you about it. But for now, find out what spooked Mark and see if it's fixable. Maybe it is and maybe it isn't, but at least you'll know instead of floating along letting life happen to you. I thought the whole point of starting over here was that you were choosing your own destiny, following your own star. So why the hell would you let Mark decide you're done if that's not the case?"

I'm silent, letting all she's said sink in. Is she right? Am I giving up too easily, letting him dictate what happens because I got my feelings hurt by his tendency to reel me in and then push me away?

The back-and-forth is hard, but from everything Mark's told me, he's maybe just as inexperienced with the whole relationship thing as I am. And maybe he's got some issues, sure . . . but maybe I just need to draw those out, listen to him, and then decide rather than go off the surface information.

I sigh, giving Marla a look. "For being damn near thirty, I feel like a teenager just learning how to date. Isn't that sad? I've been unwilling for years—years—to challenge myself and figure out what I really wanted, what would make me happy."

"Could be worse," Marla says with a snicker. "You could still be in Boise with Triple B."

"Okay, no more moping. I owe myself at least a chance with Mark, especially considering the way he makes me feel," I reply, almost smiling.

"Damn right you do. And I need all the details," Marla says with a knowing wink.

I grab Marla in a big hug. "Thank you. You are so fucking smart! I'm lucky to have you." I pull back and grin. "I think I'm going to head home, skip the fireworks. I've got some *stuff* to take care of."

Marla smiles, patting me on the back. "Go get him, honey."

I haul butt back to my place before curling up on my couch, taking a couple of deep breaths for courage. It's not like calling a guy is that big of a deal, especially considering we talked nearly every night before things went sideways, but this feels different. Before I can lose my courage, I grab my phone and search through my recent calls, pressing Mark's number.

"Hello."

I smirk to myself. Most people answer with some inflection of a question, but not Mark. Like everything else, it's merely a statement.

Without thought, I meet his statement with one of my own, meeting him declaration for declaration.

"I'm not sorry."

Since Mark wasn't privy to the jumping trails of my funnel cake–fueled therapy session tonight, he's understandably confused.

"Huh?"

"You said you were sorry about the other night," I explain. "I'm not. I'm not sorry at all. And I don't want you to think it was a mistake. That *I* was a mistake. Because it was . . . wow. You are . . . wow."

I'm rambling, a sure sign that I'm nervous, but it's worked with Mark in the past, and I can't stop the words from bubbling out of my mouth anyway.

"Katelyn," he starts, but I won't let him grab the momentum from me. Come hell or high water, I'm going to get this out.

"No, don't say you're sorry again," I order. "You're running away again, but I'm not. I'm not sorry about one damn thing we did, and I wanted you to know that. It's been on my mind all weekend."

He sighs, and it sounds like he's letting go of a weight. "It's all I've been thinking about too," he confesses. "I feel like . . . I feel like I've been in a free fall all weekend."

I think of the way he caught me as I fell apart in his arms right here on this very couch, and I know he's worth the back-and-forth, worth the work to figure this out. And I know something else—if he's falling, I can catch him too.

"Mark, come over—now. Please?" I say, the words jumping out before I can second-guess them.

CHAPTER 18

MARK

One word. That was all it took to undo all my determination that I was going to do the right thing by her.

Then . . . *please*. One word, so needy after ordering me to come over, it was like a shot straight to my cock. Normally the drive from the ranch to her part of town is about twenty minutes, so just under ten minutes later, I'm sitting in the parking lot outside her place, my fingers drumming on the steering wheel and uncertainty tearing apart my guts.

Do I turn around and go home for her own good? Do I get out and go in for my own sanity?

Maybe she just wants to talk . . .

Yeah, right. I heard the need in her voice, and she didn't call me to talk about which restaurants in town are decent besides Hank's.

We do need to talk, but that's not what this visit is and we both know it. I remind myself once again to take it easy on her. She's inexperienced and, from the sound of it, had only one partner until the other night. And that fucking city boy certainly didn't know what he had, because if he did, he'd have never let her leave Idaho.

The thought that I do know what a catch she is stirs a deeper desire inside me, one that makes me want to take her as mine, to claim her and give her all her body can handle, and maybe even a little more to push her. I want to brand her, sear her with my mark inside and out.

Steady, Mark . . . be calm, gentle. I repeat it to myself like a mantra, as if I can will the words to direct my actions. This is for her, to give her something she needs, wants to experience. And if I have to hold back, then I damn sure will.

She opens the door as I approach, not even letting me knock. She must have been watching for me. "Come in."

I don't pause at the doorway this time. We both know why I'm here, so there's no need to fight it. She has on pink yoga pants, virtually painted on her skin, and an oversize shirt that's falling off one shoulder. The soft, barely tanned skin it shows pulls my eyes to her, my mouth watering as I imagine sucking, nibbling . . . marking that skin.

Her hair is piled on top of her head, and her face is as bare as her pink-toed feet. She's dressed down; there isn't a hint of anything other than her natural self. No makeup, no perfume, nothing but Katelyn. She's never been more beautiful.

My eyes stay on her as I walk in, taking in the feminine, graceful curve of her neck, the way she's looking at me, afraid but courageous, and the way her lip looks plump, ripe for me to tug with my teeth.

She closes and locks the door behind her, the sound of the deadbolt closing sending a shock through both of our systems. I see the steadying breath she takes and know this is big for her. It's big for me too.

She said it's been months for her; it's been more than six months for me, and that was a one-night stand when I went to Vegas to watch James do his retirement bull ride and propose to Sophie. I'm not proud of it, but I was weak, and the girl was willing.

Now I have another willing woman, but this one's different. This is Katelyn, and if anything, she's the biggest danger in my life. Because it's not just a one-night thing, and it's not just a physical coupling—it's threatening to be a lot more.

"Katelyn?" It's a question, but I'm not sure what I'm asking.

She turns, her back to the door and her eyes on me. "Yes."

It's a statement, no question, and it's all the answer I need. I push her into the door, sandwiching her between the wood and my body, cupping her face in my large hands and bending down to kiss her.

She tastes faintly minty, and I realize she brushed her teeth in anticipation of my arrival. The idea that she wants this, was planning and preparing for it, readying herself for me, is my undoing. Our mouths become frantic, both of us eager and hungry for more, and I need to invade her mouth the way she's invaded my thoughts.

I feel her hands claw into my chest for a split second as she grabs hold of my T-shirt, fisting it in an attempt to pull me even closer or to keep me here. Like I'm going anywhere. She's unleashed the animal inside me, and wild stallions couldn't pull me away right now.

I look down at her hands and see her hard nipples through the white cotton of her own tee, making me lift an eyebrow.

"Princess, are you going braless?"

My voice is hard, the admonishment slipping in naturally. She bites her lip and looks up at me through her lashes. "I'm not wearing a bra," she says sassily, flirtation in every prolonged syllable. "Just this thin T-shirt."

Easy, I remind myself. She sassed me like this last time, and I'm going to keep myself under control this time. I slip my hand beneath the hem, appreciating the silk of her skin for a moment before pulling the shirt up and off.

She lifts her arms over her head to aid me getting it off her, and I love the way the gesture arches her back, pressing her tits toward me. Her shoulders are against the door, her hips pressed against me, and the curve is perfection personified.

I gather her wrists in one hand, holding them above her head against the door and running the fingers of my other hand along her sternum. It's soft, so soft and silky, and Katelyn shivers, goosebumps breaking out along her skin. I want to taste each and every one of them.

She squirms, but I press her hands to the door, stilling her. "Stay."

I let go, trusting that she'll be still, and lower slowly to my knees, trailing kisses down her chest and along her belly. I tug at the waistband of her pants, slipping them over her hips and letting them fall to her feet, where she steps out. Breathlessly, I stare at her. She's Venus, she's perfection, she's the epitome of beauty. She's . . . mine.

"Princess . . . no panties either."

I glance up her body to see she's panting and shaking her head no. "I should lecture you on walking around like a bad girl, your pussy so ready to be taken," I whisper, chastising her as my hands find the outer curves of her hips and my fingertips start to dig into her flawless flesh. "But all I want to do is show you how breathtaking you are. Spread your legs for me."

She slides her feet apart, and I can see her even better now. "Fuck, Katelyn. Look at this pretty pink slit, so wet for me. I've been dreaming of this."

I peel her lips apart with my thumbs, the heady scent intoxicating as her clit peeks out, inviting my tongue and drawing a groan from the depths of my very soul. I already know she's sweet as candy, having tasted her from my fingers before, but I can only imagine that she's even sweeter at the source.

"Me too," she says, her whisper-soft words floating to my ears and making me shiver.

I can't tear my eyes away from her glistening sex, but my voice drops to a sibilant growl as I reply. "You've been dreaming about me licking you, sucking you, devouring your pussy with my mouth? What else? Tell me."

I can feel the blush rush through her body, instantly heating her beneath my hands as her lips and clit flush a darker pink. "I dream about . . . what happened before, doing that to you. I dream about you fucking me."

She's not used to talking like this, her words stilted and awkward on her tongue as she bares her fantasies along with her body. It makes me smile. I want this honesty, this vulnerability, this woman.

I reward her bravery with a long, slow lick to her pussy, her flavor bursting across my tongue, and I can't help the groan at how delicious she is.

"Mmm . . . so good. Tell me more and I'll make it come true," I promise her. "I want to give you everything you dream about."

I entice her with another lick, and she moans, running her hand through my hair. "I dream about how you made me come harder than I ever have before, how I want to do that again and again. I wonder how big you are, how you'd feel inside me, if I could take all of you . . . in my mouth, in my pussy. I want to see your face when you come, to wipe that stoic look off your face and make you gasp out my name with your eyes squeezed shut in pleasure."

Fuck, she's getting better at the dirty talk really damn fast. She's a quick study at everything. I reward each word with more and more licks and nibbles, wanting her to get lost in the pleasure until she comes on my tongue this time.

"Hold on to me," I tell her when she starts to grind her core against my mouth. I slip my hands between her legs and sweep both knees over my shoulders, holding her securely against the door as I take all her weight onto my body, stable and strong.

"Whoooa . . . ," she cries out. "What are you—"

"I've got you," I growl, biting at the juncture where her thigh meets her pussy. It's just a reminder to us both that I'm in control, a small taste of power to satisfy my inner animal.

"I know," she whispers, her words telling me more and making me howl inside. I hold her ass in my hands, gripping her tight and knowing that I'm probably leaving fingerprints. I love the thought of her silky flesh marred with my marks. Tomorrow, the day after, for days, she's going to have rose-petal-shaped bruises as visible reminders that I held her literally in the palms of my hands.

I spread her wide so that I can lick and suck every tender inch of her flesh, memorizing her every nook and cranny and cataloging her responses as my breath fans across her skin.

"Come for me, princess. Let me drink you down. I'm fucking thirsty for you."

I devour her, not holding back, and she shudders, crying out. "Mark," she wails as she shatters in my hands. Her pussy pulses against my tongue, coating my lips and chin with her honey even as I gulp at her. "Yessssss!"

Before the last tremor stops racking her body, I stand and pick her up, spinning and laying her down on the rug.

I should take her to bed, or at least the couch, but I need to be inside her now. I rip my shirt off and unbutton my jeans, grabbing the condom I stashed in my back pocket on a last-second burst of rationality before leaving the house.

I'm rolling it down my cock, rock hard and ready, when I hear Katelyn's gasp. "Holy shit, Mark."

I look at her, a slash of fear shooting through me. Have I already been too rough? I was being so careful, watching her so closely.

But she's looking at me with something like awe in her eyes.

"You're fucking huge . . . beautiful." She reaches for me, her touch soft through the condom. "I want to taste you too."

The thought of fucking her mouth, slipping into her throat as she swallows and works me with her muscles, is almost enough to send me over. But I have other things in mind—and when she swallows me, it's not going to be with anything between her lips and my cock anyway.

"Princess, if you so much as swiped your tongue across my cock right now, I'd explode. I want inside your sweet little pussy for that. I'm gonna fuck you now, just like you dreamed."

She grins, squirming like a kitten who just saw a saucer of cream. "I'll take whatever you want to give me."

It's a reminder of before, and I groan with delight, the pressure building in my balls. If I'm not careful, I'm going to be a two-pump chump—and that's never going to happen. I kneel between her legs and tease my head along her entrance, slapping it against her swollen and sensitive clit and watching as she tenses in response, her toes curling. Her pussy pulses in eager need, the stimulation getting her closer to the edge, but it staves off my orgasm just enough for me to gather the tattered shreds of my control.

A moment later, I slip in slowly, feeding her inch by inch and enjoying the tightness of her pussy as she lets me in. She claws at the rug, her eyes widening as I take her deeper than she's ever been taken before. "Fuck, Mark. So full . . ."

"You can take me. I'm almost all the way in," I say, watching her pussy consume me. "Just a bit more."

"There's more?" she squeaks, but before I can answer, I'm balls-deep, bottoming out and bumping against her back wall. "Ahh!"

"You good?" I ask, not entirely sure if that was a cry of pleasure or pain.

"No, I need you to move . . . please . . . ," she begs. "I need—"

Both of us forgetting the rules, I do as she asks. I pull back before starting to thrust, slow at first to let her get used to the stretch as I work my way back inside, half strokes that gradually grow longer and deeper. I can feel her walls quivering already, and I resist the urge to pound into her, to make her take me hard and rough.

Still, when I feel my hips press against her and she's squeezing me, her back arching as she silently yearns for more, I pick up speed, going faster and gaining power.

She bucks against me, fucking me back, but I swat her ass gently, pressing her firmly into the carpet. "Let me."

I scoop her hips up in my hands, holding her steady in the air as I begin fucking her with long, deep strokes that send tremors through both of our bodies.

Her pink tippy toes lose purchase, and she wraps her legs around me, locking her ankles behind my back as I speed up, keeping one hand on her ass while leaning forward to balance on the other hand, looming over her. With every stroke into her, her tits bounce from the force of the impact. I watch them, hypnotized.

"Play with your nipples," I demand, my arm giving me just enough distance to watch the show. "Show me how you touch them."

She doesn't so much as blush, just grabs her tits in each hand, squeezing and kneading. She's tapped into something deeper and primal, a sexual goddess who's been suppressed for far too long. The way her pale skin contrasts with the tan of her hands is gorgeous, reminding me that her tits are just for me right now, the creamy flesh obviously never having seen the light of the sun.

She pinches her nipples, harder than I would have thought she'd enjoy, and the sight inflames me. I slam into her pussy, her muscles squeezing me like a vise as she gives as good as she gets. "Fuck, princess. Pinch yourself again. It makes your pussy clench so fucking tight."

She does it again, her velvet walls choking me, and I'm there, flying over the edge and unable to hold back any longer. "Katelyn!" I roar out.

I come like a fucking freight train, pulse after pulse of cum filling the condom to capacity as I throw my head back, eyes squeezed tight at the onslaught of pleasure. Vaguely, I hear her calling my name too, her pussy matching me pulse for pulse, and I realize she's coming again. It fills my dimming mind with pride that I was able to give her what she deserves, and even as I'm returning to earth from the high of my own orgasm, I keep thrusting, giving her more to prolong hers, draining every bit of my energy for her.

Her tremors slow, and her eyes flutter open. "Fuck, Mark." My heart stops. *Is that good or bad?* She smiles dreamily, and my heart starts once again.

I scoop her up, finding my way to her bedroom and tucking her in. She clutches the blanket, but her beseeching eyes tell me what she really wants, and I give her a kiss on the nose. "Be right back."

I head into the bathroom to deal with the condom. Running some warm water, I wet a washcloth before coming back, peeling the blanket down. "Open."

She spreads for me with a small smile, letting me wipe down her pink center, and I can't resist laying one worshipful kiss to the bare softness of her mound. She giggles, wiggling beneath my lips. The sound is music to my soul, an aural symbol of a happy, satisfied Katelyn and a sign that I did well enough with my restraint.

I toss the rag back into the bathroom and slip into bed with her. Lying on my back, I hold one arm out in invitation, and she snuggles into my side with her head on my shoulder, soft as a kitten. I wrap my arm around her shoulders, holding her close, and she throws a leg over one of mine. It's comfortable, natural, and before I know it, she's breathing slow and easy, slipping into rest.

I replay the night in my mind, studiously looking for any signs that I was too rough or too bossy or just too much, reassuring myself that I was as easy and gentle as I could be with her. Before I know it, sleep overtakes me as I comfort myself, knowing Katelyn enjoyed herself as much as I did.

Seemingly minutes later, I wake up mid-dream. I was fucking Katelyn's mouth, fast and hard as I held her by her hair, holding her still and almost on the edge of exploding down her throat. What woke me up?

My consciousness is slow to catch up that . . . it wasn't a dream. Beneath the sheet, Katelyn is hunched over between my spread thighs, and she does have me halfway down her throat. I pull the sheet aside, tightening my fingers in her hair as I begin to thrust upward into her wet, hungry mouth.

"Fuck, Katelyn. What are you doing?"

"Making my dream come true," she says, pulling off just enough to talk. "Don't make me stop . . . please."

I groan. That word is already wrapping itself around my heart, and I can't stop it. I don't want to. "I dream of you sucking me off too."

She lifts her head with a pop as she releases me from her mouth. "How? Tell me what you fantasize about."

She sure as fuck doesn't want to hear that, but maybe I can baby-step us there, just a tiny nudge, oh so carefully. "Get up. On your knees on the floor."

She grins, like I'm making her dream come true with what I'm saying. She might think she's helping me with my fantasy, and she is—but she's doing so much more. I'm still holding back, because I don't know if she can take everything I have to offer her yet, but she's a vision I never expected before. I stand in front of her, my cock bobbing with my heartbeat and excitement. I squeeze the base of my shaft, and precum oozes out to cover my head.

"Lick that. Taste me."

Katelyn nods and reaches her hands up to hold my shaft as she opens her mouth, but I pull my hips back. "No hands."

She looks at me, more curious than anything, and moves her hands to grip her thighs. It's not behind her back like in my dream, but I don't want to push when she's already so eager and handling this so well, showing me the inner vixen that doesn't diminish her cuteness one bit.

She looks like a fucking fantasy come to life, hair a mess of my doing, half-lidded eyes sparking with desire, a goddess on her knees for a monster like me. She's so proud of what she's doing, jumping past lines that she's had before, but we've still got light-years to go. She sticks her tongue out, lapping at the drop of precum, and my vision zeroes in on the pink of her tongue against my cock. "Suck me, princess."

She opens wide and takes me in one swallow, hollowing her cheeks as she moves up and down my shaft. She's not one for wild tricks with her tongue or anything crazy, and I can tell that she's relatively inexperienced. But what she lacks in experience she more than makes up for with eager, bubbly, lust-filled enthusiasm, like she's getting off on getting me off. I reach out to grab the bedpost, propping myself up, and I weave the fingers of my other hand into her hair, careful not to hold her too tight but working with her, my hips moving in time with her mouth. In minutes, I'm on the edge and try to warn her.

"Katelyn . . ."

She moans and takes me deeper, burying her nose in the close-cropped hair at my base. The vibration sets me off and I fuck her mouth, needing to come down her throat since she seems on board with that. I use her hair to control her, shoving into her throat again and again, watching for any signs that she's not okay with this. But she seems hungry for more, like sucking me is some sort of reward.

"Take it, princess. Swallow me."

As I come, I swear she takes a bit of my soul as she swallows every drop, greedily and happily letting me use her mouth for my pleasure. I sag, spent and wrung out in every way. She pulls back, smiling and wiping the corner of her mouth like she just had tea at some fancy tea party.

"Dream come true."

CHAPTER 19

KATELYN

God, I want to spend all day in bed with Mark, fucking and taking naps and then fucking again. It was more than I could have ever imagined, and I wonder why the hell I ever thought I was okay with blah, boring beige. Beige sucks.

Mark, whatever color he is, is so much better.

When I woke up, sliding under the sheets this morning to engage in a fantasy I didn't think would be half as good as it ended up, I'd been nervous that it was going to be a one and done.

My body definitely wants more of whatever it is that Mark does to it. But my heart and my brain want more of him too. And we still need to talk, that's for sure, because between rounds, we've both been too exhausted to string words together in any meaningful way.

But as he heads out the door to tend to the ranch's needs, ever the responsible one, he steals my heart with a simple stop, turning to look at me. "Come by tonight for dinner?"

I nearly jump for joy, nodding, and Mark has a spark in his eyes that has me floating on air, doing a happy dance complete with fist pumps as he closes the door, and I'm sure my happy squeal is heard through the door because he opens it again, raising an eyebrow and muttering something about prolonging the delicious torture.

I'm hoping that means he's going to tease another orgasm or three from me tonight.

~~

And now I'm doing my absolute best to not rush this wedding so that I can go get laid again. God, I'm awful. Probably the worst events coordinator in the history of ever. Even as I scold myself, I know it's not true. I'm damn good at my job and love every hectic moving piece of the puzzle from an event this big. There's just no time to dillydally today.

And the bride's wedding planner is doing a remarkably good job too, her assistance key in making sure the wedding goes off exactly as planned, and the reception is tame and tasteful. Nothing to worry about, so even before the bouquet is tossed, I'm ready to get out of here.

The bride and groom hop into the waiting limo, and I clap politely, already making my way through my mental list of what needs to happen before I can leave. I need to thank the planner and ensure she's got my card for her other brides to consider the resort as their venue; make sure the cake topper is returned to the mother of the bride, who's been concerned about the family heirloom; close out the alcohol inventory with the bartenders; check in with the cleaning crew for the ballroom; double-check that the archway has been moved back to storage by the landscape workers; and about ten more things.

Still, at the end of my to-do list, I virtually fling my clipboard across my desk and run out the door.

Not soon enough, I'm pulling up to the long line of white fence that marks the Bennett ranch property. The gate is open, so I drive on in, pulling around and into the yard.

It's still quiet when I stop and get out, grabbing the box of cookies from the seat next to me. I'm no fool; the cookies were a hit last time, so I stopped to grab another bit of insurance in the form of a couple of dozen sugar bombs before showing up this time.

There's the sound of a door opening from the screened porch area, and Mama Lou steps out, waving. "Well hello, Katelyn! Come on in. I told Mark I'd let him know when you got here. Seemed he wasn't sure how long work would take you."

I nod, smiling as the screen claps open and Mama Lou holds it for me, looking agelessly pretty in her jeans and a button-down work shirt. "Thanks, I had a wedding today, so it's always a bit of a rough estimate how long it takes after the bride and groom pull away. Everyone thinks they leave and it's done, but there's about twice as much to do after the ceremony as before."

"Ain't that the way it always is?" she says as she leads me into the kitchen. "I see you brought some more bribes for my boys?"

I set the cookies on the table, grinning. Busted. "I brought you these since you seemed to like them before."

She grins, sneaking a cookie out and holding the box open for me to grab one too. Like a couple of teenagers, we both chomp down, Mama Lou's smile morphing into a hum of appreciation. "I was hoping. Now, don't you be thinking you need to bring sweets every time you come out here. My butt and my cholesterol can't take that, but I'm not gonna argue about a good cookie every once in a while. These even have oats and raisins, so it's almost healthy, right?"

She's teasing and we giggle, but we sure do polish off our cookies with big grins. "I'm not even going to pretend. If I'm eating a cookie, I don't give a . . . hoot about the health factor," I tell her. "I'm team chocolate chip all the way."

We indulge in the cookies slowly and casually, conversation comfortably quiet as I feel like we start to connect as women.

"Can I do anything to help with dinner?" I ask, always wanting to be active and helpful. It's one of the reasons I went into the hospitality industry, after all.

Mama Lou, though, is having none of it. "Oh no, child. Mark said he was making dinner at his place. Actually, I'm taking the night off. Sophie and James are together, and Luke said he's going to grab a pizza in town."

My brows knit together in confusion, and I realize the kitchen area certainly isn't as warm as it was last time. "Um, isn't *this* his place?"

She laughs hard, and I think I even hear a bit of a snort. "Wait . . . you thought Mark was a thirty-year-old man who lived at home with his mama, and when he invited you to dinner, you said yes?"

I cringe, hearing it like that. Okay, maybe I've been a little . . . naive. "Well, yeah . . . I guess. I mean, he said he ran the place, so I guess I figured he lived here." Dawning horror breaks into my confusion. "Oh no, am I supposed to be somewhere else?"

Mama Lou catches her breath from laughing. "Well, I'm impressed that you like my boy enough to overlook that big of a red flag. No, Mark's got his own place. He just eats here most of the time because it's a family thing. My way of taking care of them, considering they bust their butts here."

I grin, still not sure if I'm at the right place or what's going on, but at least she's getting a laugh out of it.

"But relax, you're at the right place. Let me call Mark, and he can come pick you up. He's got his own pad a few acres away. Where *he* is making you dinner. Because I raised my boys up proper—they can cook and clean and take care of themselves. For the most part, they even have good manners. I did what I could there, you understand?" she says, shaking her head like they're heathens she couldn't control.

I laugh, because though they might not be perfect, they're all damn fine men, from what I can tell. "I'm sure you did what you could. If it's any consolation, Mark has been nothing but a gentleman."

She smiles, wiping her hands on her jeans. "You're a nice girl for saying so, but I doubt that very seriously. I know my sons, the good, the bad, and the ugly. But if he gets too ornery, feel free to tell him that he's not welcome at dinner until he apologizes. That's the best currency I've found with any of those boys. I make them behave by controlling the kitchen."

"I'll remember that." I chuckle.

She laughs and scoots off to call Mark.

He must've been close by, because in just a few minutes he's stomping up the back porch.

"Hey." I stand, wanting to greet him with a hug or a kiss, but I'm not sure of the proper protocol here considering his mother is in the room.

I twist my hands together to stop from reaching out to him, but he crosses the room, placing a light hand over mine, halting the nervous gesture instantly before placing a chaste kiss to my cheek. I blush, but out of the corner of my eye I see Mama Lou give an approving nod, and I entwine my fingers with Mark's, nearly floating.

"Hey," Mark says gruffly, his eyes saying about a hundred times as much. "Thank you. We're off for dinner, Mama. See you tomorrow."

I think she tells us good night, but I'm not sure because my focus is locked on Mark. He looks great as always, but as I sit in the Gator beside him, I realize what Marla was talking about. Mark smells like a man, a combination of sweat and sunshine, leather and animal. I'm not sure if that's his base scent or from being around the horses all day, but it makes me want to climb in his lap and bury my nose in his neck, inhale and taste his skin.

He drives over a hill in a direction we didn't go the other day, and suddenly a small house is visible. "This is your house?" I ask stupidly. *Well duh, Katelyn. I doubt he lives in a tent.*

Still, Mark just nods, looking at the long single-story soft-blue house with pride. It's cute, with white trim around the windows and door, and I can imagine a few flower boxes underneath the one big window, which is obviously the living room. It's simple and plain, more functional than flash.

After a moment he pulls around the back, where a screened porch stretches the length of the house. As soon as I see it, I know this is the porch where he often talks to me at night on the phone. He's told me this is his favorite part of the house, and now I think it's mine too.

It feels like I have another piece of his puzzle in my hands, like being here tonight instead of on the other end of the phone line is a big step for us both. It's like I'm being let inside a secret place, trusted with something most people don't even suspect Mark has.

He parks and we go inside, the back door leading into the kitchen, just like at the main house. Wood cabinets and white appliances surround a small central worktable, and off to the side a round four-seater table looks unused, at least for dining, considering there's a small assembly of mechanical parts spread atop it.

"Working on something?" I ask, poking around at the pile of steel gears and other stuff. "Looks . . . complicated."

"Just tinkering with some old farm gear. It's not really usable anymore, but I like to try to fix it sometimes. It's a . . . challenge."

I smile at that, imagining him sitting here in his spare time and puzzling out fifty-year-old machines. "That is so you."

His eyes light up a bit, so I'm taking that as a good sign. He pulls out a barstool from the island and gestures for me to take a seat. "Sit. Let me throw the chicken on the grill. Be right back."

I settle in, watching with delight as he rummages in the fridge, well stocked from what I can tell, and walks out the back door with a plate of chicken that looks to be seasoned and marinated already.

As the screen claps him in the butt, I call after him, "Anything I can do? I'm actually pretty decent in the kitchen and happy to help."

He comes back in, grabbing a plate of skewered veggies. "You can set the table for us. I like the grill."

I glance at the tractor-part-covered table, and I swear his mouth twitches in another laugh. "Not that one—the one on the porch. Plates, glasses, silverware," he says, pointing at two cabinets and one drawer. "Nothing fancy, but it'll do."

He disappears back outside, and I gather the supplies, setting the table on the porch. He's right, his kitchen's not fancy, but the white plates and steel silverware are sturdy and look like they'd survive a small war without a single scratch.

Delicious aromas start coming from the grill as he expertly flips the chicken, and I lean against the porch railing, watching him quietly. It's nice, like a secret peek into his life, while at the same time it makes me feel cared for that he's cooking for me.

The evening is comfortable and quiet, the sun setting lower in the sky and the crickets starting to sing around us. Soon enough, he plates our dinners, uncorks the wine, and pours us each a glass. "To quiet dinners on back porches with beautiful company."

I blush even as I smile, the words a small reassurance to the lingering questions about what the hell we're doing. "It does feel like we're in a private world, all on our own out here."

Mark sips the wine, looking out over the acres of green. "That's what I was going for when I asked Pops to let me build a place out in this corner of the ranch. My own sanctuary."

I smile, trying to imagine how that conversation went. "So I guess I should tell you this before your mom does, because she got a pretty good laugh out of it . . . I thought you lived with her."

He looks at me, face immobile like he doesn't get the humor. "I mean, you never said otherwise, just 'my house' and 'my room,' which could've been there. And I didn't see any other structures besides the barn and ranch house when we went out to see Demon and Cobie. So how was I to know? When she said you were taking me to your house, I was so confused."

I stop, realizing I'm talking in circles, and I start laughing, the embarrassment replaced with good-natured self-mockery. His lips twitch, and I can feel him holding back from laughing at me. But even that sliver of a smile means so much, considering his usual stoic outer shell.

"What'd Mama say?" Mark asks as I calm down, his eyes twinkling. "I bet she laughed a bit."

"Oh yes. She told me she was impressed I still came if I thought that." I laugh more, sipping my wine. "But really, has she met you? I don't think I'd care if you lived in the barn. I'd be coming over for dinner all the same."

And then it happens.

His face breaks into a stunning, white-toothed smile. He's gorgeous when he's serious and straight-faced, but this . . . this is something else. And oh shit, he's got a dimple. An actual, God's-honest-truth dimple in his right cheek.

I want to dive into it, live in it and keep it a secret from every other woman in the world because it's mine. He just gave it to me, and I'm keeping it for myself.

I take a mental snapshot at the same moment I say, "You shouldn't do that."

His brows knit together, the dimple disappearing in a flash. "Do what?"

"Smile like that. It's not fair to all the other guys in the world. Because you are gorgeous already, but that"—I say, pointing at his mouth and the disappeared dimple—"that is an unfair advantage the world isn't ready for. God knows, I wasn't. My heart is fucking racing, and I want to keep all your smiles for myself like a greedy little bitch."

I grab at the air in front of him, pretending to encircle my arms around his happiness and clutching it to my chest. "Mine, all mine!"

He does it again, and I swear I do swoon. I'm buying a lottery ticket on the way home, because it must be my lucky day.

He seems pleased with the compliment, amused with my silliness, and I fall a little more for him.

CHAPTER 20

MARK

Dinner is excellent. Yes, the food, but more so the company. I like having Katelyn here in my space, imagining that she's mine and this is our simple nightly routine of dinner and snuggles on the back porch. Maybe it's a little domestic, but it's a thought that keeps running around in my head.

I was pleased with her reaction to my house, admittedly worried that she'd think it small and plain. I've never been one for fussy decorations, or hell, any decorations at all. Even the two throw pillows on the couch are more functional than pretty, and they came with the couch, so it's not like I chose them.

But when she looked around, it seemed like she'd taken everything in with a spark of delight in her eyes, like she was learning about me by cataloging the rare picture, tractor junk, and this morning's coffee cup in the sink.

At first it felt vulnerably revealing, but then I accepted it. I'd done the same when I visited her home, feeling like I could peek into her inner psyche by evaluating her couch, artwork, and bed.

Katelyn's place was bright and soft, just like her. Everything seemed comfortable, feminine, and with that little frill somewhere that still somehow invited me to relax even though I worried about leaving mud stains behind.

My place is simple and functional, a place I can kick my feet up—boots off, Mama raised me right—and enjoy the peace and quiet. And now, reclining back on the chaise lounge on the back porch with Katelyn laid back between my spread legs, her back to my front, I can fully appreciate the functionality of the piece of furniture I relax on every night.

Although this evening I'm anything but relaxed. Her hair falling across my chest and her curvy body pressed on mine is making every muscle in my body twitch with the need to consume her. Despite my best efforts at being a gentleman, I'm sure she can feel that I'm rock hard in my jeans. We both ignore that fact for now, though, as I let my fingers trace lines up and down her bare arm, connecting the few freckles I see with lines of wispy touch.

She's kicked off her heels, and I can see her bare feet, crossed at the ankle, wiggling as she enjoys the affection.

A happy sigh escapes her lips, and I memorize the sound, wanting to make her re-create it every day. That sound is going to be my new favorite part of the evening in my imaginary nightly routine with my princess.

"Mmm, Mark?" she asks, her voice low like she's afraid to disturb the beauty of the quiet night. I grunt in response, and she squirms against me, giggling a little. "I can feel that vibration in my back."

I do it again just to please her. "Is that all you feel?"

She snuggles against me again, almost purring. "Definitely not all." But then her voice grows more serious. "And as good as that feels, I feel like we need to talk."

My hand stills in its perusal of her arm, and I wrap my arms around her, squeezing her tight like I can stop her words by hugging her.

No luck. This girl's damn bullheaded when she wants to be. "I mean, I know you told me from the get-go that you're not interested in dating or anything serious, but that was before . . ."

Her voice trails off like she's not sure how to complete that sentence. I lean down a bit, whispering in her ear. "You mean before I fucked your sweet little pussy like it'd never been fucked before? Or before you screamed my name as you came all over my tongue?"

She presses her thighs together, my words turning her on and her reactions turning me on. Katelyn still wants to talk, though, nodding her head as she refuses to look back at me. "Mark—"

"Are you asking if I want to do it again? If I want to fill you up, pound into you until you scream my name as you drench me with your cream? Is that what you're asking?" I rumble, sliding a hand around to cup her breast. Her nipple's already pebbly, and her back arches, pushing against my touch as she turns, pressing her lips to mine. She tastes like the wine we had with dinner, complex and fruity, making me want to sip at her lips to savor the flavor. And I'm a beer man.

She sighs again, and I swallow her exhaled breath before taking the plunge. "Or are you asking something else . . . maybe more?"

It's a gamble and I know it. She's just out of a relationship, being friends was her idea although it was more of a compromise to my stubbornness, and I've already pushed her limits both emotionally and physically.

I should take what I can get, play it patient and slow, keeping her distracted and sated with orgasms so that she doesn't realize that I'm already thinking of her as mine.

She sits up and turns to face me, her legs bent beneath her as she rests back on her heels. The position is sexy as fuck, bringing all sorts of filthy things to mind, but I push them down, focusing on her.

She bites her lip, her eyes fixed on me. "I guess I'm asking what you want. I don't want to play games or wonder what we're doing. Considering where we're at right now, I don't think it's friends, or at least not *only* friends. If you want casual, I think I can do that. If you want not casual, I'm good with that too."

She's so transparent, or at least she is to me. She doesn't want some casual fuck-buddy situation, but the fact that she's willing to do that if it's what I want speaks volumes. It's what makes me realize that I can do the same for her, give her what she wants, even if it's less than what I dream of.

I haven't felt like this in a long time, like a woman might be worth putting forth the effort to be in a relationship. And honestly, I already feel way more for Katelyn than I ever did for Nicole. The thought of my ex, of how ugly things got with her, puts a small damper on my mood, so I force it from my mind, especially considering that Katelyn has already been more, done more, and handled more than Nicole even considered.

Relationships are built on compromise, so I can lock down the full depth of my desires, meet Katelyn's needs, and that will be enough. I'll make it be enough, because she is my best chance at happiness. And I'm a selfish bastard who'll take that opportunity for myself, but I'll make it worth it for her too. So worth it.

She's so beautiful, delicate, and feminine, and even though I'm more of a bull in a china shop, I want to be able to step lightly with her. For her, as long as I can.

I look back into her eyes and place my hands over hers. "So this 'not casual' option—what does that look like?"

She smiles, and I can see she's already excited that I'm considering it. "What do you mean?"

I'm not considering it—I've already decided—but I want her to spell it out for me so that I can give her exactly what she wants. No fucking around, no guessing. I'm never good at that anyway. "Well, we talked about friendship, and you told me it was texts, phone calls, and pizza-movie hangouts. What now?"

There's a smirk in my voice, but not on my face. She notices, which pleases me. She wiggles back and forth a bit, almost dancing, as she laughs lightly. "Well, those things still, obviously, because . . . pizza," she says dramatically. "No offense, but I don't think Mama Lou makes pizza."

"Of course not," I agree, slipping a strand of hair behind her ear. "What else?"

She taps her chin thoughtfully, tilting her head so that it presses against my palm gently. "And dates, like this . . . dinner, dancing at Hank's, or whatever. Hey, maybe you can teach me to ride too?"

"I'd like that," I say, making mental notes of everything she says, the lighthearted conversation belying how seriously I'm taking this. "And sex?" I ask, running my hand up her thigh, from her knee toward her core. Her legs part a little, giving me access, and I knead her muscles, marveling at the soft skin.

She whimpers a bit, nodding. She reaches down, pressing my hand higher on her thigh, sighing as I get closer to her core. "Yes, and sex."

I give her a hard look, silently demanding her attention. "And, princess, no one else. Just you. Just me. This pussy is mine . . . you are mine."

She nods, agreeing and setting my mind aflame even though she doesn't realize the full depth of how I want to possess her. "On one condition," she says, trying to maintain her calm even as my thumb strokes the edge of her panties. "You're mine too."

"Easy. I think I've been yours since I bumped into you with that door and caught you in my arms."

"So are we . . . dating? What do I call you? *Boyfriend* sounds rather juvenile, don't you think?" she asks, gulping as I caress her through the silk of her panties and her eyes go wide in arousal and pleasure. "I feel like I don't have the right words. I haven't done this before, at least not since I was a teenager, and I don't want to say something stupid."

I can hear the insecurity in her voice, and though the same thoughts plague me, considering I haven't dated in years, I reassure her, hoping my own heart takes note too. "I haven't either, Katelyn. So don't get caught up in words, and don't ever worry about looking stupid to me.

We can call it whatever you want—dating, boyfriend, whatever—as long as it's clear to us that you are mine and I am yours."

It's the slightest hint at what I want, but she seems delighted with it, and it soothes the beast in my center. She smiles a soft smile, her hands coming up to rest on my chest. "I like this . . . us."

"Me too," I agree, almost shocked at the words. If it was anyone else, I would be running. If someone told me that they felt like this after only a few weeks of conversations, even though it's been more than daily, I'd tell them to slow down, that there was no rush.

But it's not someone else—it's Katelyn. Yeah, she's all City Barbie, cute and soft, sweet and naive. She's an heirloom rose in a crystal vase. And I'm just a country boy, too rough and warped, hard and unyielding, like one of the dirty tractor parts tossed on my table. But this feels right. In fact, it feels more right than anything ever has. And that scares me, because there's a little voice inside me that says it'll come to an end at some point.

I don't want it to end, though. Katelyn's shown me so much, that she wants more and more of me every time we're together. She sees the parts of me nobody else does. She makes me feel things inside. Maybe I'm not quite the stone-cold asshole I believed I was.

And she's more open to sex the way I need than anyone has ever been. My biggest fear is that I'm not going to be able to hold back, to keep my foot off the gas and avoid pushing her too far, too fast.

Sooner than I'm ready, she'll realize I'm not the good guy she thinks I am. She'll want more from me than I can give. But that day isn't today, and I'm going to enjoy this moment like the heartbreak won't ever happen.

I move quickly, turning to place her under me on the lounge and covering her with my body, not pinning her but caging her with my arms and legs. I hold her head still, one hand on either side of her face, plundering her mouth and devouring her to the point that I don't know if the air between us is hers or mine—it's simply something we share.

Within moments, our clothes are strewn about the porch and we're bare, the cool breeze of the night tickling our skin. I bury myself in her slick heat without any warning or foreplay, knowing that she's ready to take me. I give her a few soft strokes, coating my sheathed cock in her juices as she adjusts to the fullness, and when she moans, I give her more.

I grab her hips, my fingers digging in for purchase to hold her still, and I press her into the cushion of the lounge. "Is this what you want?" I ask.

She grabs at my hands, and for a split second I think it's to lessen my hold, but instead she claws at my forearms like she never wants me to let her go. "Yes. Fuck yes, Mark."

"That's it, princess," I rasp. I bare my soul with the words, "Mark me up, make me yours."

She cries out, nails digging in to leave half moons carved in the flesh of my arms. The pain is exquisite, and I don't stop, stroking into her with fierce thrusts of my cock, fucking her into the cushion beneath her and making her bounce against the invasion despite my tight hold.

She arches, her head thrown back and the tendons of her neck highlighted in sharp relief against her creamy skin. I cover her, hip to hip, chest to chest, and lick along the length of her neck, tasting that which is uniquely Katelyn. There's a hint of salt from the sheen of sweat dotting her skin, and when I reach near her ear, I can smell her rose scent. I inhale deeply, needing it in my every pore.

I suck along her skin, greedily wanting it all for myself and driving her wild, judging by the incoherent mumbles pouring from her mouth.

I lick back up to her ear, pumping harder as I nibble at the soft pink shell. "Fuck, Katelyn. You feel so good. Come for me and make your pussy milk me."

At the first hitch of her cry, I bite the spot where her neck becomes her shoulder, holding her in place like the animal I am and sucking her delicate skin. "Yes! Mark me, too, make me yours," she says, throwing my words back at me, and it's all I can take. "Mark!"

I don't know if her last word is an instruction or if she's crying my name, but the thought of her wearing my mark, crying out from the pleasure I'm giving her, and the incredible way she's contracting around me is more than I can handle. I come hard, the explosion starting in my spine and rushing through my whole body.

"Katelyn!" I roar, sealing our mutual pact—our promise to date, her destiny to at some point want more, and my fate to break when she realizes I'm not the hero in her happy ever after, just the beast she has to survive.

I don't care, accepting it all. I'll take all the pain and heartache of later to have the present with Katelyn today, and I let the thoughts of the future go, determined to enjoy the moment of contentment I've been gifted with right now.

An amazing woman in my arms, sighing with delicious happiness from the pleasure I've given her, and who hasn't so much as flinched at my rough treatment of her body since that first night. And it'll continue, as long as I hold back and give just what she can handle.

The thought rests heavy, a reminder to take extra care and be cautious, with her body and my heart. But I fear it's already too late for the latter.

CHAPTER 21

KATELYN

My to-do list is in front of me, and I look through each bulleted item.

The easiest are the Keller, Smithson, and Frederick brides. The thank-you emails for them choosing the resort as their venue are sent; now we're just waiting on the responses to set a date to sign the contracts.

There's the Elliott birthday and the MarioCorp dinner that I have to follow up on as well. We're pretty much smooth sailing on the birthday, only waiting to get the timeline set in place, but I still need to meet with Bethany about MarioCorp's selections, so I make a note.

Lastly is the Wilson wedding. The horses are sourced, and the signed contract has already been sent to the Bennetts.

This one gives me pause even as I mark it off. It's been days since I had dinner with Mark, since we redefined what we're doing.

I still find myself doing a happy dance every time I think about it, and I've been dreaming of that dimple in his cheek, almost as sweet a surprise as his willingness to date. I even did the toothbrush boogie this morning in the mirror, looking like the world's happiest rabid dog as foam dripped from the corners of my lips, but I couldn't stop.

Even now, a sappy smile works its way across my face as I mentally replay our conversation and his words, the stilted way he admitted that he liked "us," too, almost like he was afraid to give the words the weight of being spoken for fear they'd fall flat.

But I'd caught them and held them tight, let them ring through my heart and fill the cracks left by my past.

Somehow Mark's slightest commitment to date feels more significant than anything I've ever had before, definitely more than living with Seth ever was.

My reverie is broken by Marla's slightly amused, mocking laughter. "Okay, Katelyn, spill it right now."

I look up, startled and refocusing my eyes on her. "Huh? Did you say something?"

Marla rolls her eyes, drumming her fingernails on her desk. "Don't play dumb with me. Only one thing makes a woman look all fuzzy-eyed like that—a man. And I'm guessing that man is one tall, broody cowboy named Mark Bennett. Now spill, because these invoices are boring the shit out of me."

I grin, knowing she's right but teasing her back. "Maybe I'm just thinking about work stuff—you know, visualizing tonight's wedding to see if I missed anything," I joke. "So I can get you more invoices."

Marla stands up, planting her hands on her hips and giving me raised eyebrows. I get a visual of what she must look like in Mom-mode to her girls when they're in trouble. She's a bit terrifying, in a bulldog puppy kind of way. I crumble beneath her glare, laughing as I confess, "Fine, you're right. I was totally thinking about Mark."

She plops her butt into the chair in front of my desk, propping her elbows up and resting her chin in her hands, ready for the details. She hangs on every word as I tell her about my date with Mark. "So you two are officially dating now?"

I nod, leaning back in my chair. "Yeah, it was awkward at first. I've never had to have *the talk* with a guy. I guess that was kind of the problem with Seth—we never discussed where we were going or what we wanted. So I decided you were right. I pulled up my big-girl panties and dove into the conversation, though I was blushing hard the whole time. But it felt good to tackle the elephant in the room, not avoid it. I figured 'lesson learned,' and it would be better to know once and for all where Mark stood with everything—and he was on board with more."

My voice cracks on the last word, just how much more Mark said echoing in my mind. And on the heels of that, how much more he gave me right afterward. Not just one or two, but three orgasms before he was done. I barely stayed conscious on the drive home.

Marla narrows her eyes suspiciously. "What are you not saying? What's *more*?"

I try to duck my head a bit, but then I realize that I'm proud of what Mark and I are, and I don't want to hide it, least of all from my best friend in town. After a moment I square my shoulders and look Marla dead in the eye. "Well, I told him that 'boyfriend' sounded a bit juvenile—"

She interrupts with a giggle. "Whoa, I can't imagine anyone calling that man a boy-anything."

I giggle with her, thinking of just how much man Mark is. "Exactly! So he said we could call it whatever I wanted because I am his and he is mine. And then we . . . you know. It was so . . . possessive. Almost primal."

Marla's grin drops from her face, and she exhales sharply, fanning herself like she's about to pass out. "Daaaaaamn. That's hot."

I don't even try to stop the smile that spreads my mouth wide, feeling some heat myself. "I know, right? I'm in so much trouble, Marla. I am falling so hard, so fast, but damn if I can stop it. Not that I want to."

Marla's smile changes, from heated to supportive. "I'll admit it seems fast, but there's nothing wrong with that. And I wasn't lying when I said that Mark doesn't date . . . like at all. So it means something that he wants to date you. My bet is that he's falling just as fast and hard as you are. Sometimes you just know."

Her smile reassures me, because I am so in over my head, but instead of feeling like I'm drowning, I feel like I'm flying. Finally free in his arms. "Thanks. I appreciate the 'come to Jesus' talk the other day. It was hard to hear at first, but I definitely think I needed the wake-up call."

She wipes imaginary sweat from her brow. "Whew. Glad that worked."

I sit up, pointing a mock-stern finger toward Marla's desk. "Speaking of work, we'd better get back to it. I need to meet with Bethany on the MarioCorp dinner."

"Ugh, better you than me," Marla says coldly. "I'd rather do invoices. She gives me itchy hands."

I cock my head, confused. "Itchy hands?"

Marla grins evilly. "You know, she's like the queen of the back-handed compliment with a superiority complex to match. Makes my hands itch to smack some sense into her, maybe a bit of humbleness too. She ain't nothing special, grew up right here in town, but you'd think she came to Great Falls by way of Buckingham Palace."

I grin. "Well, I'll have to refrain from smacking her for you. Hostile work environment and all that, you know? Need anything while I'm running around the property?"

"Actually, I'd literally kill for a Diet Coke right now. You mind grabbing me one from the vending machine?" she asks.

She's already fishing quarters out of her purse before I even respond, knowing I don't mind. "Sure thing. I'll bring you one, if only to prevent a murderous rampage. Need any chocolate to go with it, especially if it's that dire of a situation?"

She grins and flashes me a big thumbs-up. "See, that's good looking out for us peons, boss lady. Way to think ahead. Some peanut M&M's might do me good."

She drops a big stack of quarters into my palm, and I promise to have them back as soon as possible. As I leave, she feigns melting to the desktop. "I'll try to hang on until you get back, but no promises."

I laugh at her melodramatics and head out, planning to hit the restaurant before grabbing Marla's snacks. After all, if I'm going to bring the girl a drink, it might as well be cold.

Walking into the restaurant is like walking into another world. The deep colors and welcoming vibe of the lobby give way to a sea of white tablecloths and tapered candles in shining gold holders.

Each table is surrounded by slim-lined high-back chairs so that the intimacy of each table seems absolute. Just standing in the doorway, you know that this is a realm of excellence. It's impressive and inspiring, and I know we're going to have those stars for it ASAP.

As I sit down with Bethany, it feels like we're in a private cocoon divided by the table.

Marla's words loop in my head as I explain the table settings to her, demonstrating with my hands. "So, lilac tablecloth, leather die-cut placemat, silver charger, white plate. And they'd like a pocket fold for the floral napkins, with a single lilac bud placed in each. The florist will deliver the buds and the centerpieces three hours before cocktail hour begins. Whew . . . I think that's everything," I say with a grin. "Any questions?"

Bethany looks up from the notes she's been meticulously taking. "Sounds like you have things well coordinated, but isn't that going to look like a Mother's Day tea luncheon, not a Fortune 500 corporate dinner?"

Though her comment is snarky, bordering on bitchy, her tone is more curious. It's nothing new to me. Some folks have a narrow mindset and vision, and their work looks cookie-cutter because of it, regardless of how professionally they do it.

It takes a special creativity to take clients' ideas and make whatever preferences they have suit their event. Rainbow unicorn glitter cookies . . . for your grandmother's seventy-fifth birthday? Sure, I can make that look classy.

Matronly wallpaper roses for your baby shower to welcome your . . . son? Yep, I can do that, too, and you'll love it.

"The hostess and CEO is a particular fan of purple—it's sort of her trademark. It'll be lovely. I promise."

Bethany looks around the restaurant, and I can see that she's trying to imagine it. "If you say so."

Her comment is said warmly, but I hear the challenge in her words. And have no doubt—challenge accepted. I can feel what Marla is talking about. Bethany says all the right things, but it feels slightly off somehow.

My hands aren't itchy, but she does set me on alert a bit. That sensation is strengthened when she narrows her eyes at me and says, "Katelyn, can I ask you a personal question?"

I lift my brows in response, giving permission but unsure where she's going with this. "Are you seeing Mark Bennett? He called you *princess* the other day in your office, so I'm curious."

I can see more than curiosity in her eyes, but like with Marla earlier, I'm proud of whatever this is with Mark, definitely not hiding anything but not stupidly volunteering information for the gossip grapevine either.

"I am," I say matter-of-factly.

Her lips thin, but her voice takes on a calming tone, like she's breaking bad news to a clueless victim. "I thought so. Katelyn, I know we're not really friends, but I do feel like someone should warn you. Mark Bennett is known for being a bit of a perpetual bachelor, I'm afraid. He's that stubborn, quiet, chunk-of-ice type that many a woman in Great Falls has tried to land, even though I'm sure it'd take some work to rehab him into anything relationship-worthy. Like the bad boy every woman thinks she can tame. He's not really a bad boy, but you get my point. I'd just hate for you to get hurt by the likes of him, especially when you're new to town and don't know his reputation. He's simply not worth your time and the considerable effort it would take to sustain a relationship because it'd all be on you, and then he'll likely simply walk away when he's had enough. He's done it before."

Her words are all coated in saccharine, like foul-tasting medicine disguised in sweetness to help it go down easier. But there's nothing she's saying that I'm not aware of. I know what this town thinks of him. Everyone in Great Falls, according to Marla, seems to think he's cold as ice, but he feels like blue flames to me, just on the verge of combustion and barely restrained by his force of will.

I wonder if anyone knows him at all. I somehow doubt it, considering I'm not sure he even admits that to himself. His magnetism is powerful, and he's protective, almost to a point of possessiveness, something that I've never experienced.

If you'd asked me before, I would've said I'd hate that, consider it antiquated and disrespectful, and I suspect I still would . . . if it was anyone besides Mark. But he manages to make it feel gentlemanly, even in its harshness. He makes me feel like nothing bad would ever happen to me, because he simply wouldn't allow it to.

I notice Bethany still looking at me, and I realize she's waiting for some kind of response. Putting on my most polite but icy smile, I give her a nod. "I appreciate your concern, but it's ill-placed. I assure you that I have no desire to change a single thing about him or, as you said, 'rehab' him. We're dating, and I prefer to enjoy that rather than plan for a future breakup that may or may not happen."

Bethany seems taken aback by the barely veiled venom in my words. She smiles wanly, backing down. "Oh, I'm sorry. I didn't mean to offend you. Just a friendly warning. If I was new to town, I'd want someone to tell me if I was making a misstep. Just extending that same courtesy."

By the time I head back to my office, I've forgotten Marla's snack and my palms are definitely itchy. "Well?" Marla asks.

"Everything seems pleasant and polite on the surface with Bethany, but I can't help but feel there's another layer to every word that comes from her mouth, like what you see is definitely not what you get."

"That's her. One of the Mean Girls for sure," Marla replies. "Hard part is, somehow she manages to turn it so that you feel bad for judging her poorly."

I nod, thinking about how Bethany is charming and manipulative enough that I doubt my own read of the conversation. I may not be sure about her, but I am sure about Mark. I have no doubt there that we're discovering something much bigger than either of us expected.

Needing that connection, I pull out my phone to send him a quick text.

Ugh, rough day at work. Miss you!

It's only minutes later that my phone dings with a reply.

Trade you "rough days." Miss you, too, princess.

The text is followed by a picture of Mark sweaty and dirty, with James and Luke sitting on the pen fences in the background. It looks like the two of them are smiling, but Mark's Mark, straight-faced and solid. But I can see the spark in his eyes, the relaxation of his jaw, even if he is surrounded by a sea of brown-and-white cattle.

I trace a line of sweat running down Mark's neck in the picture, biting my lip. Yeah, it's only been days, but I'm enjoying the hell out of dating him, exactly as he is—gruff, quiet, possessive, growly, and best of all . . . mine.

CHAPTER 22
Mark

The next week is hell on earth. Texting, phone calls, and a few hours together before one of us has to go home are not nearly enough. I'm letting myself go short on sleep to have every extra minute with my princess, but I know I'm sleepwalking through parts of my day, either because my body is shutting down or because my brain is replaying the moments with her in my arms.

I understand both of our busy schedules, but I'm desperate for more. By Friday, I'm damn near throwing stuff at my desk, not giving a damn where it lands just so I can get the hell out of here and peel out for town. I've already arranged for the chores to be taken care of tomorrow, and I can soak in Katelyn's warmth all night.

I hear a chuckle from the door and raise my eyes to see James not even bothering to hide his huge grin. "I guess it's only fair, after all."

I don't have time for his games, which are definitely designed to delay my departure, but I can't help but take the bait. "What's fair?"

He scratches his lower lip, pausing dramatically before answering. "Well, remember when I was dating Sophie, how many times did you cover for me so I could stay over at her place instead of getting up before dawn to leave her? Because I tell you, brother, leaving a sleepy woman who is trying to snuggle up to you is a damn crime."

I consider giving him some version of a "work hard now, play hard later" speech like Pops might have done, but I recognize two things. One, that'll only delay me further, so I simply agree with him to short-circuit the discussion. Second, though, he's right. Tearing myself out of Katelyn's arms to come home or to let her leave is torture. I swear one of these days they're going to have to hook Cobie and Demon to my ankles to pull me out of her bed.

"You're right," I simply reply, though, before smirking. "I covered for your lazy ass enough, and I'm cashing in on the favors. If you'll excuse me, I'll see you late tomorrow."

I push past him, but he stops me with a hand on my shoulder. "Sunday. Make it Sunday night. I'll cover for you all weekend."

I freeze, warring with myself. I want that time with Katelyn—in my arms, underneath me, learning her mind and her body, owning her pleasure and earning her light, letting it fill me. Hell, two nights in her bed would be finer than sleeping in a luxury resort.

But the responsible part of me, that huge boulder on my shoulders, knows that it's irresponsible of me to ditch my chores and leave them for James.

He must see the battle raging in my mind because he adds weight to the scale, his voice losing all traces of joking as he looks me in the eye. "Do it, Mark. You'd do it for us, man. Hell, you have. Let me do it for you. I ran away from this for too long. Let me help repay the debt I owe the ranch, the one I owe you."

A knot pulls tight in my chest, and I have a moment of almost fatherly pride in my little brother. He'd make Pops so proud with his mature life choices now. "You know it ain't like that. You left because you needed to. And when you were ready, you came back. None of us hold it against you. We're proud of you . . . champ."

He nods, his lips twitching in a smile before he sobers again. "Champ . . . don't matter what title I won, I still feel bad about not carrying my weight here. Maybe I hold it against myself, but I want to earn two other titles instead. Husband and father."

His words are heavy, so much unlike James, but he's totally serious. "You will be. I see it in the way you take care of Sophie."

James nods and leans back against the doorframe. "Hope so. I just want you to know that I see it . . . see what you've accomplished here, what you do for the family. If I can make it a little easier for a minute, help you get something you want, I'm ready and willing to do that."

I swallow the lump working its way up my throat and nod. "Thanks, James. Okay, I'll see you Sunday night. Let Mama know, will you?"

He grins, serious James gone and the wild child back. Shaking his head, he drawls, "Aw, hell no. I'll do your chores, but you'll have to tell Mama yourself that you're spending the weekend at your girlfriend's house."

I feel my lips twitch up at James's casual use of the word that gave Katelyn pause, although I agree that boyfriend and girlfriend does sound woefully inadequate for what I consider her. We're in that middle ground, that space where nobody really has ever come up with the right word in English.

"Alright, but I'm calling her once I'm on the road," I reply. "No sense tempting her to ground me to my room like I'm fifteen again."

James laughs, pushing off from the doorframe and guiding me away from the office. "You know, she might surprise you. Mama was shockingly cool about Sophie coming over when we were dating. And you're practically ancient, so she'd probably just be excited that you might actually get married and give her grandbabies one day after all."

"Don't get ahead of yourself. Or worse, encourage Mama in that vein," I warn him.

"One summer. That's all it took for me to know Sophie was *the one*. Seems like you're halfway through summer already, Mark," James says with a chuckle. "You'd better jump on it. Or are you so old that you need to take your time so the Viagra can kick in?"

"Only kicking I'm going to do is kicking your ass," I reply as he winks, but it's not with the same jocularity. Inside my head, the timer running in the back of my mind tick-tocks a little louder. How long till she realizes she deserves better than me? Until she sees I'm not relationship material and runs for the hills? Too soon, however far from now it may be, so I should take advantage, treasure each little moment she gives me while I can. "But I'll have to save that whooping for later. Better head out now. See you Sunday."

In less than ten minutes, I'm flying down the two-lane dirt road that connects the ranch to the main road back to town, twin plumes of dust spewing from my tires I'm so desperate to have Katelyn in my arms.

It won't be enough, it'll never be enough, but I'll treat every moment like the precious jewel it is, knowing that I'll never recognize the last time until it's too late.

~~

Too soon and not soon enough, I'm curled up on the couch with Katelyn, remnants of a pizza and a bottle of wine on the coffee table while a movie neither of us is watching plays in the background.

By threat of death, I couldn't tell you the name of it or a single actor, but I could draw a map of the freckles on her nose or re-create the flecks in her blue eyes like a record of the constellations.

Our conversation is easy—chatter about our day, the events she has coming up, and various ranch happenings.

"Well, we gotta drive the cattle across the ranch into the new pasture on Monday," I reply, thinking about the move.

Suddenly, Katelyn turns, grinning.

"Wait, like a real cattle drive?" she asks, giddy like I told her Santa was coming early. "Are you going full cowboy on me like in a movie?"

I chuckle, remembering that despite her small-town roots, she's not *that* country. "Sort of. We move them around on a schedule to keep the grass regenerating. This time we're crossing five pastures to get them back to the far west side."

She flops back against the couch, arms spread open and a wide smile on her face. "What are you grinning at, princess?"

"Sshhh," she says as she closes her eyes and purses her lips before grinning some more. "I'm picturing you on a horse, hat pulled down low as you direct the cattle this way and that, like some big boss cowboy. All sweaty and dusty from working."

My lips twitch to hold back the grin, while at the same time I resist the urge to wrap my hands around her stomach and pull her against me to show her another way to get sweaty. "You do know I kinda do that every day? This is just a longer move. And though we do ride, sometimes we use ATVs too."

Her pink bottom lip pouts out slightly. "Do you take Sugarpea or an ATV?"

It's hard not to laugh, and in my head, I know I split my time between horse and machine, but based on the look on her face, I'm damn sure not telling her that. "Sugarpea loves it," I reply seriously. "He gets extra treats, a dip in the pond at the end of the day, and a big, long rubdown. No way would I even think of cheating him of the joy."

She can hear the hint of teasing in my voice and kicks out a pretty pink-tipped toe toward me, laughing. "You're lying. You totally take the Gator, don't you?"

I catch her foot in my big hand. "Maybe. But if you want to come watch some of the drive this time, I'll ride Sugarpea just for you. Wouldn't want to mess up your fantasies, now would I?"

She opens her mouth to smart off, but I cut her off by digging the pad of my thumb into the arch of her foot. Instead of a sassy response, I get a groan of delight. "Oh God . . . do that again."

I oblige, massaging and kneading one foot and then the other.

"You have no idea how good that feels. I swear I get pedicures not for the polish—because I can do that myself—but just so someone will rub my feet. It's heavenly . . ."

Her voice drifts off into moans, making me think filthy thoughts. "Do you make those sounds when you get a pedicure? Like you're on the edge of coming? If so, I'm gonna have to kill every person who's ever touched you. I think this might be my new job, although no promises on my polish skills."

She grins, full of sass as always. "No, I usually hold back the noises. It freaks them out if you start yelling out 'Yes, yes, right there.'"

I reach down, smacking her hip lightly as her toes stroke my cock through my jeans. "Brat. Be nice or I'll stop."

She closes her mouth, miming like she's locking it and throwing away the key. "That's better, princess."

I resume my ministrations, finding every ticklish spot and every place that makes her groan with pleasure as she lazily rubs along my cock, the two of us building something that's going to be white-hot before too long. I move higher up her legs, memorizing her calves, her knees, and up to her thighs with my fingers, searing each pleasure point into my brain forever.

As I cross her knee, I feel a slight bump in the skin and realize she's got a scar. "What's this?"

"High school," Katelyn says with an eye roll. "I tried out for the cross-country team. That lasted all of one meet when I tripped and fell, got a rock right in the kneecap. So ended my high school athletic career." I kiss it better, even though it's long since healed. She's wiggling for me the higher I go, the relaxing massage turning into something more heat-filled. "God, you're making all the aches and pains go away."

"You know those damn heels are the reason your feet hurt, right?" I growl, both hating that they hurt her and loving the way she looks in them.

"I know, but I love them," she admits. "They make me feel badass in a way, like I'm in charge and can conquer the world. Plus, *someone* told me they make my legs and ass look fabulous."

I let my hands move even higher, grabbing a handful of her ass and kneading it too. "They do. How about now that your muscles are all relaxed and massaged, you go put on your favorite pair for me . . . and nothing else."

My sudden order ignites the building fire between us. Her eyes light up as she bites her lip, and then she literally jumps up and scurries down the hallway.

I let my head fall back on the couch, considering taking off my shirt for a moment, but then I decide I'll let Katelyn do it for me. A chuckle bubbles out at how excited she is to get dressed up for me.

Well, not up—more *undressed*. I hear shoes clicking behind me before soft, rose-scented hands cover my eyes. "Close your eyes. No peeking."

I squeeze my eyes shut behind her palms, and she releases me, the click of heels telling me where she's moving. I hear a rustling, and then she speaks again in a breathy, sexy voice that sends tingles down my body to my toes even before she's got the words out.

"Okay. Open."

I open my eyes to a fucking vision. Katelyn ditched the casual and comfy shorts and tank that have been teasing me for the last few hours and now stands before me in sky-high black leather heels . . . and tiny black silk panties.

I take the moment to enjoy every detail, from the way she's standing, one knee bent with her foot turned so I get a view of both the front and side of her heels, to the flush on her cheeks, to the bright flashes in her eyes. I whirl my finger in the air, and she obeys, spinning in place.

"Damn, princess. I'll rub your feet every day if this is the reward, because you are a fucking treat."

She preens under the praise, her eyelashes fluttering as she glances down, tilting a leg for me and making her calf muscle pop. "I know you said just the shoes, but I bought these panties specifically because they matched the lacing on the heels."

She points to the back of the shoes, where crisscross leather straps lace up the heels, and then to the hips of her panties, where silk laces mimic the X-pattern, letting her tanned skin peek out and giving me a new appreciation for the design of fine women's lingerie.

"I can take them off, though," Katelyn says, slipping her fingers into the waistband of the delicate silk.

"No. Leave them. And bend over the arm of the couch." My voice is harsh, but I can't temper it. She moves to the arm opposite me, eyes on me the whole time as she bends over.

I wait a beat, letting the tension build before getting up. Katelyn swallows, her gaze still locked on me, following my progress toward her. I squat down behind her, my fingers tracing the skin along the edge of the leather before moving higher along the length of her leg.

"Mark?"

"I did say heels and nothing else, didn't I, princess?" I growl, watching her squirm. This is her punishment—but it's a good punishment. "I guess we'll just have to leave these on for now. See if you can come from me rubbing you through them, see if you can drench this fine silk."

She whimpers, wiggling her hips in front of my face, and the black silk is like a red cape in front of a bull.

"But first, you might need a little spanking for not following directions." I let a bit of tease into my voice to soften the suggestion, even though I'm completely serious. She arches her back, thrusting her ass out, begging for my hand. "You like that? Want my hand to pink up your ass?"

I'm testing the waters pretty hard here, my urges rising and bubbling to the surface, but I'm stepping delicately, watching her closely until I know that she's fully on board. I cup her ass, running my hand along the flesh gently.

"Katelyn."

I wait for her to look back and meet my eyes. This is important. Once I have her full attention, I pause my hand before continuing. "Who's in charge?"

She smiles softly, an angel and a princess and more all in one look. "You are."

There's more question in her voice than certainty, and I know she's answering the way she thinks I want her to. I stroke her skin, shaking my head as I bare my soul a little more to her.

"I think we'd both like to think that, but no. You are. My badass princess, in heels or out, you're in charge. You may not have conquered the world yet, but you have conquered me. Let me give you what you want, what you need, even if you don't know it yet."

She bites her lip and nods, thrusting her ass out once again. I grab a firm handful on each side, loving the feel of her in my hands. Squeezing tightly, I let go, loving the way her flesh is already pinking up from my rough handling.

Without warning, I rear back and smack her, sharp but soft, watching the rebound through the taut muscle and letting her cry quench my soul.

"Fuuuuuck, Mark." She groans.

Her voice is breathy, obviously aroused and not freaking out. The knot at my center relaxes by a millimeter, until she wiggles, silently begging for more. My gut tightens again, ready to give her all she wants. Always.

I smack the other cheek, watching it match its partner in delectable pinkness. "Now you've got matching handprints on your ass. You like that, princess?"

Katelyn moans. "Yesssss . . ."

I bend down behind her once again, and I can see that the answer to one of my earlier questions is obvious. She's drenched through the silk, leaving a dark outline of her pussy lips where it clings to her. I run a finger up her inner thigh to her folds, inching closer and closer to where she wants me, judging by the way she's bucking and moving to get me there.

"Princess," I whisper, some combination of warning and reverence in the single word.

She stills instantly, and when she speaks there's so much strength in her voice I almost have tears come to my eyes. "Mark, I can take it. Whatever you want to give me, I want it . . . I want you."

For a split second, I think she knows, has realized that I want so much more with her, body and mind and spirit, and I damn near roar and weep with the joyful relief.

Then my brain clicks into gear, and I realize she's giving back the words I gave her that first night. She's agreeing to take what I give her. But I know she doesn't understand. She thinks this is a scuba dive, when it's really like taking a sub to the bottom of the ocean. She doesn't understand the pressure, the depth, the intensity, and she has no clue it even exists. But she wants to try. She's so good, so much better . . . I have to keep trying. And though a thread of disappointment weaves its way through my gut, what's she's offering is enough. It has to be.

I remind myself to be easy, but I take control of her, grabbing firmly around her waist and holding her securely against me. My other hand slips between her legs, rubbing her through the silk until she's crying out, begging for more as my fingers find all the places that I already know, stroking her not until she screams my name, but until she forgets to breathe. I let it build as long as I think she can take it, edging her again and again, before whispering the order in her ear.

"Come, Katelyn."

Her shudders of pleasure echo in my core, my joy coming from hers as the melody of her moans washes through me like the sweetest music I've ever heard. I drop my pants down my thighs, slip a condom on, and shove into her heat in one smooth motion. She doesn't stiffen but pushes back, squeezing herself around me immediately as she gives in to my power.

"Ahh, yes . . . Mark."

Her plea spurs me on, and I fuck her deep and slow, each stroke slamming in balls-deep and then pulling out slowly until barely the tip remains. It drives her insane, her head thrashing back and forth as she tries to get more, looking back at me over her right shoulder and then her left, trying to get a better view.

I run a finger down her spine, caressing each vertebra like living sculpture and loving the swish of her blonde locks over my arm. The next time it comes around I gather her hair in my hand, holding a loose ponytail and helping her see me. Her eyes are hazy, half-lidded with sex, but I know mine are clear, flashing with barely controlled heat.

"You good, princess? Want more?"

Her bottom lip disappears behind the white of her teeth, and my hand tightens reflexively on her hip, creating divots where my fingertips dig in.

She nods, her eyes fluttering as I push in hard again before pulling back. "So good. More . . . more . . . more . . ."

The word is like a prayer, and I'm not sure she even knows what she's asking for, but I give it to her. Every thrust is a delicate balance—easy for her, hard for me as I fight the urge to go faster, wanting us both to feel every inch of heat. I find that sweet spot, making Katelyn cry out gutturally, and I can feel my balls tighten as I work her body higher and higher before I overwhelm her. I tug oh so gently on her hair to get her attention.

"Go again for me, princess. Come with me . . . now."

With a final savage thrust, we do, falling apart and falling together in one beautiful moment, more one being than two.

CHAPTER 23

KATELYN

Only half teasingly, I'd told Mark that driving the Gator for the cattle drive was perfectly acceptable as long as I got to come along for the ride. He agreed, although that might've been because I'd had him halfway down my throat and he'd been on the verge of coming.

Yeah, dirty trick, but it was all in fun. And negotiation's all about making your offer at the right time. The memory of his gruff agreement, more growl than spoken word, makes me squeeze my legs together again as we rumble across the pasture.

From the driver's seat, he reaches over, laying a rough palm along my thigh, and I curse the layer of denim separating my skin from his. It's hot and sunny, and I want my skin to be kissed by the sun just so that I can feel his touch on it.

"Having fun?" he asks, like he's worried that I'm bored.

I nod quickly, grinning as I adjust the cowboy hat Mama Lou lent me. "So much fun! I love seeing everyone working together, and there's a part of me that wants to pet the cows."

He shakes his head slowly, but I see his lips twitching as his eyes go back to the herd. "If this was a dairy herd, that'd be one thing. They're trained and used to human interaction. Beef herds, though, spend a lot more time independently. You gotta be more careful with them before you go petting them like a puppy."

I giggle at the image of me, surrounded by cattle like some Cowgirl Cinderella. "Noted—don't pet the cows like puppies. See, I'm probably halfway to cowgirl already!"

Mark's eyes do a slow roll from my ponytail, to my tied plaid shirt that hugs my tits, over my denim-covered hips, and down my legs to my feet, encased in my new boots.

It probably looks more like a cowgirl costume than functional workwear, but I wanted to make an effort to fit in with his brothers today since I kind of intruded on their workday.

"You don't look like any country girl I've ever seen."

If anyone else said that to me, I'd have a flash of insecurity, but Mark's complimentary intention is clear.

"And don't you forget it!" I sass, winking at him playfully.

He lifts the right side of his mouth, gifting me with a quick shot of his dimple and rendering me speechless. But his words are dead serious as he leans over to whisper in my ear. "Don't get those new boots too dirty today, country girl. Because I'm gonna fuck you in them, and nothing else, later. I want those boots up over my shoulders, my cock buried in you, and you screaming my name."

I swallow, the image coming to life in my mind. "Hell. Yes."

I pull my feet up into the seat, then decide they might be safer behind the plexiglass of the windshield and put them on the dash. It makes me lean back, and I know I'm pushing my tits up, but that's fine by me. Let my man watch them bounce around when he's not checking the cattle. He might call it a distraction; I'm calling it foreplay.

The slightest chuckle escapes Mark's lips, and I watch his chest swell with the sound. He puts his hand back on my thigh, giving me a firm squeeze that promises so much more later.

We drive around, directing cattle here and there and working with James, Luke, and a ranch hand named Carson. It feels like we're all a team, moving cogs with the same goal. James is on a pretty spotted horse named Polka Dottie, Luke's on Duster, and Carson is riding an ATV, patrolling the line and making sure the gates are all set for the route to the proper pasture.

My respect for everything Mark is in charge of deepens as I watch him give instructions to the crew, directing the whole thing.

"You're kind of like an event coordinator, just instead of brides, you've got stampeding cows," I tell him after he sends James after a couple of stragglers. "And instead of weddings and events, you've got drives to different pastures. Suddenly, our jobs feel rather similar."

Mark cuts his eyes over to me, then snorts a little in amusement. "Might be a bit of a reach, but I guess I can see it. I bet your team smells better than mine," he jokes. "I think mine are a lot more predictable than your bridezillas, though."

In contrast to his words, James draws our attention by thundering past at a full gallop while whooping and whipping his hat over his head, laughing like a fool.

"If you say so," I deadpan. "So, tell me about the cattle . . . about the herd, moving them around, selling them, buying them, all of it."

Mark looks surprised. Well, that's what I take the slight lift to his brows to mean.

"Why?" he asks.

I grab his face in my hands, bringing his eyes to mine as he stops the Gator. "It's what you do, and it's important to you. And if it's important to you, it's important to me. So tell me all about it."

And that's how the day passes, trundling past the pastures behind the herd of cattle as Mark gives me a basic rundown on ranch operations.

"Well, the nice part about the cows themselves is that as beef cattle, they tend to take care of themselves in a lot of ways. They're pretty hier-archical. There's a queen bee in the herd who has her little clique, and she's the leader of the whole group. Then there are the new mothers.

You gotta be careful with them because they're real skittish about their babies."

I hum, watching James get another mama with her calf back into the group. "So the cows take care of themselves, how—?"

"Mostly because cows will get stupid shit in their heads, and then you've got about one ton of hardheaded pain in the ass to deal with. So you have to constantly watch for holes in the fence, making sure they haven't torn up the lines to the water troughs we have out here for the dry season. And, of course, health checks, stuff like that. Pops used to say that cows are a lot like kids. They'll get themselves in trouble if you let them."

We continue, and as we do, I find it fascinating to learn more about him. There are constant challenges, and juggling them all is key to having a profitable year. It's amazing, and Mark's borne it all—along with leading his family—since Pops's passing.

Even though I already respect the hell out of him, my admiration grows as I realize just how brilliant he really is to run a successful ranch, considering all the factors working against "small" ranchers nowadays.

After the drive, dinner with the Bennetts is a loud and noisy affair, dishes passed around and compliments to Mama Lou's cooking flowing freely. I'm surprised by how hungry I am considering I just rode in the Gator, but I'm famished, and Mama Lou looks more than happy to let me pack away the roasted veggies and juicy pot roast like it's nothing.

There was a momentary awkward pause as we all sat down and realized that there wasn't room at the table if we left Pops's chair empty. Mama Lou gave Mark a nod, and he slowly settled into Pops's chair after pulling out the chair to his right for me.

Though his face stayed stoic, I saw the stiffness in the hold of his shoulders.

Luckily, food seems to be a steady distraction, especially after the day of hard work, and as we all dig into Mama Lou's feast, he seems to calm slightly, though he's rubbing at a small groove in the table. I've seen similar grooves in wooden furniture before; my grandfather had a hollow he'd worn in the armrest of his favorite rocking chair that was nearly a quarter inch deep.

Without thinking, I place my hand over Mark's, soothing the tension and stilling the stress-induced motion. He catches my hand with his, bringing it to his lips and laying a soft kiss to the back of my hand before turning it over and kissing my palm. His eyes meet mine, a silent thank-you communicated seamlessly now that I'm better able to read the nuances of his every tiny expression.

Suddenly, I realize the cacophony of noise from the rest of the table has stopped, and all eyes are on Mark and me. I blush, trying to pull my hand from Mark's, but he holds on firmly, placing our joined hands on the tabletop between us, the message clear. In his own way, he's claiming me loudly to his family.

My heart races, nerves ping-ponging through my body, and my hopes lift as I look to Mark's people for their reactions. James and Sophie have matching shit-eating grins on their faces, Luke seems to be studying Mark closely, and Mama Lou is both smiling wide and seems to be close to tears.

She clears her throat, breaking the lengthening moment. "Do you boys remember how that scratch first happened?"

Mark's lips rise into a real smile, his dimple proudly on display. "I do. I thought Pops's head was going to explode."

She laughs, nodding. "Honestly, I did too."

"What happened?" Luke asks. "I don't remember this story."

Mark leans back, glancing up at the ceiling. "Well, I must've been about five or six."

"Five," Mama Lou clarifies. "Summer before you started kindergarten."

Mark nods and continues. "Five then. So, I decided I was man enough to have my own pocketknife. Pops didn't agree, not one bit. Told me I had to be at least eight. But I was determined to show him I was ready. I got his off the dresser, no dinky kid's knife but a full-fledged Spyderco. It wasn't huge, but it still had a wicked-sharp four-inch blade that could do just about anything Pops ever asked of it until I got ahold of the darn thing."

"What happened?" Luke says. "Did you break the thing?"

"More or less," Mark admits. "I snuck out to the tool barn and sharpened it. Well, I thought I did, but I guess I dulled it more than anything. Then I tried to whittle some wood right here on the dining table. He came in and caught me, and his yell made me slip. I sliced my finger open, and it was a gnarly uneven cut because I'd messed up the blade so badly, and then the blade dug right into the tabletop."

He rubs at the line in the wood, and Mama Lou takes the story over. "I don't think I'd ever heard him holler like that. And he had a vein in his forehead that wouldn't quit throbbing."

At my nervous look, she gives me a smile and a small shake of her head. "Don't get me wrong. He wasn't a hotheaded man, but fear can so easily masquerade as anger. And you scared the dickens out of him, son," she says, her attention turning back to Mark. "He didn't know you'd messed up that blade, and he told me later he could see you taking half your thumb off with the way you were holding that stick. He felt bad about your cut, but he was more scared than I'd ever seen him before."

James and Luke take it all in, probably thinking their father had never been scared before. He seems like he was larger than life, to hear them all talk about him. Luke turns to Mark. "Did you get to keep the knife?"

Mark snorts, shaking his head. "You must have spent too much time in the sun today—you're crazy. I didn't get one of my own until I was eight, just like he said. Funny thing is, when I opened the box, there with the knife was the block I'd been carving on three years before. He'd saved it for me, said it was a reminder that I'd get what I needed when I was ready for it and not a minute sooner. He made me set that wood chunk on my dresser from there on out as a reminder. It's on my nightstand at home right now, though I haven't thought of that story in a long time."

Mama Lou smiles, her eyes glistening. "I didn't know you still had it! Pops would like that."

Mark nods, rubbing the groove again. "Me too. Still got that first knife, too, though it's in a drawer. But after that, whenever one of us boys started to annoy Pops, I would see him rubbing at this scratch, I guess reminding himself that boys do stupid things."

The story feels like another piece of the puzzle, and I yearn to kiss the scar from the knife from so long ago, whichever white ridge on his working man's hands it might be.

After that, family dinner is comfortable, and I feel like I've been taken into the fold. Sophie and Mama Lou end up talking wedding stuff again, which makes sense since the wedding is mere weeks away and the last-minute rush to the altar is in full effect.

I listen and add in tidbits where I can, but mostly I try to remind them that they have a good plan and not to tinker with it too much. Just relax and let the moment come, because it's going to be magical regardless. It's like my time with Mark.

Over Mama Lou's apparently famous peach cobbler, I find myself just enjoying the moment with him and his people, thankful for the insight into the boy he once was and the man he is now.

CHAPTER 24

MARK

"You almost here, woman?" I growl into my phone, making Sugarpea snort. "I'm waiting."

Katelyn laughs lightly, her voice echoing slightly because she's on speakerphone. It's high and casual, like she's not as crazed to see me as I am to see her. "You ready for me? Turning on your road now."

She's trying to act like it's no big deal that she's driving out here after work, but her leaving after dinner with my family had taken both of us damn near an hour of kisses and touches and quiet words to let go. And that had been in the shadows of the barn, pressed against her little girly car.

The only reason I hadn't thrown her over my shoulder and carted her back to my place to give her what we both wanted was because I knew she had an early morning the next day. Not as early as mine, but I would've happily pulled an all-nighter for her. But I wouldn't compromise her that way, so I'd reluctantly released her and spent all night tossing and turning, wishing she was in my arms. And now it's been a week of stolen moments here and there when our schedules aligned. But it hasn't been enough. I want more.

Tonight, that's exactly what I'm gonna get. I see the cloud of dust billowing up and follow it to its source to see her white Bug flying down the road. Literally, she hits a little bump about a hundred yards from our gate, and I can see daylight under her car and the shake as she bounces before she brakes and stops at the gate.

A grin breaks across my face, which feels awkward but good. That's happening more and more frequently these days.

"Who's in a hurry to see who now, princess?" I ask the wind, but it doesn't answer. I urge Sugarpea forward, going to open the gate for Katelyn. I pop my head in her window for a quick smack that's not nearly enough to ease my need for her, but at least it reassures me that she's here, back with me where she belongs.

"Follow me. You can park and then ride with me to the barn," I say as I remount. Sugarpea's taken a liking to Katelyn, which goes a long way in my book. Sometimes horse sense is the best sense.

Once she turns the car off and steps out, she grabs a small bag, twirling it around for me to see. "Should I leave this for now or bring it?"

I wonder what she's got in her bag of tricks this time. Her last overnight, just a few days ago, had almost verged on a booty call, a late arrival after an evening wedding and an early departure for both of us to get to work in the morning. But because it's us, I loved every second of it and saw many layers of meaning to it all.

And I definitely wasn't complaining about the sexy bra and panty set she'd worn, barefoot this time, with her hair casually knotted on top of her head. It said volumes to me when I'd complimented her copiously and she'd blushed, finally telling me she'd never made that much of an effort with Seth, just a few failed attempts with a Valentine's teddy that he hadn't appreciated. I had to shake my head. Before, I would have chased the stupid fuck down to kill him for making Katelyn think she's anything less than the beautiful creature that she is.

Now? Now I want to send the man a thank-you note for his stupidity at not knowing what he had.

I made damn sure Katelyn knew I appreciated her efforts by worshipping every inch of her body . . . and then I took off the sexy lingerie to do it all again. I recognize the blessing Katelyn is, and I want her to know that too.

"Go ahead and bring it with us," I finally reply. "We can stop by the house and drop it off."

She slips the straps over her shoulder before approaching me and Sugarpea, pausing to rub along his nose as she does some version of baby talk to my big, strong horse. If anyone else did it, I'd be pissed, but he crumbles the same way I would.

"Who's a good horse? Is that mean cowboy making you work too hard today? I promise I'll get you an oat cookie later to make up for it. Okay, baby?"

Sugarpea stomps at the ground, tilting his head to get closer to Katelyn's magic fingers, and I can't help but snicker inside. This horse is gonna end up spoiled; I already give him too many carrots and snacks as it is. "Alright, that's enough, or you're gonna turn my workhorse into a lazy pet."

There's no reprimand in my voice, especially since she's well aware of how much I treat Sugarpea like a favored friend. "Who says I'm going to let you keep him? Maybe he's my horse now?" Her eyes sparkle as she talks to Sugarpea in a high falsetto while scratching up to his ears. "Aren't you, baby?"

I shake my head, smirking at her, cocky as can be. "He's been my horse since I graduated high school, so I don't think you're gonna lure him off now with cookies. He's as loyal as they come." A big grin is her only response. "Come on up here."

I take her bag, throwing it over my shoulder, and offer her a hand. It's not that hard a move, but I still love the slight effort of pulling

Katelyn up after she's slipped her foot into the stirrup I temporarily abandon before she pulls her other leg up, climbing to sit in front of me. It's a tight fit. Though the saddle is a decent size, I'm a big man and don't leave Katelyn much sitting room. She ends up partially in the saddle and more in my lap. I love it. One more quick kiss, and we're off.

"So you ready to ride again today?" I ask as I wrap my arms around her to hold Sugarpea's reins. "You did really well the last time out, although I still swear you're shitting me that you've never ridden before."

She preens under the praise, but it's warranted because she took to riding like a natural. "Nope, I've ridden all of two times, both with you. I think today, though, can we just ride around like this . . . together? Instead of on two horses?"

She snuggles against me, her back to my front, her ass pressed dangerously against my cock making me ache in my jeans. A hard-on is *not* what you want when riding a horse. I swallow and shake the reins, directing Sugarpea on. "Whatever you want, princess."

We stroll through the field toward my back porch, and when we're close, I hold her bag out. "Anything breakable or fragile in here?"

"Nope, just clothes for tomorrow," she says. I nod and toss it onto the lounge chair. It lands with a soft thud, safe and secure, just like she is with me. "Let's ride, cowboy."

The ride is perfection, like something out of one those chick flick movies I tell her I won't watch, but always end up sitting through anyway because they make her happy. I think I've seen more of Hugh Grant than I've ever wanted to recently.

But I'll do anything to keep my princess happy, including a sunset ride across my family land on my favorite horse. This moment is more than I ever dreamed I'd get in life, and I appreciate every bit of it, while trying to keep a firm hold on the reins of my heart.

Doesn't matter—it's too late and I know it.

I'm in love with Katelyn.

Deeply.

Madly.

Crazily in love with her.

God, I sound like my own chick flick at this point, maybe a cowboy one with Sam Elliott giving some sort of deep-voiced rumbling advice. Something about how it's too fast, too stupid on my part, right before telling me that a man's gotta do what a man's gotta do or something like that.

But it's the truth. And I want desperately for her to love me back, to love me even though I'm a cold asshole who wants to possess her.

Almost as if she can hear my thoughts, she wiggles a bit, looking back at me. "Can I ask you a question?"

I let Sugarpea keep his pace even though my heart falters, a kernel of unease blooming in my gut. In my experience, anytime a woman says "can I ask you a question," you're not going to like what it is. Still, I have to let her. "Anything. Of course."

"You're like . . . perfect," Katelyn says, laying her head back on my shoulder. "A gorgeous, sweet gentleman but with just enough growly, brooding bad boy to make you feel a little dangerous. I was right about you—you're definitely not beige."

The description reminds me of her words when we first met, something about her ex being "beige." I swallow a lump at her sweet words, thinking that no one has ever really taken the time to describe me so succinctly. "Thank you."

I remember that she led with asking if she could question me, and I know there's more coming. "But?"

"But with all this amazingness you have going on, I guess I'm wondering why you're not already married off? I mean, I'm certainly glad, because now you're all mine, but surely I'm not the only woman to breach the wall you have erected around yourself, right?"

She sandwiched me, a trick she'd told me about when we talked about her tools of the trade in dealing with crazed clients. I wonder if she even knows she did it, or if it's just how her thoughts organize after so much experience.

For a split second, I consider playing it off by giving her a light, blasé answer and hoping she'll let it go. But she's told me all about that idiot Seth and how she felt blah about everything, but was unwilling to make a change until something truly spectacular gave her the push she needed.

She deserves more than a brush-off. Hell, she deserves it all. The full truth.

But if I tell her that, she'll run screaming, and I'm not ready for that.

Maybe I can give her just enough to satisfy her curiosity, but not share everything? I can at least answer her question about if there's ever been anyone else. It seems only fair after her confessions.

I take a deep breath, praying for strength as I try to delve into one of the worst moments of my life and make it palatable for the one person I hope to never scare away.

"Her name was Nicole. We dated for a while, our senior year of high school, and we tried to keep it going when she went off to college. It was hard to maintain the long-distance thing when she left for school. Still, we managed well enough. She was a sweet girl, talkative when I was quiet, friendly when I was reserved. The yin to my yang in a lot of ways, I guess. She was my first . . . everything, and I was hers. We learned about love together, experimented with sex, and I thought we were going to get married."

I look around the fields surrounding us, remembering the fantasies I'd had back then of little mini-Marks running around the house and riding horses, the next generation of Bennett boys. Back then, it seemed so easy, and that I'd have plenty of carefree years where I could just learn at Pops's side while I taught my sons, three generations on the land.

I hear Katelyn's soft voice cutting through my reflections and pulling me back. "What happened?"

I huff a cynical laugh and swing off Sugarpea to look up at her. "I happened."

She doesn't pry, just waits patiently, giving me the time to find the words I need. After a moment, she adjusts in the saddle, but I keep the reins in my hand, leading Sugarpea as I try to explain. "She came home that first summer and I guess we were both a little more grown up than we had been previously, more adult and less teenager. She'd had all these grand adventures at school, been exposed to all these different things, and I was still just . . . me. A ranch-working guy with too few words, too much dirt, and a mind that focused more on the practical than discussing the philosophy classes she'd been taking."

I take a shuddering sigh, shaking my head. "She begged me for more, wanted me to share my thoughts, my feelings with her, but I was so confused because I thought I had been. We argued, about our past, about our future. Somehow it turned physical . . . not like that," I quickly explain, realizing how bad the words sound as they leave my mouth.

"What do you mean then?" Katelyn asks, her face neutral.

I plunge in, realizing that regardless of her opinion of me, the story could be taken poorly. "I mean, our words, the anger . . . we had 'mad sex,' I guess you could call it? It was rougher than usual, for both of us. By the end of it, she had bruises from my fingers and I had claw marks down my back. She'd left a hickey on my neck bigger than a half dollar, and I'd pounded into her so hard, she was puffy and swollen. It was like nothing I'd ever experienced. Her either, I guess. But while I felt reborn, powerful, and pleased that I'd driven her that wild, she was horrified. She'd scrabbled up from the floor, covering herself from me and looking at me like I was a monster, even though she'd been with me the whole time, giving just as much as she was taking. We broke up pretty much immediately after that."

I risk a look at Katelyn, scared to death to see that same fear in her eyes. But her pupils are dilated, big black pools surrounded by a barely visible ring of blue.

Her breath catches, and she swings off Sugarpea to grab my belt like I'm about to run away. "Oh, Mark, there's nothing wrong with fucking like that."

The dirty words make blood rush to my cock, but more importantly, they create a balm that soothes the pain in my heart. I let go of Sugarpea's reins, and he gives us a curious look before wandering a few steps away, content to munch on some nearby sweet grass.

"Say it again," I whisper, not able to stop the hint of begging in my voice. I just need to hear it, those words that say I'm not a monster, not a freak . . . or if I am, that I'm with someone who is just as monstrous as I am.

She takes my face in her hands, her eyes burning in the dimming light as she strips away the scar tissue from my soul. "Mark Bennett, you are a remarkable man who has shown me amazing things, both in and out of the bedroom. And there's not a damn thing wrong with some rough fucking if that's what we both want. For God's sake, grandmas are reading *Fifty Shades of Grey*. A little grabbing and spanking is basically par for the course these days. It was just a different time, and Nicole was a different woman."

"And you?" I ask. "I . . . I need you to say it."

"I'm your woman," Katelyn whispers. "And right now, I could use a hard fucking more than anything in the world."

I attack her, devouring her lips to taste her reassurances, her filthy words.

There's more, so much more to the story, and maybe I'll tell her more later, but what she's already accepted is overwhelming.

I never had a chance to explain how the powerful sex with Nicole so many years ago had opened my mind and heart to so much. Even in its awfulness, it became a defining fork in my road. After she left, I realized that not only was I hard to be with because of my quiet ways, but that my baser needs weren't the norm. Between the two, I'd shut myself off—from friends, from family, and definitely from women.

But this little dip into my psyche hasn't scared Katelyn off, and that's more than I could have ever hoped for.

Whatever she wants, whatever she can handle, that's what I'll give her, and I'll be so damn happy with that. With her because she's . . . everything.

CHAPTER 25

KATELYN

"No, really. It's totally fine. It's James's bachelor party. Go with your brothers and have fun," I assure Mark. "I'm going to be at work late anyway, setting up everything for Sophie and James's big day."

"Are you sure you don't need help?" Mark asks. "I could come move tables or chairs or something."

I laugh, shaking my head. "While I appreciate the offer, if you come here, I'll have two problems. First, I've got a bunch of guys who get paid hourly to do stuff like that, and you'd have them pissed because you did half the work. Second, and more importantly, I wouldn't get a damn thing done because I'd be too busy ogling you, especially if you start moving furniture around and charming the ladies."

He chuckles gruffly, knowing he can't argue with that. "Fine. I'll go with the boys."

He sounds resigned, like he's being forced to do something he doesn't want to. We've already had this conversation about the bachelor party once, when Mark confessed that he was uncomfortable with the public spectacle aspect of the party. "You know James needs you there, right?" I ask seriously. "This is a big deal to him, and you're like the stand-in for Pops to your brothers. It's a lot to ask and a heavy weight to carry, but if any man can be that strong, it's you. Go, represent the family with Luke, and for the love of God, keep James from doing something stupid that'll mess up the wedding."

I soften the pressure of my words with the light joke, knowing that James, while he has a reputation as a bit of a wild child, has happily shed that skin to emerge as a budding family man. The wildest that particular horse has gotten recently was going ATV racing in a back pasture and popping a tire after landing a jump.

"You're right. And I want to be there for James, you know I do," Mark replies with a sigh. Since our sunset ride, he's opened up more, chuckled more easily, smiled more. James isn't the only one budding and blooming. "I think I'm afraid tonight is going to be a clusterfuck of epic proportions, and I'd rather have a quiet evening on the porch with you than go drinking with my brothers and a bunch of rodeo guys I don't know. Even some of Sophie's family and friends will be there. Her brother told me they have some weird bachelor party traditions too. I don't know what that means—he just said he'd take care of it. Like that doesn't stress the control freak in me right the fuck out."

"Well, they're a part of James's past and future, family and friends. You'll be fine, and it'll be fun."

Mark snorts. "Either way, lunch today wasn't enough."

He's right about that. He'd stopped by for a lunch visit, a rare moment of escape from the ranch in the middle of the day, to come make the final payment for the wedding tomorrow, and we'd had a picnic on the resort grounds. Neither of us had wanted it to end, but duty called, in the form of Marla for me and Luke for Mark, both needing our respective help ASAP.

"Relax," I assure him. "You'll get me all weekend after the wedding. Just behave yourself tonight."

"You know I will, princess," Mark says, his voice dropping to a sexy rumble that even through the phone gives me goosebumps. "Maybe I can come see you after?"

The idea of a late-night visit from Mark . . . mm-hmm. But we did agree beforehand that tonight was for others, both of us having roles to fill. "I'm tempted, babe, so tempted, but no. Tonight is about you and your brothers. And I'm going to be busy until late and have to wake up super early. It might be your brother's wedding, but this is a huge deal for me too. I don't know if you're aware of this, but your brother is famous and his sister-in-law-to-be is super famous. Like, I've had to make sure the photog and staff working the thing all have NDAs on file so nothing leaks out. I want everything to be perfect."

"It will be," Mark assures me. "Pissing off a bunch of cowboys isn't a good idea. Besides, you're amazing at your job, and the planner should be there to help out too."

His compliment tells me everything I need to know, and I smile. "You're pretty amazing yourself. Now, let me off the phone so we can both go do what we need to. I'll see you tomorrow?"

There's a pause, and I think he's already hung up or we got disconnected, but then I hear his voice, deep and serious. "Katelyn."

I wait for him to say more, but I nervously fill the lengthening silence. "Yes?"

"I . . . uh, I . . ."

Oh my God, is he doing it? This man has never stuttered or been at a loss for words a day in his life. He may not speak often or to many people, but he is eloquent when he chooses to be.

My heart soars because this is the moment I've been waiting for.

Over the last few weeks, I've fallen more and more for Mark, and the realization that I'm in love with him has been a bursting bubble of joy surrounding me while I wait for him to say it first.

I'm not exactly the best judge of what's typical, but I'm well aware that this is fast. That doesn't dissuade my heart in the slightest. It's fully and entirely *his*.

I don't want to scare him, though, so I'm following his lead, like so many times before, trusting that he'll get there eventually too. I can wait for him.

"Yes?" I ask, holding my breath and closing my eyes in anticipation.

"Uh, never mind," he finally stutters. "Yeah, I'll see you tomorrow."

My breath escapes out of me, and disappointment rushes in to the vacant places the oxygen usually fills. "Okay, see you then," I reply, unable to hide my disappointment. "Good night."

"G'night, princess," he says softly.

There's a weight to the moment, both of us knowing that he backed out on what he was going to say. He's never been a man afraid to bear anything, and three little words have him twitchy? But they mean so much, and I don't want him to beat himself up. He's given so much to me, and I want to reassure him that it's okay; I'll wait forever if that's what it takes.

"Mark . . . ," I start, but before I even get the word out, the line goes dead. I consider calling him back, but decide I need to try to shake it off and give him the time he needs. I don't know that he was going to say those three magic words; that hope was all in my head. Still, it had felt so real, like we were on the cusp of clasping hands and jumping off the edge into something deeper, grander, and scarier than anything we've done before. To hell with gravity—we'd let our feelings keep us soaring.

And as we stand on that edge, we haven't jumped yet. But we will, I know it. I just have to wait for him.

~~

Wedding prep keeps Marla and me busy all night long, well into the wee hours of the morning, and we're both slamming Red Bulls by the end of it. Marla sets up the groom's room with a local whiskey and a tray of crystal tumblers while I set up the bridal suite with ginger lollipops and organic sparkling juice.

I consult the planner's instructions as we count chairs and do a measurement recheck to confirm the correct aisle runner was sent.

The arbor is already in place, and Marla and I get to work wrapping it in white tulle. The florist will arrive in the morning to add greenery and flowers to the design, so while it still looks bare, I know it'll be fine.

We spend hours in the ballroom, blaring an old '90s rock station and jamming to Bon Jovi, Soundgarden, Nirvana, and more. Admittedly, Marla knows all the words way better than I do, but I do a decent job of dancing along to her quietly screamed solos.

Suddenly, she stops, setting her steam iron aside. "Okay, what's up?"

Confused, I gesture all around us to the half-finished tables. "Uh, a big-ass wedding is what's up. Hello, you're with me, right? Or are you getting loopy from too much caffeine?"

Marla grins, reaching over and downing her third can like it's nothing before shaking it and tossing it in the big garbage bag we've set up to keep the mess corralled. "Girl, I know what's going on with the wedding. Damn near as well as you do! I meant, what's up with you? That was a mighty long lunch break you took today. Need me to have Security Steve erase the tapes for any area in particular, say from noon to one thirty?"

I laugh, pushing her shoulder while blushing. "No, of course not. Besides, I'm pretty sure security tapes have gone the way of the dinosaur. Whatever footage they have would be a digital file."

"Ooooh, so there is footage? What might that footage show?"

I grin. "It would show a perfectly polite and respectable lunch, that's what."

Marla pouts, her lip stuck out almost all the way to her chin it seems. "Pssshaw, that's no fun. What a waste. Is he going to sneak over tonight, maybe a late-night rendezvous?"

I smirk but shake my head. "No, I told him not to since we'd be so late. And he's got the bachelor party tonight too. Someone's got to keep an eye on those rodeo boys."

Marla laughs at my weak excuse and picks up another white table-cloth. "You've got it bad, boss lady. I can see it in your eyes. Can you at least tell me he's just as gone for you?"

I hesitate, wondering if I should share with her. It feels so personal, but I could use a sounding board for this. And Marla was instrumental in helping me get my head out of my ass early on about Mark, so maybe she can help now too.

"I don't know," I admit before hurrying on. "I mean, I think so. Though we haven't said it exactly, not those three words. I thought he was going to on the phone tonight, but then he didn't. I'm waiting on him."

"Chicken!" Marla teases, clucking at me and folding her arms into flapping wings. But she sobers to ask, "But for real, does that mean you love him?"

I duck my head a bit, but my voice is steady. "I do. I completely and utterly do. I don't think he's there yet, but I'll wait."

Marla shakes her head. "He may not have said the words, and let's be honest, the man hardly speaks—"

"Not true!" I jump in, defending him. "He talks all the time to me!"

Marla grins, raising an eyebrow. "Okay, so he talks to you, but for the most part, he's quiet. The question is, does he show you that he loves you with his actions? That's what matters, not some simple words that are easy to fake. Actions count for more than words sometimes, especially with a man like Mark."

"You're right," I admit, wondering if Marla's got a fast track to my inner thoughts or something. "He does show me, from the picnics to teaching me to ride to . . . other ways."

Marla squeals, dropping her tablecloth and ignoring it as it flutters to the ground. "Tell me about that—the other ways. And if you say lights-off missionary, I'm going to DiNozzo smack your head for being a liar."

I blush, not sure what to say. "I'll just say . . . definitely not beige," I finally admit. "It's like Technicolor vibrant of every shade of the rainbow with Mark. He's amazing."

Marla nods and picks up her tablecloth, letting me keep some semblance of my privacy. "I figured that with the way you've been smiling twenty-four-seven lately. Congrats, girl."

"Thank you. We still have a long way to go. I think he's pretty spooked about relationships in general, for good reason from what he's said. I can feel him still holding back some, but we're doing really well."

"Well, keep on talking and *not* talking, and you two will figure it out in due time."

"Thanks, Mar."

Her words are the same thing I've been telling myself, but the repetition of them strengthens the resolve in my heart.

I'll wait for him to figure it out and say it, and then I'll tell him that I love him too.

In the meantime, I'll do as he says and take what he gives me. Happily.

CHAPTER 26
MARK

After last night and James's half-drunk, tearful monologue about how Sophie makes his life complete, all I could think of was Katelyn, which is why I'm here so early. I don't want to disturb her; I know she's busy. But I need to see her, just lay eyes on her and maybe snag a quick kiss before I head upstairs to get dressed in my suit.

I find her near the site of the ceremony, and I lean against the doorway, sipping the smoothest whiskey I've ever tasted from a heavy tumbler as I watch her. Sure, it's a little early for whiskey, but it's after noon, and if there's any time day-drinking is acceptable, it's the day you stand up for your baby brother while he marries the love of his life.

Katelyn takes my breath away. She's wearing a gray skirt and heels, along with a blouse that's the same color as the blush on her cheeks when I say sweet things to her. But she's not blushing now. She's totally in charge, a powerhouse keeping an assembly line of people moving in a choreographed dance of make-ready.

It's sexy as hell, knowing that this powerful, intelligent woman is giving herself to me of her own free will, and I watch raptly as she approves the archway outside, a checkmark to her clipboard. I see her scan the white iron chairs, mentally adding up the seats, and another checkmark. She's a general, not in the military sense, but commanding all the staff with a smile and quick charm before they scurry off to do her bidding.

I know the feeling, because I'd do damn near anything she said too. Vaguely, voices behind me break into my consciousness.

"Yes, ma'am, the ballroom is completely ready—tables and chairs, place settings, and centerpieces. And rather gorgeous, I must say. Excellent choices by you and the bride."

I don't turn around, not caring about some staff member talking to what sounds like the wedding planner Sophie hired. I think her name is Ramona. Instead, I keep my eyes on my princess, her badass in-charge attitude a sexy call for my attention.

But the voices behind me come closer, and I can't help but listen. "The kitchen has the menu all prepared—house salads with balsamic vinaigrette, a selection of beef in red wine reduction or chicken with asparagus and herb sauce, duchess potatoes, garlic haricots verts with bacon, and strawberry sorbet with mint leaves."

"Wait . . . what?" Ramona says, the alarm apparent in her voice. "No, no. The dessert should be lemon sorbet, not strawberry. James has a friend who is highly allergic to strawberries, so that simply won't do."

I hear Bethany—that's who I've realized is talking to the planner— reply. "Oh no. I'm so sorry. I don't know how a mix-up like this could've happened. I'm certain Katelyn said strawberry, and I know I saw the chef preparing the strawberry sorbet today."

My ears perk up further at the mention of my princess's name. I'm fully listening, even though I don't change my posture or turn around. My brows knit together as I sense the danger Katelyn is in.

"Let's check with Katelyn," Ramona says, obviously pissed but holding a tight control on her voice.

"It's fine. I can correct this," Bethany says, and a moment later my radar's blipping again. "She's terribly busy, and this is her first wedding of this size. A few mistakes here and there are to be expected, but she's really doing an awesome job. Glad we caught this."

I look to Katelyn, who seems to be directing a landscaper and is making a sweeping motion. He looks a bit chastised and walks off, leaving an electric blower by her feet and picking up a broom before he starts doing it the way she wants.

I don't have time to wonder what that was about as Bethany continues. "We actually served lemon sorbet in the restaurant last night, so I know we have some freshly made. We'll simply switch for the evening—lemon for the wedding and strawberry for the restaurant. Problem solved."

Ramona lets out a sigh of relief, and out of the corner of my eye I see her put a grateful hand on Bethany's shoulder. "Thank you, Bethany. I think I'll go check in with Katelyn and make sure every last detail is taken care of with the utmost care."

I'm furious, though I probably shouldn't be. Katelyn made a simple error, and one of the other staff members corrected it before it was an issue. That's a good thing, and it's what a team is supposed to do. But something about the way Bethany made Katelyn sound inept pisses me off.

Everyone makes mistakes; hell, we do on the ranch from time to time. And while I might ream James or Luke out over a mistake, I never do it in front of the other—and I'd die before doing it in front of an outsider. For Bethany to be so flippant to Ramona sets my teeth on edge. Katelyn's a damn fine event planner and has done a phenomenal job on James and Sophie's wedding.

I grind my teeth and squeeze my glass a bit tighter, forcing myself to stay still and keep my mouth shut, not saying anything or gulping the last of my small drink. The last thing Katelyn needs is me defending her at work, on her turf where she's the boss. Instead, I school my face into the mask I wear so often in public like this—uninterested, uninteresting, with a decent dose of "fuck off."

It's a delicate balance, and I've perfected it; I could walk through the county fair and not get a single pitch on the midway. Except Bethany seems immune as she comes over, popping out from behind my right shoulder to stand in front of me. I look down for a moment, a bit shocked to see her.

She notices and smiles widely. "Well hello, Mark. Aren't you a sight for sore eyes? You excited for the big day today?"

Small talk, one of the things I hate the most, but Mama raised me to be polite, and I try sometimes.

"Yep," I answer shortly, my eyes roving the ceremony space because in the one second I looked to Bethany, I've lost sight of Katelyn.

"James and Sophie are adorable, obviously deeply in love," Bethany prattles on, oblivious to my disinterest in her waste of words. "May they have many years of wedded bliss."

"Yep."

"Maybe you could save me a dance later at the reception?" she asks.

God, this woman doesn't take a hint. I cut my eyes to her, my face hard, my lips sealed tight. Her chin is tilted down, and she's looking up through her lashes, practically batting them at me. She's a practiced vision of flirtation, feigning shy innocence, but I can spot a fake a mile away, and she's definitely playing angles to see what works.

"I don't think so," I reply evenly, considering telling her that I'm with Katelyn, but I don't know what Katelyn has shared at work beyond her daily conversations with Marla. I don't want to mess with her position at the resort, especially considering the conversation I just overheard.

Bethany lays her red-tipped hand on my arm, and I have to suppress a shudder. It feels wrong, foreign to have someone other than Katelyn put her hands on me. "You know I had such a crush on you back in high school. Can you believe that?" she giggles. "Funny how we all grew up and things change. Just a dance for old times' sake?"

She's leaning closer, sending every green-light signal, but my brain is shouting, *Red, red, red, get the fuck out of here.* I'm about to tell her no—fuck politeness, because she's all up in my space and not the one who should be there. There's only one woman who has that right, and Bethany ain't her.

But as I open my mouth, I hear Katelyn's voice from a few feet away.

"Mark."

I'm not doing anything wrong, but I still jump a bit, which makes Bethany laugh a little. She swats at my chest, her voice light and flirty still. "Oh, she's not that scary, big guy."

I swing my eyes to Katelyn to watch her look ping-pong from me to Bethany to me again. Before I can say anything, she speaks, her voice professional and clipped. "James is looking for you. Said he needed his big brother for a toast. Luke tried to step in, but I think it's you he wants."

There's no emotion in her voice or on her face. She might as well be a robot—or me, for that matter. She gestures with a hand, like she's fucking Vanna White, and every fiber of my being wants to grab her hand as we walk into the hotel, heading toward the waiting rooms. Before we're three steps away, I hear Bethany behind me.

"I'll find you for that dance later."

I swear Katelyn's pace picks up, and I lengthen my stride. Once we're in the hallway, I do grab her hand after making sure we're alone. "Hey, slow up."

"What?" she asks, turning to me with stone-cold eyes.

She's furious; I can feel it coming off her in waves. I try to smile, failing. "You know nothing is going on with Bethany, right? She came up to me, and—"

"Not now," she says, cutting me off. "Not here. I'm at work, and this is the biggest event this resort has ever had. I will not fuck it up."

She's right; whatever reassurances I need to give her that Bethany was coming on to me and I was solidly not into it will have to wait. Although I hate that she thinks for even a second that I would consider anyone else when I have her. She's all I need, all I want, and I'm scarily obsessed with her. If she knew how I felt, she'd definitely never doubt my faithfulness, but she would see the monster I'm hiding and run anyway.

"Okay, later then." The words are serious, a promise that this conversation isn't finished. "Hey, by the way, I overheard Bethany and Ramona. I guess there was a mix-up with the sorbet. Bethany seems to have straightened it out and made sure the lemon went to the wedding and the strawberry went to the restaurant. Just wanted you to know, because it seemed like a big deal. Some allergy or something."

"What?" she exclaims, obviously stressed. She shakes her head, then nods briefly. "Thanks, I'll take care of it. Now you, go do the toast for your brother."

"Consider it done. But we're talking later."

She lifts her chin and spins, striding off down the hall. I watch her go, the sway of her hips mesmerizing as always. It's not until she turns the corner that I realize she didn't kiss me.

There's not a soul in the hall besides us, so we definitely could've gotten in a quick peck. I try to tell myself that it's because she's worried about making sure everything goes off without a hitch, not because she's angry about coming up on me with Bethany like that.

But it rings hollow, and before I can choose between chasing her down and my toast, Luke opens the door. "Fuck's sake, Mark, get your ass in here before James has a heart attack!"

CHAPTER 27

KATELYN

The ceremony is picture-perfect gorgeous. The whole space is filled with tulle and flowers, hopes and dreams. Roxy knocks it out of the park with her singing, and there isn't a dry eye in the garden as James and Sophie exchange vows, though there are a few giggles at some of the personal promises, especially something about whistles and watering holes.

I'm doing a good job keeping up with it all, but the reception is well underway by the time I have half a chance to catch my breath. I've just been so worried, because it's been such an oil-and-water mix on the outside that I didn't know what to expect.

On one side, Sophie's family is *money*. There are tasteful flashes of wealth, from diamonds to Rolexes, an air of elegance surrounding her people. I imagine they'd all be comfortable at a black-tie fundraising gala. On the other side, James's friends and family are wearing starched jeans and their cleanest Double H boots. It seems like they'd be right at home at a rowdy hoedown in the back pasture.

But the two groups seem to have found a middle ground of respectful celebration, James and Sophie uniting them all for the evening.

I feel a little like a cowgirl myself as I help the staff herd everyone to the reception, imagining it's my own fancy version of a cattle drive. I care about Sophie and James a lot after the past couple of months, and I'm happy to have had a hand in making their dream day come true.

As we reach the ballroom, my eyes drift to Mark for what has to be the thousandth time, and though I can tell he's on the verge of stomping over and carting me out of here, he restrains himself, letting me work like I asked. I appreciate it, even though I'm chomping at the bit to talk to him about what I saw with Bethany.

As the festivities get into full swing, dinner complete and the dance floor filling, I step over to Ramona, the wedding planner. "May I speak with you for a moment?"

She looks over, also obviously relieved that so far things are running well. "Of course."

I lead her into the kitchen and introduce her to the people I wanted her to meet. "Ramona, this is Stefan, our chef, and this is Brianna, one of the resort owners and the previous events coordinator."

I wait while they all shake hands and exchange pleasantries. "Ramona, I wanted to follow up with you about a concern I was informed about. In our previous meetings, we discussed the menu at length, including lemon sorbet with a single mint leaf. Correct?"

"Yes, yes. And it was lovely," she says, more to Stefan than to me.

I feel my lips thin, but I'm going to be professional about this, because I don't think Ramona is anything more than confused. I turn to Stefan, checking my clipboard. "Stefan, in our meeting, we agreed on lemon as well, yes?"

He nods, looking confused about why we're having this conversation. "Of course, Ms. Johnson."

"When was the last time you made strawberry sorbet?" I ask.

Stefan, for his part, looks horrified. "Oh no, we talked about the guest with an allergy, and the kitchen staff took the utmost care to prevent any cross-contamination. We do have strawberry sorbet made, but it's from two days ago. That's why we kept the lemon for tonight in a different freezer. Did something happen?"

"No, everything was lovely," I assure him, watching his shoulders sag in total relief. "No issues at all. Just to clarify, you and the staff were aware that tonight's menu included lemon sorbet and took every precaution for safety."

He nods vigorously, still looking confused. "Yes, of course."

That settled, I turn to Ramona, who now looks confused as well. "I understand that you might have been led to believe there was a potentially dangerous mix-up in the kitchen with the menu. I wanted to reassure you that our communication was appropriately shared with the kitchen and that in no way was there ever a food risk. Your instructions and the party's wishes were carried out explicitly and carefully."

Ramona hums, nodding her head. I can see the wheels turning. She looks to Brianna, who has been quietly watching the exchange, seamlessly stepping into her ownership role in the middle of an event at which she's an invited guest. "I appreciate the follow-up. It does seem that I was misinformed, or rather possibly intentionally misled. I will say that Ms. Land's quick thinking to address the issue was appreciated, but it seems that the situation itself may have been fabricated to highlight her in a positive manner."

I didn't intend on having Bethany shanked in such a public way. My main concern was the resort's impeccable reputation as a venue for discriminating brides. And considering Ramona's clientele, I definitely want her opinion to be positive after working with us so that she will recommend us again in the future. And though my goal was to maintain utter professionalism, I'll admit to the tiniest sliver of retribution at the karmic justice Bethany's sneaky behavior is bearing.

Brianna's expression hardens around the eyes, but her voice is kind as she offers a hand to Ramona.

"Thank you for understanding. We've greatly enjoyed working with you and look forward to doing so again in the future. Please rest assured, we will make sure this is a one-time incident."

Ramona looks to me, nodding her apology. "I feel confident that Ms. Johnson has things well in hand. Today was beautiful, and she and her staff have handled the unusual nature of this wedding with graceful ease. Now, if you'll excuse me, I'd like to get back to make sure the dancing hasn't become too rambunctious. I did make a promise to Mrs. Bennett to keep her son off tables," she quips with a laugh that says she's not sure if that's a real risk or not.

In an instant, Ramona disappears while Stefan makes himself scarce, muttering something about checking the freezer. When we're alone, Brianna turns to me, still angry inside but totally not at me. Thank goodness. "Great job tonight, Katelyn. The wedding was lovely, and besides this drama, everything seemed to go perfectly." I smile at the praise, but I know there's more.

"I'll talk to Bethany and make sure this doesn't happen again. She put our reputation on the line in an attempt to look like some sort of guardian angel. That's unacceptable in my book and hugely unprofessional. She should feel lucky that I'm in a good mood and she still has a job."

I nod. "Thank you, Brianna."

"Also, in the future, any communications with planners will go through you, nobody else. There was simply no need for Bethany to even speak with Ramona today, and a single point of contact would clear up any potential *miscommunications*." She says the word with the smallest hint of scorn. "Think you can handle that?"

I'm still processing everything, so her question throws me for a moment. "Yes, of course," I answer, nodding.

I want to throw in that Bethany should keep her lying hands off my man, but that seems rather unprofessional, so I bite back the words, knowing I'll have to settle that myself later.

I don't have the chance to enjoy any of the reception, and when I get home to my apartment, it's very late. Still, my heart lifts when I see a light on in my living room, and I know Mark is here, just like we'd arranged. I unlock the door, and when it swings open, I can see that he's sitting on the edge of the couch, hair a mess like he's been running his fingers through it over and over again.

Before I can say a word, he looks up, pain in his eyes. "Katelyn, I swear, she was coming on to me, and I was trying to get out of there politely so I didn't cause a scene in the middle of your work."

He's reassuring me, like he's worried I don't believe him. It's so clear, and the realization hits me right in the chest. For all my ability to read his straight face and subtle mannerisms, he can't read mine. Compared to him, I'm all big emotion, big words, big . . . well, everything.

And because of that, he's been worried on what should have been a day of joy for him. I let the cool professional facade I've had to wear all day fall, slamming the door behind me and running to him. Now isn't the time for soft words or tears. Maybe later, but this is a time for big actions, for concrete steps and clear statements.

I pull at his shirt, yanking a button free. "Get this fucking thing off. She touched it, and I need it off your skin. Now. I want to burn it."

He looks confused for a second, but I have to give the man credit—he recovers quickly. "Anything you want, princess. Anything at all."

Sitting up and creating a little space between us, he grabs his shirt and yanks, Superman style, buttons flying around the room and pinging off my television. I help him get the cuffs off his wrists before pushing him back, looking at his chiseled torso.

I climb onto his lap, straddling him as my skirt rides up high on my thighs, and I greedily kiss him hard, plunging my tongue into his mouth. As we plunder each other's mouths, my words are driven by the force of desire coursing within me.

"I want your fingers buried in me. I'm going to claim them as mine so that her touch is obliterated, covered by my mark." I don't know where these dirty words are coming from, and I've never been jealous or possessive like this, but right now, I feel like I need to stake my claim on every inch of Mark, yell from the rooftops that he's mine so no one ever dares get too close again.

"Fuck, princess," Mark moans, his hands cupping my ass and already pushing my panties down. "You're not pissed?"

I pull back, running my fingernails down his chest. Bethany's not the only one who got a manicure for today's wedding, and I smile at the scratches my pink nails leave on his skin.

"Oh, I'm mad as hell. But not at you. I could see how uncomfortable you were. I'm mad that she dared touch what's mine."

"Mine," he echoes back. I'm not sure if he's agreeing with me or claiming me, too, and I don't care. I just need him—filling me, claiming me, marking me as I do the same to him.

In a heartbeat, the fire between us flares like it's been doused in kerosene, mouths hungrily devouring each other, clothes flying through the air like forgotten kites, and a symphony of primal sounds. Mark swipes his fingers through my slit, groaning at the wetness. I'm already ready, and I want more, so much more. Desperately.

"Hands and knees," he commands, reading my mind when I whimper my desire. I nod, quickly kneeling down on the rug.

Before I can even arch my back, he's there, naked and sheathed, ready for me. He slams into me, bottoming out on the first stroke so hard that I bounce forward a bit. He grabs my hips, pulling me back, yanking me onto his cock without mercy.

I cry out in pleasure, the fullness completing something in me I didn't know was empty. Mark suddenly smacks one ass cheek, then the other, the sting a hot reminder that I'm his.

He doesn't stop his punishing pace, pounding into me with an animalistic ferocity, hitting my cervix with each thrust. "Reach back, spread yourself for me," he demands, his voice low and full of gravel. "I want to see your pussy taking all of me."

I press my cheek to the floor, freeing my hands, and I reach toward my ass, spreading myself. He presses in deeper, and I'm on the delicious edge of pleasure and pain, where I swear he might split me in half, but fuck, do I want that, right here on the edge for the rest of my life. This is the man I want, and to die from impalement on his cock would be the purest way to go.

But not yet. More . . . I need more. As much as I want to leave my mark all over him, body and soul, I think I need this more. His raw power, beautiful and wild and feral. On some level, I recognize this is what he's been holding back, and it brings tears to my eyes. Ones of relief and release that finally . . . finally he's with me. Fully, powerfully, authentically . . . mine.

Mark reads my mind again, or maybe it's my incoherent cries egging him on, pleading with him for more. He grabs my waist in his rough, powerful hands and pulls me back as he thrusts forward, using my body for his pleasure and riding me hard. I can feel the dimple each of his fingers makes in my flesh, like he's holding me together by sheer will because I feel like I'm expanding, too big for my skin to contain me as he takes me higher and higher.

Every few seconds, I'll feel his hand let go of my hip and have a split second of anticipation before he spanks me again. Or scratches along the backs of my thighs, his stubbed nails sometimes raking my skin and sometimes grabbing handfuls of the shaking muscles. It's exquisite agony, not because I don't want it, but because I want it *all*. The overload of sensations, rough and hard and *everything*, is an unbelievable experience I've never imagined. I'm thrashing beneath him, hips bucking wildly, when his finger, wet with my cream, circles my asshole, where I'm spread wide for him. I've never done this, but I trust him, and the tingly feeling as he rubs over my tight hole makes me want more. I whimper, pulling myself wider for him, and Mark groans.

He fists my hair, turning my head to the side a bit, and I side-eye him, trying to see his face through the loose strands of my blonde waves. He presses his teeth to my shoulder before growling in my ear, "Take it, princess. Fucking take it."

I try to nod, but his grip keeps me still as he presses his finger in slowly, even as his thrusts into my pussy stay mercilessly hard and fast.

Every smack of my thighs on his hips lets him slip in a little farther until he's fully seated, cock in my pussy and finger in my ass. It feels odd but good. I'm fuller than I've ever been and totally in his control, now and for always.

I feel him everywhere—in me, on me, surrounding me. His free hand roams my body, kneading, scratching, pinching, holding. Every touch an extra incentive toward whatever maelstrom he's building inside me with his punishing strokes in my pussy and ass, the depth he reaches surprising and delighting me. He fills me completely and then retreats, leaving me empty and greedy for more. Again and again.

The combination is my undoing. In seconds, I'm trembling, something about being at his mercy, taking all the pleasure he can heap on my body as I'm spread wide beneath him, knowing he's watching raptly as he gives me everything. It triggers me in a way even our sex before has never touched.

I come like a banshee, wailing and crying, overcome with the massive waves of pleasure from the carnality of how he's taking me. My defenses are nonexistent, my filters useless as my mouth lets loose the words I've been holding so tightly.

"Fuck, Mark . . . I love you! Oh, yesssss . . . I love you."

There's a big gush between my legs as I come, and distantly a tiny part of my brain whispers what just happened. I've never done that before. Hell, I thought it was a freaking myth. But Mark just drew it out of me, demanded it from my body, and I'd obeyed.

Mark roars, slamming deep into me, and all cognizant thought leaves my mind as I soak in his every drop of pleasure, letting the heat he's spilling inside me burn me to ashes. It's glorious, it's primal, and it's everything I never knew I wanted.

And then I hear him growl, "I love you, too, princess. I love you too."

The words make me come all over again, collapsing flat to the floor as the spasms rack my body. Mark rides me hard through each lingering shudder, powering deep inside me, pushing a cry of ecstasy from my throat with every thrust.

Too soon, I feel Mark pull out, but I'm too boneless to move.

Until I hear his tortured words and quick steps. "Fuck. Fuck. Fuck."

I have a thought that maybe the condom broke. I wouldn't be surprised, considering the workout we just gave it, but then I hear a rustle and realize he's pulling on his pants.

"Mark?" I ask, my voice shaky and hoarse from my cries. I look up, and he's got his pants already on, trying to zip what I'm pretty sure is a broken zipper. "What are you doing?"

He freezes but doesn't look at me at first. Slowly, like he's forcing himself, he lifts his chin. His eyes are wide, panicked. And I think I see tears trembling in the corners, and it makes my heart break.

"I'm so sorry," he pleads, still confusing the fuck out of me. "Shit."

Without another word, he grabs his boots, not even bothering to pull them on, and he bolts for the door.

I sit up, confused. "Mark! What's wrong?" I call out. "Mark?"

But he's already gone. I'm lying naked on the floor, apartment door wide open, frozen as I hear his truck peel out of the parking lot.

To the empty room, I whisper, "I love you . . ."

CHAPTER 28

KATELYN

I sit on the floor in shock for several minutes, unsure about what the hell just happened.

Well, I know part of what happened—Mark just gave me the fucking of my life and said he loves me before running out the door like the hounds of hell were after him.

The first tears come slowly, but once they do, it's like a faucet's been turned on inside me, burning hot as they rush down my cheeks, completing my humiliation at his rough dismissal of me after such an intense mating.

The way he left was so much more hurtful than any of the forcefulness he used while we were fucking. His apology was a blade to my heart, bleeding it dry with every hiccupping moment that passes.

I see his eyes, the panic and horror written so clearly on his face that anyone could read it. The confusion swirls inside me, a riot of questions begging for answers. Part of me wants to hide, to say this is too much, that whatever the fuck is going on with Mark, I can't take it anymore.

It's just so hard. Being with Mark means that there's pain, that there's effort. And not just effort like a hard day at work. I mean that out of the blue, I might have to grab the world and heave it onto my shoulders, to pick it up without warning and haul the whole thing up a hill.

You mean like Mark's done every day since his father died?

The voice stops me in my tracks. It's true; Mark had the weight of his entire world dropped on his shoulders. And since that moment, he hasn't had it easy. He's had to pick up his entire family, the good and the bad, and keep it going. And yet somehow he found the courage and the energy to let me in. To let me love him, even when I could tell he was scared.

He found the courage to love me.

It's scary, knowing just how powerful a man Mark is. And what I may be in store for if I go after him. The girl I was, the girl who lived with Seth for that short stint in purgatory, she'd have run.

But I'm not that girl any longer. I'm Mark's princess. I'm not the girl who just meekly, blandly . . . *beigely* goes through my *beige* middle-class life, finding a *beige* middle-class guy, only to be miserable by the time I'm forty-five.

No. Fuck that. Even if it destroys me, even if it's painful and angry and as black as the deepest pits of a coal mine, I'm going to find out the fucking truth. I've spent years not rocking the boat, but for Mark, I'll capsize the whole damn ship.

I know he's been holding back from me—his words, his heart, his story—but I've been taking the crumbs he's offered as he shared them, letting him take his time. No longer. Whatever secret it is that he's had locked inside him, whatever it is he's ashamed of, I don't care—he needs to tell me. I want it all, and I want it now.

He keeps saying that he'll give me anything I want. Well, let's start with the truth. All of it. He said I was a badass and in charge? He hasn't seen anything yet.

I get dressed as quickly as I can, grabbing a pair of cotton shorts and a tank, more pajamas than clothes but I don't care right now. I slip them on, jamming my feet into a pair of untied sneakers, no socks, and hit the highway out of town before I call Mark's number.

It goes straight to voice mail. The same thing happens the second and third time I call, and I'm tempted to leave a message, but this isn't something I can say to a damn machine.

I growl into the heated late-summer-night air and press the pedal of my Bug a little harder, for the first time wishing it was built for horsepower and not practical fuel economy.

When I get to the Bennett ranch, the front gate is closed up tight, but I refuse to be deterred. I lay on the horn, not giving a shit that it's creeping up on midnight and the jarring sound will echo across the flat fields for probably a mile. I demand entry.

After a full minute, I don't see any movement.

"Fuck it," I grumble, switching off my engine and getting out. "If I have to climb the fence, I will."

My fingers are on the rail when I hear a long sliding sound, and I recognize it as the steel gate to the mechanical barn. After spending time out here with Mark, I'd recognize it anywhere. Cupping my hands around my mouth, I call out. "Mark?"

The voice that replies is sleepy, and not Mark. "Katelyn? What the hell are you doin' out here raising hell at oh dark thirty?"

"Luke," I reply as his silhouette comes into view and I can confirm it's him, "let me in. I need to talk to Mark. Now."

Luke runs a hand through his slightly shaggy hair, waving me down. "Alright, hang on a second. Damn, woman, keep it down. We've got neighbors and shit. Kind of."

The Gator is louder than I was, but I don't bother mentioning it, just jetting through the gate as Luke opens it. I stop in the driveway, and Luke pulls up beside me. "Get in and I'll take you down to Mark's place."

I climb in the passenger side, taking a moment to look over at Luke. "Thanks, Luke. Sorry to wake you up."

Instead of replying, he's looking at me with shock on his face, his hands dropping off the steering wheel. "Holy shit, Katelyn! What happened?"

I smooth my hair down, thinking I must have some seriously freshly fucked locks if they're making Luke look at me like that. I didn't look in the mirror before I left, just made up my mind and set out as fast as possible.

"I'm fine. Mark just ran out, and we need to talk."

Luke's teeth clack together as he snaps his mouth closed and his eyes narrow. His voice is tight and silky with restrained violence. "Mark did that to you? Motherfucker, I never . . . I'll kill him myself."

I can feel the anger in Luke as his tension rises, and I'm confused. "Luke, what are you talking about? I'm not here to kill him. I'm here to talk to him."

Luke looks at me, incredulous. "Katelyn, I saw it in the headlights—there's a bite mark on your shoulder, the backs of your thighs are red and purple, your hair is a mess, and you have mascara running down your face in black rivers. What the hell? I need an explanation before I take you to see him if he did this to you."

He shakes his head, the anger still coiled tight. Dawning realization hits, and I take a deep breath, putting my hand over Luke's. "Luke, you've got it all wrong. Nothing bad happened. Well, not until he walked out suddenly. It's not what it looks like. The rest of this was . . . um, all good."

I blush fiercely. This is certainly not a conversation I thought I'd ever have, and definitely not with the brother of the man I love. Luke seems unsure, but he takes a deep breath.

"All good?" he asks skeptically. "Katelyn . . ."

I can hear that he's about to go off again, but I'm done with the conversation. I don't have time for more explanation. My voice is firm, hard, brooking no argument. "Yes, all good. Now, are you going to drive me over there, or am I walking?"

To emphasize my point, I step a foot out of the vehicle, ready to hop to the ground. Luke sighs and shakes his head. "Fuck. No, I'll take you. Get back in."

Luke rolls down to Mark's house quickly, and I'm half expecting him to be sitting in the outdoor lounge, but everything is dark as we pull up.

"Stay put. Let me make sure he's even here," Luke instructs me, turning the Gator off and heading toward the door.

Maybe the old Katelyn would have listened, but as soon as Luke steps out, I jump out the other side, running for the door. Luke hollers at me, but I pay him no mind.

"Mark Thomas Bennett, where the fuck are you?" I demand as I burst into the kitchen. Country living, no locks on the doors.

I scan the kitchen and living room areas in one sweep, and I almost miss him. He's a big man, but right now he's curled into himself, sitting on the couch with his head in his hands, a bottle of whiskey on the table in front of him.

My fury ices over at seeing him broken this way. I don't know what happened, but it's affected him just as much as it did me, maybe more. I go to him, kneeling beside him, my voice calm and steady.

"Mark?"

He shakes his head, refusing to meet my eyes. "Fuck, Katelyn. I'm so sorry."

Luke clears his throat, and I look to him, silently communicating with my eyes that he needs to get the fuck out. This is between me and Mark, and we don't need an audience, especially one of his brothers, for whatever breakdown this is.

"I'll head back to the barn for a bit. Think I'll stay up and read," Luke says, speaking to me but clearly meaning it as a warning to Mark as well. "Give a holler if you need anything. It'll carry out here. I'll hear you."

I nod tersely, thankful for his willingness to stand up for me, but I just need him to go so I can be alone with Mark. After a final glance, he does, and I wait for the sound of the Gator to fade before I begin. Kneeling in front of Mark, I take away the whiskey bottle and put my hands on his knees.

"Mark, look at me."

With a sigh of misery that has the weight of years, he does, and the pain reflected in his blue eyes guts me. "What happened tonight? Please tell me."

He reaches to touch my hand where it lies on his thigh, but he pulls back, like he can't trust touching me. His brow furrows, the words tumbling out in a ramble, something I've never heard him do.

"I'm sorry, princess. I swear I didn't mean to hurt you. You attacked me, and your possessiveness just broke all my restraint. So fucking sexy. You got me so deeply, so worked up I got . . . carried away. I wasn't gentle like I promised myself. I said I'd never hurt you, and I did."

"You didn't hurt me, and I'm confused. Why are you trying to be easy? I thought we were *not* being gentle most of the time."

Mark growls, standing quickly to pace around the room. Anger pierces through every movement, every breath, and every syllable that comes out of his mouth as he harshly turns to me, his eyes blazing with self-hatred.

"Fuck, I knew I was pushing you, but I thought I'd know when it was too far. Easy . . . is that so fucking hard?"

His words seem to be more to himself than to me, and I get up, getting in his way to bring his attention back to me. He needs to talk to me, not the demons he's fighting.

"Mark! Talk to me," I beg, but my pleas go unanswered. His sadness has morphed into madness, rage pouring from him like a physical force as he turns away to resume pacing back and forth in front of me. I'm tempted to shrink from the weight of it, retreat and preserve whatever fragile hold I may have on him and try again tomorrow.

But the truth hits me like a bolt of lightning, and I bring my hand up to my lips, my fingers trembling in the weight of my realization.

"You're scared."

There's no response from the beast before me. Instead, he just keeps cursing himself out. I can't let this continue, so I step in front of him again, and when he doesn't stop, my hand flashes out, my palm shakily pressed to his chest, physically forcing him to heed me.

"Stop and listen!" I yell, minding my volume because I know Luke'll be down here at a sprint if he hears me. "You're scared. This is fear masquerading as anger."

The words mean something to him, connect something in his past to something happening right now. He blinks, his fists closing and opening with every inhale and exhale.

"I'm both. I'm fucking furious at myself for hurting you and so damn scared that I've lost you." The words are spit out, like the raw honesty and pain tastes sour to his tongue.

Now that I have his attention, I need to break through to him. I take his hands in mine, weaving my fingers through his and shaking my head. "I'm not hurt, at least not physically. But you did hurt my feelings by saying I love you and then bolting for the door. And this"—I gesture between him and me—"whatever this is right now, hurts. I need you to talk to me."

"I can't!" he snarls. "I don't know what to say. I'm not that guy."

He's shutting down, I can see it, so I do the only thing I can think of. "Fine. Don't talk. Don't say a single word because I'm going to say my piece."

I see a flash of pain shoot across his face, and I realize he thinks this is the point where I walk away. But I'm not. I'll follow this man to the ends of the earth if I have to, but he's going to talk to me, and I'm going to talk to him. Brutal honesty, it's the only way.

"Mark, when I met you, I was swept off my feet by the quiet giant who lit up my mind, body, and soul in a way I'd never dreamed of. And then we became friends. I hated every single minute of it, because the whole time I wanted more with you. The first time you touched me . . ." I see him flinch, but I press on, determined to lay it all on the table. "The first time, I realized how much I'd been missing out on. I was so mad at myself for settling for so long. You opened my eyes to the world. It felt like I'd been living in black and white, and suddenly there was color, so much color, everywhere, but it was all centered around you."

Mark shakes his head, trying to pull his hands from mine, but I'm not going to stop, not going to let go.

"And there were movie dates, horse rides, and phone calls that lasted until our morning alarms went off. I was desperate for it all, every bit of you I could get, like treasured trinkets as I solved the puzzle of your every expression, mood, and word. And I realized that I love you. I've been waiting—God, I've been waiting to tell you that. I didn't because I was afraid you'd freak out. But tonight, all my defenses crashed, and the words slipped out. Even though you said it back, I don't think you meant it, judging by the way you ran out of there."

Mark stops, shaking his head and looking at me with shocked eyes, but even though I'm starting to cry again, I press on. "So, Mark, if you're not there, it's fine. I'll wait however long it takes, because I want you. You're mine. I'm yours. Remember?" I'm blubbering, ugly-crying as the emotions pour from me as much as the tears do.

It's all I have, every bit of my soul served up on a silver platter for his acceptance or refusal, no charm or finesse, just pure, raw . . . love. Mark blinks, his mouth opening and closing wordlessly before his face crumbles and he collapses to his knees at my feet, grabbing around my waist tightly and pressing his cheek to my belly.

"Katelyn."

The gut-wrenching emotion of that single word takes me aback. This mountain of a man is kneeling . . . for me. I run my fingers through his hair, comforting him as he starts to weep, and I hold him dear.

"Mark, talk to me. What happened tonight?"

He gulps, and I feel the movement of his Adam's apple as he fights the words. I don't know if he's forcing them out or forcing them down. "Say it one more time," he rasps, his voice choked. "I need to hear it."

I push his head back, looking into his eyes, confident and clear. "I love you, Mark Bennett. With all my heart, with all I have."

A sob escapes his throat, low and rough. He buries his face in my stomach again, the words coming slowly. "I don't do relationships. I'm not good at them. But I've been trying so hard, and tonight, I sat on your couch thinking you were going to come home and be pissed at me. I was prepared to handle that. But you came in like a hurricane, all possessive and wild. It was so fucking sexy that I lost control. The words slipped out, and I meant them. Dammit, I love you, princess." He squeezes me tighter with the words, the emphasis not just in his words but in his body.

"But I didn't mean to be so rough. And when it was over, I realized what I'd done. I didn't want to see that look in your eyes when the high left and the realization set in that I'm a monster . . . that I left marks all over your body, tears pouring down your face when I didn't even realize you were hurting. I thought I'd know, I swear I did. But I couldn't go through that again, didn't want anyone to look at me like that, but especially not you, so I ran. But I swear I can do better. I swear it."

He squeezes me tighter again, like he thinks I'm about to step out of his arms. But how could I? His words are what I've been waiting to hear. He does love me. He freaked because he thought he was too rough, that I would run out like Nicole, not because I said those three little words. Hope burns bright in my soul, and I stroke his hair again, bending down to kiss the top of his head.

"Wow, she really did a number on you, didn't she?" I ask quietly. He looks up at me, and I hold his face, not letting him look away from this, wanting him to see the truth in my eyes. "I am not Nicole. In one moment, she fucked up your head real good. But listen to me, Mark

Bennett. *I am not Nicole.* I don't think you're a monster, not at all. Every single time we've been together has been amazing."

"Really?" he asks, hope dawning in his eyes incrementally.

"Mark, up until you, I'd basically only had missionary sex, and it was a banner day if the lights were on. Beige, blah, bland, boring. You told me once that you were definitely not beige, and you're right. But I'm learning that I'm not either—I just didn't know any better. You're red, orange, blue, pink, black . . . the whole damn rainbow. And tonight was fireworks, glitter exploding and filling me with so much pleasure I thought I'd burst. You know what I see when I see the marks you left behind?"

He shakes his head slowly, still not believing me fully, his brows pulling together questioningly.

"I see your passion, *our* passion on my skin. Every kiss, every touch, every sucked bruise, every handprint—passion." I softly trace the muscles on his chest with my fingernail, watching as his eyes flutter closed, reveling in my touch. "I love you, and I love the way you take charge of my body, showing me things I never knew were possible. I want to keep doing that. If you do."

Mark stands up, his calloused hands taking my face the way I'd held his, forcing my attention on him, as if I'd look anywhere else in this moment. "Fuck, Katelyn. I want that too. So much. You have me, heart and soul. I want to have you, to give myself to you . . . to have a future with you. I love you."

Our lips crash together, the desperate need to connect physically after the emotional display filling both of us. Mark's teeth nip at my lip to demand entry. I open happily, just as hungry for him as he is for me. We seal our words, our commitment with this kiss that's fire and sweetness together as we go back and forth, giving and taking equally, pouring ourselves into the caress. There's no breath, and when we break apart, he crushes me to his chest, holding me tight, and I feel the shudder run through his body.

I feel a huge release of worry from my heart, my body taking strength from the man holding me in his warm embrace. I snuggle in deeper, reveling in it, basking in the moment. But I feel a tautness to his muscles; he's still holding on to tension, fear. Everything I know about this man, everything I've learned from watching him, tells me there's another question to ask.

"There's more, isn't there?"

He looks at me, shaking his head. "No, this is it. Us. This is what I want. What I need."

But I can read it; even after this short time together, I know he's only telling me 90 percent of the truth. He does want us, he wants to be the man for me, and I'm all he needs—I can feel the honesty in his words. But he's holding back still. And I can't let him. I need every last bit of him, no holdouts. This is a turning point for us, but maybe more so for him. He's got to let himself free.

"Mark. Tell me. I want it all—the brutal, real truth. That's the only way this works. I want you, all of you. Whatever it is."

Mark releases me, the thread between us pulling tight with tension once again. He gestures to the nearby chair, his voice stronger but still quavering slightly. "You should probably sit down."

Shit. He's scaring me. But whatever it is, for him, I'll handle it. I can be the badass he thinks I am, the badass I'm becoming. I sit in the chair, folding my legs under me.

He sighs, crossing his arms over his chest and rubbing himself as if chilled. "I don't know where to start. I've never had to put this into words, you know?"

I nod, knowing that he's struggling, but he's trying so hard to tell me. "Take your time. Choose your words as carefully as you always do. I'll wait while you collect them to explain. I need your truth because I'm giving you all of mine. I deserve that gift. More importantly, I think you need to give it, have been waiting your whole life to speak it, hoarding it like a treasured marble too pretty to take out and play with."

"It's not pretty, that's for damn sure," he spits out. "More like the ugly center you hide. The truth you dress up for public consumption so it's easier and more palatable. But alone, you let the facade fall away, the work of pretending not worth the energy when there's no one to see."

I shrug, not quite sure what he's talking about, but wanting to encourage him. "People are just people, different in some ways, alike in others. Everyone has their public face and their private self. Tell me what you're hiding. I swear I'm worth the risk of your honesty."

Mark inhales deeply, looking at me with total devotion. "You are. I know you are, princess. It's just hard to tell you this. I don't want you to see me differently."

"But I do," I counter. "I want to see you for who you are, nothing more and nothing less. Just let the words come. I'm not going anywhere, Mark. I love you."

The promise seems to give him strength, and the words begin to trickle out, slowly becoming a steady flow. "It's about the framework of what I want, what I need. No, more than that. It's the foundation of who I am."

He nods, like the words feel right, and I feel like we're getting somewhere. I don't dare interrupt him; this is a fragile moment.

"What I need isn't a partnership, but a mutual possession. So embedded in one another that there is no you, no me, only us. A depth where there are no walls between us, not ever, about anything. A trust so complete that it is pure submission, where you know that every solitary thought I have is for your betterment, your pleasure, your happiness, and you give that back to me unquestioningly as well. Because I am just as purely submitting to you. Where the word *love* is grossly inadequate to describe what we feel."

He takes a deep breath, like the release is lightening his load, syllable by syllable, and he can't stop throwing off the stones that have weighed him down for so long.

"It's not about sex, or at least not *only* about sex. It's more than that. It's when I know every nuance of what you need, where communication is done with hearts and breaths, not words and minds. That connection that lets me read you without negotiating boundaries or safe words, but a life where you give to me fully as I give complete care to you in return. Where I can tear you to pieces, split you in two with violent thrusts, my hand in your hair as I give you more than you think you can handle. Or tenderly worship you for hours with soft caresses, giving attention to every bit of your body and soul . . . and you lust for that, knowing that I'll always take care of you, that I'll put you back together once again, filled with my cum, my love, and my soul. And I take yours too."

I'm breathless, the poetry of his words hitting me like darts straight to my soul. My heart races as I stand, his eyes warily watching my approach. I've never felt more like prey to his predatory gaze. I can see the rise and fall of his chest as he fights for breath, waiting for my judgment, my reproach. But there is none forthcoming.

When I'm close to him, I place my hand to his chest, feeling the solidity of the muscle there and the matching rhythm of his speeding pulse. "Yes."

His eyebrows shoot up, eyes going wide as saucers. "Huh?" he gasps.

"Yes," I repeat. "I don't know how to do or be all that, and I don't care at this moment because we'll figure out what it means to us on a day-in, day-out basis. I want to be what you need, the way you are what I need. But you'll have to show me. We'll have to talk . . . a lot. And each word has to be honest . . . always, no matter what. The good, the bad, the ugly—we'll have to be willing to share it all."

His mouth opens and closes, at a sudden loss for words after the rambling explanation that is likely more words than he's ever spoken at once.

Finally, one word escapes. "Princess?"

The vulnerability in the question is more unguarded than he's ever been with me.

Finally.

The crux of this man. His deep, dark center, surprisingly so well matched to the one inside me that I didn't even know existed. Perhaps he simply willed it into being, creating a kindred spirit in me.

All I know is that I want it all. With him.

"Mark, I love you. Just as you are." My hand clenches his shirt, crumpling the fabric in my fist as I pull him down to me. "Mine."

I press my lips to his, the promise one of the heart, not words. His hands reach down to cup my ass, and he lifts me up. My legs wrap around his waist as he moves toward the bedroom.

I kiss down his neck, and from above I hear his reply, the words unneeded but music to my ears. "Katelyn, I love you too. Just as you are. Mine."

He emphasizes it with a squeeze to my cheeks and I whimper, not in pain but at the memory of how he took me so wildly. I buck against him, searching for more. He lays me down in the center of his bed, kneeling between my spread thighs.

"Princess, I need to worship you. Kiss the marks I carelessly made."

I pout a little, my lip popping out, and he smirks, his dimple a shadow in the lamplit room. "But that sounds so *beige*." The word is a denunciation of my previous life.

"Princess, hard or soft, rough or gentle, I don't think we'll ever be beige," he says with a lift of one brow, daring me to disagree. I don't—I definitely don't. "I'll mark you up again," he growls, "but this time it will be careful and intentional."

He runs a finger from my ankle to my inner thigh before lifting my leg into the air and retracing the line with his lips. I moan at the onslaught from the barest touch to my oversensitive skin.

"We'll see," I tell him, every bit of sass in my voice I can muster, but it comes out breathy. He chuckles against my skin, and I wiggle beneath him. His eyes flash to mine as his tongue peeks out, touching my calf.

"Take it, princess."

I still instantly, and I can see the joy in his face, the utter relief at being completely open with what he wants for the first time in his life. And I do my best to give it to him as he worships me, taking his gifts of pleasure and giving in return.

All of me.

All of him.

CHAPTER 29

MARK

My morning is broken rather awkwardly as Luke comes down just after dawn, knocking on my door loudly. I guess it's to check on Katelyn. He got protective of her last night, something I can both understand and appreciate since I feel the same way.

"Luke, come on in," I tell him, still wiping the sleep out of my eyes as he helps himself inside.

Katelyn tries to hop up from my lap, probably to give us a minute of brother time to get some shit straight. But I hold her steady, running my thumb along her thigh soothingly, and she settles in for the duration.

"Good morning," Luke says carefully, coming into the kitchen slowly. "How's everything?"

I grunt, having met my quota for words for approximately the next six months.

Katelyn smiles warmly, though, as she grabs a piece of bacon from my plate and offers it to me before smacking it up herself. "We're great. You?"

He helps himself to a cup of coffee and sits down at the table across from us, eyes evaluating as they flick between Katelyn and me. Though her face is scrubbed clean now, Katelyn still looks freshly fucked, hair in a messy pile on her head, wearing my T-shirt that barely brushes along the marks on her thighs. My bare chest, scratched from her nails, and the hickey on my neck add to the overall effect. My gut clenches at how my little brother is going to react to all this. Last night and this morning is a lot to ask him to overlook.

"Doing well I guess. Although I might need a bit of a nap today," he says with a wink. "I'm a total pain in the ass if I don't get my eight hours."

Katelyn sighs, looking a little sheepish. "Yeah, sorry about waking you up last night. Thanks for bringing me down, though."

I give him a nod of appreciation too. I know he and I will talk about this later, but Luke's fears are put to rest.

Katelyn looks back to me, running a hand through my hair. "It was a rather eye-opening night."

I smile fully, feeling lighter than I have in forever. Katelyn touches a light finger to my dimple, letting me know without words how much she likes it, and then lays a soft kiss to my lips. Luke chuckles, downing the rest of his coffee.

"So basically, you two are kinky as fuck? Is that what we're going with here? Should I keep an eye out for the whip in the barn disappearing?" he asks laughingly.

Katelyn laughs and I growl, "Get the fuck out, Luke."

A shit-eating grin breaks across his face, and he gets to his feet, putting the coffee cup in the sink. "Fine, I'm going. Wish I could say that I'd take care of your chores today, but with James gone, you're on your own, because I'm busy with the horses. You can take care of the herd check your damn self."

"I know. I'll be up soon," I say, already turning my full attention back to Katelyn.

Luke opens the back door but pauses and looks back. "You two look happy," he says sincerely, "so no matter what, I'm happy for you.

You deserve it, Mark. Both of you. Just don't hurt each other." He smirks, his eyes twinkling. "Well, unless you're into that, I guess."

I grab a biscuit from the table and toss it toward his head. Luke snatches it out of the air and shoves it into his mouth, grinning as he mumbles around the crumbs that tumble all over my clean floor.

"Thanks, Mark. I needed a snack. Good looking out."

"You, too, Luke," I say loudly enough for him to hear. He throws up a two-finger wave of acknowledgment, and then I'm alone with my princess once again.

Katelyn smiles, turning to me. "If you don't mind, I need to go home and shower and get changed for work. I can't show up in pj's."

By the time we finish breakfast, both of us really have to get going, but I don't want to let her go. I have a knot of fear that once she's out of my sight, she's going to come to her senses and realize how fucking crazy this is. I run her up to her car in the Gator and try to kiss her senseless, muddy her thoughts so that she won't think clearly even after she's left. She's leaned back against her girly car in Mama's driveway, my tongue exploring her mouth, when I hear a voice behind me.

"Excuse me, you two."

We break apart, and I press my forehead to Katelyn's, my eyes already apologizing, because if I thought Luke coming to breakfast to check on us was awkward, it's nothing compared to my mother interrupting a morning goodbye with my woman, especially when she's wearing next-to-nothing shorts and a barely there tank top. I'm especially grateful that our position against the car hides the marks on the backs of her legs. The thought of the bruises brings equal parts cringe and pride to my heart; I'm still amazed at how accepting of everything Katelyn's been. Let's hope that streak continues right now.

"Morning, Mama," I intone.

Katelyn, though, of course is all sass and respect, giving Mama a sweet smile as if our compromising position is no big deal. It definitely is, especially to Mama. "Good morning, Mama Lou."

"I don't want to interrupt, but I wanted to invite Katelyn to dinner tonight," Mama says, her grin telling me she is probably up to something.

Katelyn nods, putting an arm around my waist. "I'd love to come to dinner. What time should I be here?"

"Well, I'm making fried chicken," Mama says, "so why don't you come around five, and you can help me? If you can get here by then?"

"Nothing's going to keep me from that," Katelyn says happily. "I love good fried chicken."

Mama gives me a knowing look, and I know how important her seemingly innocent question is. It makes me smirk, and once Mama goes inside, Katelyn turns to me, smirking as well.

"Okay, mister, what did I miss? Because you two were making all kinds of eyes at each other."

I tuck a loose lock of hair behind her ear and hug her gently. "Don't freak out."

She laughs, rolling her eyes. "Seriously, after last night? This is what you think I'm going to freak about? It's just fried chicken!"

"No, it's not *just* fried chicken," I reply very seriously. "And you'd best keep your voice down, because you do not want Mama to hear you call it that. It's her secret recipe. She guards that thing like there are spies coming to steal it at the first opportunity. She's only let one other person ever make fried chicken with her."

Katelyn's eyes are getting wide, the gravity of the situation sinking in. "Who?"

I lean down, whispering the answer in her ear. "Sophie."

Katelyn's breath leaves in a whoosh as the full meaning hits her. "Oh shit. What do I wear? Should I bring flowers? Cookies! I'll bring cookies. She loves cookies."

She's losing it, rambling again. It's fucking adorable, and I love it. "Just bring you, no cookies required. It'll be fine, princess. Breathe."

Her eyes stop zipping around and lock on mine as she takes a deep breath. "It'll be fine. I can make fried chicken, with your mom, using her top-secret recipe she's only shared with James's wife."

Her voice is a little higher than usual, but she's mostly calm-ish. I nod and open the door to her car, helping her in. "Okay, okay. Bring the cookies, but only if you get me a peanut butter one, okay?"

My lips twitch, and she swats at my arm, her eyes still wide. "You're the worst. I'm freaking out here."

"Seriously, after last night, this is what you freak out about?" I throw her words back at her, and it does the trick. She dissolves into giggles and leans out the door to kiss me.

"You're funny. Thank you for talking me down."

I don't think anyone has ever accused me of being funny, never in my life. And I've never *talked* anyone down. But she gets me in a way no one ever has before. It's more than I could've ever hoped for. It's everything.

CHAPTER 30

KATELYN

It's been almost a month of discovery for both of us. Conversations have long since moved beyond stilted words and blushes, and instead we delight in sharing fantasies and thoughts. I've never felt more adored, and my body . . . oh, the things that we've done leave me tingling for hours afterward.

Mark takes care of me physically, mentally, and emotionally. He listens to me like no one ever has, whether it's about work or a story from my childhood or something I want to try in the bedroom.

In return, he's opened up to me, letting me inside his brilliant mind and letting me care for him, too, something foreign to the man who's been used to taking care of everyone else. I kind of laugh a bit when people describe him as a quiet asshole now, because to me, he's anything but.

He's funny and talkative and sweet . . . for me.

Some nights we haven't even had sex, just sat on the porch lounger, lost in conversation for hours until we have to part so I can sleep for work. Other nights, we'll spend hours making love. Sometimes gentle, sometimes not. I'd had to reassure him at first that I liked—no, loved—the "glitter sex" where he's more beast than man, not always but sometimes. I love it just like every other color of the rainbow with him—fiery red passion, cool blue tenderness, warm leisurely yellow, and whatever else feels right for us in the moment.

This weekend, I'm giving him one of the fantasies he's shared with me.

Luke told me Mark would be out in one of the far fields until dinner, so I told Mama that we'd be skipping dinner with the family tonight. I've been cooking all afternoon, all of Mark's favorites, including lasagna and homemade peanut butter cookies.

My phone rings, playing a prearranged ringtone once, the signal from Luke that Mark is leaving the barn after putting Sugarpea up for the night. I've got three minutes tops to finish up, and my heels click on the floor as I cross the kitchen, turning the oven on low to keep dinner warm.

I hurry into the bathroom, checking my makeup before going to the kitchen. I kneel down on the floor, cross my hands behind my back, and wait.

A minute later, I hear Mark's boots on the back porch, and a smile of anticipation sneaks across my face.

"Princess?"

I say nothing, letting him cross the porch in three steps before he opens the back door, the creak frozen halfway through as he sees me. "Holy fuck," he whispers hotly.

I look up at him, loving the way his eyes caress every inch of my skin, bared just for him.

"You look stunning."

"Thank you," I reply, watching as he shudders. "Like a fantasy come to life?"

It's all the prompt he needs, but he looks around, realizing that dinner will be served here tonight, for just the two of us.

"Thank you," he says, the last soft words he'll offer as a change takes over him and he becomes something different. He's still my Mark, but more—rough, hard, dominant. I can't wait. He comes close, not offering me our usual hello kiss. Instead, he stands in front of me, unbuckles his belt with a soft whisper of leather, undoes his jeans, and shoves them down along with his boxer briefs.

His cock, thick and already rock hard, bobs in front of me. Mark grabs the base, giving it a tight squeeze, and a drop of pearly precum leaks from the tip. My mouth waters. I want it, but I know better than to take it without permission. The delay makes me squirm, heat pooling between my legs.

Oh so slowly, Mark slips his head along my lips, and I get a hint of his salty-sweet taste.

"Open."

I let my jaw fall wide, beyond ready for him. Mark weaves his fingers into my hair, holding my head still, and then he thrusts against my tongue, a slow torture for us both. He knows I want more, want him in my throat, but it takes me a moment to relax enough to take him, so he gives me what I need over what I want, taking care of me even as he lives out his fantasy.

Finally, we find our rhythm as he fucks my throat, holding me tight against his belly for a second as I take him to the hilt, the *gluck* sound from my throat as I swallow him repeatedly sexy as hell.

He waits just long enough, watching me closely and letting me retreat for oxygen just before I really need to, keeping me able to go back for more time and time again. My moans vibrate against him, triggering his growls.

"That's it. Suck my cock down your pretty little throat."

I nod, and his fists tighten in my hair as he fucks my mouth. I never would've imagined that letting him use me this way would give me so much pleasure, make me feel so powerful, but kneeling at his feet, choking on his cock makes me feel loved. It doesn't have to make sense; it's simply true.

It only takes a handful of strokes and he's spasming, his cum pulsing deep in my throat, and I swallow over and over, not wanting to spill a drop.

His shudders stop, and he pulls out of my mouth, immediately bending down to lift me up.

"Over the table?" I ask, knowing that's the next step in his fantasy.

But Mark shakes his head, his eyes swimming with emotions. "Will dinner keep?"

I bite my lip, wondering where he wants to take this. "It's on warm."

Mark nods, scooping me up and carrying me down the hallway, depositing me in the middle of the bed. "Changing the plan for tonight, if you don't mind?"

I shake my head, on board with whatever he wants.

He slips the belt from his jeans and orders, "Hands."

His command galvanizes me, and I hold my hands out to him, watching as he wraps his belt around both wrists at once. It's not tight, more symbolic than actually restraining me, and I could easily get out if I wanted to.

But I don't. Instead, I let him do whatever he wants, wiggling in anticipation. I'm aching, my pussy wanting to know how he plans on taking me. "Spread."

I open my legs wide, my honey already coating my thighs. Mark licks his lips, taking me in. "Fuck, you look so pretty. Good enough to eat."

I moan as his tongue touches my lips, the barest hint of stimulation, but I'm already creeping up on the edge because he has me so turned on.

"Please. Lick me," I beg.

My breath is taken from me as he doesn't just lick me, but his entire mouth devours me, his tongue dipping into my core as he sucks me fiercely.

I cry out, my back arching, and he rewards me with a nibble to my clit, the zing shooting through me. I reach up, pressing the palms of my bound hands against the headboard for leverage, my legs shaking against the bed as I push up to grind against him.

"So close, yessss . . . ," I whisper, urging him on.

He stops, and I moan with need when he sits up, kneeling between my thighs to look at me. His eyes take their time, moving from my raised hands, to my desperate face, to my flushed body, to my dripping pussy.

He traces a fingertip along my skin, not enough and not where I need him to be to send me over, but it feels good.

"I never thought I'd have this, Katelyn. I was resigned to a life of solitude. You've changed all that."

I thrash, chasing his touch as the words come out in little gasps. "You changed everything for me too."

His finger finally centers over my clit, giving me more and taking me higher and higher. "I'm a greedy bastard. I want this for always."

"Always," I promise as his weight pins my right leg down, leaving me unable to move and forcing me to take just what he offers me. "I love you, Mark."

"Look at me." His finger circles my clit, harder and faster, driving me wild, but I force my eyes to focus. His blue eyes are dark with need. "Princess, Katelyn . . . marry me."

There's a frozen moment of time where his words reverberate through my mind, joy already singing through me. Then the time warp rushes in with a whoosh, and he dives for my pussy, sucking my clit hard, battering it with his tongue.

My body bows as I cry out. "Yes . . . yes . . . yes!"

I'm lost in space, floating in happiness, but I know that Mark is my anchor, my strength as I shatter and am reformed into his princess once again. I'm still pulsing when he shoves into me, bare skin on mine, bared heart and soul visible in his eyes. As he begins to thrust in earnest, filling me as he pins me to the bed, I remove the belt to wrap my arms around his neck, pulling him deeper into me.

"Say it again."

He growls behind clenched teeth, thrusting deep and slow. "Marry me."

"Yesssss!" I moan, digging my fingernails into his shoulders.

We crash together again and again, until too soon the physical pleasure and emotional joy become a tidal wave and we both come again. Together. More one being than two.

~~

Hours later, we've raided the lasagna and garlic bread for sustenance, and I sit in Mark's lap as we feed each other cookies. I giggle, still not believing that he asked—no, that he *ordered* me to marry him mid-sex while I was semirestrained. Whose life is this?

The reality that it's mine makes bubbles of joy rise in my heart. A smile breaks across my face, and Mark kisses at my lips like he's tasting my happiness. He stands, setting me back in the chair and going to refill my wine glass and grab himself another beer.

He leans against the table casually. "You know, I might not have thought this through. Isn't the first question women are going to ask you is how I proposed?"

I look up at him thoughtfully and shrug. "Yeah. But I wouldn't change it. It's our story. It's who we are."

"The fact that you say it's who *we* are—and not who *I* am—brightens every corner of my heart," Mark admits. "There's not much darkness left there. You've filled in every nook and cranny with your love, but sometimes you take my breath away."

I smile, thinking I'll never get used to the sweet and poetic way he loves me.

"Katelyn." He drops to one knee, holding out a ring as he looks at me with a sparkle in his eyes. "Last chance, princess. Once this goes on, it ain't coming off. Will you marry me?"

Tears stream down my face as I nod my head. "Yes. I already said yes."

He slips the ring on my finger. It's gorgeous, a square pink diamond with a halo of sparkling diamonds surrounding the center stone. "Oh my God, Mark. I love it! It's perfect."

"Just like you. A girly ring for my girly princess. Diamond-hard and badass."

I lunge at him, tackling him to the floor, and I end up straddling his lap as he sits on the floor. He cups my face, his voice soft. "I love you, Katelyn."

"I love you too. And yeah, you're probably right—I'll tell everyone this version of the proposal story. The other one is just for you and me. *Ours*."

EPILOGUE

Mark

Four weeks may not seem like a lot to most people, but to me it's been a season in paradise. Only four weeks since Katelyn agreed to marry me, and my life's done a complete one-eighty, and today just seems like the surreal cap to that change. Three days of rain earlier this week had folks worried, but yesterday the sun came out, and now the large central area that surrounds the pond has been transformed. It's fall now, so while the grass is still green, the trees in the mountains have started to change into a fiery riot of colors, orange and yellow and red. It's a picture, a painting, and I love it.

A mishmash of chairs, hardly any matching another, are lined up in rows. The arbor from the resort has been set up and covered with white fabric that billows in the mild breeze above and below the twine ties.

It's exactly what Katelyn said she wanted. The plan was simple, small, and no stress, considering what she does every day at work.

She and Marla handled it like the pros they are, taking care of everything in record time. I'm grateful to Marla for her help, both with the wedding and the pushes she gave both Katelyn and me. I give her a nod as she and David sit down to wait.

Meanwhile, I stand here, my brothers by my side and Mama sitting in front of me next to a seat with Pops's picture in it. A hawk cries out in the sky above us, and I am struck with awe at how things have changed. I'm not scared that I'm broken any longer, destined to be alone and unloved. I'm not scared that the only thing I'll be able to care for is this land surrounding me.

Now it's different. *I'm* different. Not in my true self, but in accepting who I am and being okay with that. It's funny, Katelyn swears I've opened her eyes, but I think she's the one who truly took my blinders off. And though we already know that she is mine and I am hers, irrevocably, today is a public recognition of our private bond.

A violin begins to play softly, and from the hill, I can see Katelyn walking toward me, her dad on her right and her mom on her left. Once I'd apologized for not asking her dad's permission before proposing, we'd been fine, and so far he seems like a really great guy.

Although the thought of me asking permission for anything had triggered a giggle fit for Katelyn, and I'd had to pinken her ass after they left.

I didn't mind. She didn't either.

As she comes closer, I get the full effect of my bride, my princess. Her white gown is molded to her curves, flaring out by her knees, and as she walks, I can see her boots kicking from the hemline. It's the only compromise she's had to make, though I offered to carry her all day if she wanted to wear her heels. In the end, she went with the boots that would let her walk down the aisle and dance during the reception.

She comes to stand beside me, and it's all I can do to hold myself back from kissing her now, protocol and manners be damned. But the preacher begins, and we move through the ceremony. I don't hear half of what he says; I'm lost in Katelyn's eyes, reveling in her smile.

Luke coughs, and I realize he's reminding me when I have to open my mouth to say something. Finally, we're to the vows. Katelyn smiles and leans closer to me.

"You can do it," she whispers, knowing I was nervous about this part in front of everyone, even if it's just our closest family and friends.

I clear my throat and take her hands in mine as I begin. "Katelyn, you are the worst friend I've ever had."

Her lips tilt up, the laugh threatening to burst free as Luke hisses behind me and I hear his quiet snarl. "What the fuck, man?"

But I continue, knowing that Katelyn gets it and that's what matters. "When we decided to be just friends, it was torture. Because I wanted more. I wanted everything. The problem was, I didn't know how or if I even deserved it. You demanded more from me than I ever thought I could give, and in return, you've given me a gift I will cherish forever—your heart. Pops once told me that you get exactly what you need when you're ready for it."

I chance a glance at Mama and Pops's picture, knowing he's here with us, smiling down at his fool boy finally living the legacy he'd dreamed.

"I didn't think I was ready, didn't know if I ever would be, but you are exactly what I needed. And I'm ready to spend the rest of my life with you. I love you, princess. I am yours. Always."

She smiles, even though tears are running down her face. I pull the handkerchief from my pocket, dabbing at her cheeks so as not to ruin her makeup. I press the cloth into her hand and nod as everyone shifts their attention to her. From the corner of my eye, I see Mama crying openly now, something I've seen less than a handful of times in my life.

Katelyn takes a deep breath and begins. "I wasted a lot of time, floating aimlessly and carelessly, and when I finally found the courage to stand on my own two feet, I fell. For you. Literally. But you caught me then, and you continue to catch me anytime I stumble," Katelyn continues. "And no matter how many times I discover a new challenge, you support me while encouraging me to be strong. I'm brave because of you. I'm badass because of you. I'm brilliantly iridescent, every color of the rainbow reflecting through me, because of you. I love you, Mark. I am yours. Always."

I don't wait for the preacher to give me permission, because I can see that Katelyn needs it as much as I do and I'll always give her what she needs, so I pull her to me, wrapping my arms around her and kissing her as properly as I can in public.

Inside me, though, the simple fact that she's my wife burns in my soul, igniting a fire I wasn't anticipating.

I don't think I succeed in appropriateness, because I hear Luke laugh quietly behind me.

"That's enough, you kinky fuckers," he whispers.

But it'll never be enough.

Not for my princess.

ABOUT THE AUTHOR

Wall Street Journal and *USA Today* bestselling author Lauren Landish writes books that have garnered a legion of praise from her readers. When she's not plotting how she'll introduce you to your next sexy-as-hell hero, you can find her deep in her writing cave, furiously tapping away on her keyboard, writing scenes that would make even a hardened sailor blush. The author of the Irresistible Bachelor Series and *Buck Wild* in the Bennett Boys Ranch books, Lauren lives in North Carolina with her boyfriend and fur baby. To find out more about Lauren and her worlds of rock-hard abs, chiseled smiles, and men with deep, fat pockets, visit her at www.laurenlandish.com or on Facebook at www.facebook.com/lauren.landish.